With over twenty million copies of her books in print, **Heather Graham** is one of the world's most widely read and best-loved novelists. In *A Magical Christmas*, she tells her most heartwarming story yet, an unforgettable re-creation of a love that neither time nor war could destroy . . . and a family renewed by a special kind of miracle. Nobody ever said love was easy—but oh, what a special kind of wonderful it is.

A Magical Christmas

"Unique . . . magic . . . surprisingly different."
—*Rendezvous*

"Swift-moving. Appealing."
—*Library Journal*

"Heather Graham is an incredible storyteller."
—*Los Angeles Daily News*

A Magical Christmas

by

Heather Graham

A TOPAZ BOOK

TOPAZ
Published by the Penguin Group
Penguin Putnam Inc., 375 Hudson Street,
New York, New York 10014, U.S.A.
Penguin Books Ltd, 27 Wrights Lane,
London W8 5TZ, England
Penguin Books Australia Ltd, Ringwood,
Victoria, Australia
Penguin Books Canada Ltd, 10 Alcorn Avenue,
Toronto, Ontario, Canada M4V 3B2
Penguin Books (N.Z.) Ltd, 182–190 Wairu Road,
Auckland 10, New Zealand

Penguin Books Ltd, Registered Offices:
Harmondsworth, Middlesex, England

First published by Topaz, an imprint of Dutton Signet,
a member of Penguin Putnam Inc.
Previously published in a Topaz hardcover edition.

First Mass Market Printing, November, 1997
10 9 8 7 6 5 4 3 2 1

Ⓣ REGISTERED TRADEMARK—MARCA REGISTRADA

Printed in the United States of America

PUBLISHER'S NOTE
This is a work of fiction. Names, characters, places, and incidents either are
the product of the author's imagination or are used fictitiously, and any
resemblance to actual persons, living or dead, events, or locales is entirely
coincidental.

To Cynthia Bethe,
for her real estate prowess

To Father Dennison (St. Augustine's)
& Father Moras (St. Theresa's),
for understanding Christmas
all year

&

To Jason, Shayne, Derek,
Bryee-Annon & Chynna Pozzessere,
for being the magic
of my Christmases,
always!

Prologue

Christmastide
Northern Virginia
1862

Darcy Gannon leaned against the library door of the Oak River farmhouse, a small plantation now held by the Federals and housing a number of Confederate prisoners. Cavalrymen, soldiers known as "Mosby's Men."

They were men who had infuriated a very young Union brigadier general, a certain George Armstrong Custer, with their ability to raid supply wagons, sabotage Union lines, steal Union horses, medicines, ammunition, and more.

Custer had sent out a stern warning: Those caught would be hanged. The sheer outrage of it had rung clearly throughout the mountains, throughout the Shenandoah Valley, to Front Royal, and all the way to Richmond. But there wasn't much to be done about such an affront—this was war.

Sergeant Darcy Gannon, his ear pressed to the glass in his hand, which was hard pressed to the wood of the door, listened to the verbal dispatches being relayed in the foyer beyond the library.

Darcy winced, eased the glass from the door, and turned to his companions. "Captain," he said, looking to their leader, a slim, handsome man in worn butternut and gray, "that damned Custer, he does intend to do it. Five of our number. Five of us are to hang. Only five 'cause of the holiday, but those five will be hanged—right on Christmas Eve."

The captain acknowledged that information with a nod. Not a shudder, not the slightest paling of color betrayed his emotion at the news. "Well, now, five of our number. We knew this was war, gentlemen, and we knew we risked all when we rode with Mosby. Not that I'm anxious to die, but there's no finer man in the Confederacy to die for than our Mosby, and no finer state to fight for than Virginia."

"Here, here!" came a murmur from the men, but the sound of it was somewhat weak. And as he looked around the room, the captain saw as well that the faces surveying him were ashen. Sickly. Around their campfires, they had sung sad but hopeful ballads, wishful lyrics about soldiers going home for Christmas. Now, once they accepted the dire truth of their situation, they'd be singing with grim humor about soldiers being hanged for the holiday instead.

"Five of us, eh, Sergeant Gannon?" the captain inquired. He looked over what was left of his company. Twenty-four men. He himself made twenty-five. One-fifth of their number. Hanging only five of them probably was what Custer would consider a generous concession to Christ's birth, considering how bitter Custer was because of Mosby's abilities to ride circles around him and rob him blind. Custer was an ambitious man, and Mosby's boys sure made him look bad to his superiors. "Five," the captain murmured again. "Naturally . . ." he began, then found himself at a loss for words, a major obstruction seeming to have lodged in his throat. He didn't want to die. He wanted to go home. To her. Even if they had parted in anger. Especially because they had parted in anger. She had warned him, pleaded with him, begged him to leave the service. He had served far longer than he had ever intended, but she simply hadn't understood that a man, a captain, didn't just walk away in the middle of a war.

She had been weary of the war, raising their crops alone, raising their children alone—even if only their daughter remained now. His son's determination to lead his own life was another blade of steel that seemed wedged within his heart now—they'd had such terrible differences between them! How awful now to wonder if he'd ever have the chance to say, *I love you, and I respect the way that you have stood up for what you have believed in.*

Yet, *she* lived with all the fear, daily, on her own, worrying alone, ever mindful for the time when Union troops just might come marching through. . . .

Well, the Union troops had come marching through. But thank God in heaven above for small mercies; his family wasn't here. They had gone down to spend the holiday with her sister at Front Royal.

Thank God, thank God. . . .

If he could only see her.

Oh, God, no, that would be worse. She might cry, and he might not be given a single instant to touch her, and it would be so hard then to be the captain, the leader of his men.

But to think that he might die without touching her face again . . .

After the way they had parted . . .

The irony, of course, was that he was a prisoner in his own home. And that he would be hanged from one of the huge oaks he had climbed as a boy. Because naturally, as he was trying to tell his men, no matter how desperately he wanted to live, how terrified he was of the hangman's rope and the hanged man's death, he would be one of the five. He was their captain.

Oh, God. Oh, God. He was afraid. He didn't want to die. He had faced death frequently enough, but always with the belief that he could survive. He'd refused to believe that he might be among the fallen, and yet . . .

If he would have been killed in battle, it might have been mercifully quick. No time to ponder the things he had left undone, unsaid. While to hang . . .

Hanging was the worst death for a man. Ignoble. Pathetic. God be with him.

God give him courage.

"Naturally," he said briskly then, "I will be one of the five. My friends, I've never ridden with finer men. I'd die for all of you if I could."

"Captain—that ain't right," old Billy Larson said. God alone knew just how old Billy was. He'd hailed from a small town just down the creek from Oak River Plantation, and he'd been an old man when the captain himself had still been climbing trees.

"That's right," Darcy agreed. "You just can't decide you're going to be one of the ones to die, Captain. You got a wife, a family."

"We all have families, Darcy. Every one of us has someone, wife, mother, father, brother, sister, child. And God knows, this war has been no quick picnic like we all thought it would be when the Rebs crushed the Yanks back at First Manassas. They've all been hurt enough."

"I ain't got no one," Billy Larson said. He started to spit tobacco on the floor, then seemed to remember that it was their captain's library—even if the Feds were keeping them prisoner here. He edged on over to the spittoon. "My wife died of the smallpox in fifty-three, my boy died the day he was born. They'll take me, for one."

"Hell, now, Billy, don't you go being noble that way," Pierce Roswell protested. Pierce was one of the older men in their company as well, a graybeard nearing sixty, but a man with the agility of a boy.

"Hell, we're Mosby's Men, we're all noble!" Jake Clary, a grinning twenty-four, informed them. Laughter rose.

From everyone but Jimmy Haley.

Little Jimmy Haley. They hadn't really wanted the boy with them. He was just thirteen—their mascot, and he'd wound up with them because his ma had died alone in the mountains and his pa was either dead or fighting somewhere and Jimmy didn't know where. And he might have starved to death in winter, left up on that mountain, so he'd come with them as a drummer boy. He'd been in uniform with them, and he'd been taken with them. And now, it seemed that Jimmy knew, just like everybody else, that he had a one out of five chance of dying, and he was damned green.

"Don't be afraid, Jimmy," the captain said.

"I ain't afraid, Captain," Jimmy said. He tried to smile. "Ain't no Yankee gonna scare me, sir. And I ain't afeered of dying, Cap. They can count me in, just like the rest of the men. I'm one of you, right?"

"Sure, Jimmy, you're one of us." The captain looked at Darcy across the room. They wouldn't let Jimmy die; that was for certain.

"Hell, those of us who don't die will be going to a prison camp," Lem Smith said. "Like as not, it will be better going by a rope than a slow death in one of those wretched Yank camps."

The captain held silent. They all knew that the Southern camps were more wretched. The Northern blockade was slowly strangling the South. The South couldn't feed her own men, much less her Northern prisoners. In the North and the South, there were prisons that were really bad, and prisons that weren't so bad. Like it or not, a lesson was being learned across the divide of the states. Good men were Yanks; bad men were Rebs. Bad sons of bitches were Yanks—and their counterparts could be found among the Rebs as well.

"It's going to be a draw," Darcy said. "It ain't gonna matter none which of us wants to die. We're going to draw lots."

"Lots?"

Darcy shrugged. "I don't know exactly what that means, but it's going to be the luck of the draw. That's what Custer's man said to the guard out there, anyhow."

"Well, gentlemen, we'll have to see what unfolds, and deal with what happens as it comes along," the captain said.

Later that afternoon, after watery stew and moldy hardtack—the Yank stuff admittedly better than what they'd drawn as rations lately from their Confederate depots—the Rebs were taken outside for exercise. The snow was inches deep on the ground, but it had stopped falling. The day was crystal clear, the sky beautifully blue. The cold felt good.

The captain could close his eyes and see times gone past. This was his home; he could see Christmastides gone by. Smell roast goose cooking in the oven, see his wife's face, beautiful, flushed from the work she insisted on doing herself in the kitchen. The house would be decked out in holly and evergreen branches. The warmth would envelop him, along with the aromatic scents of their holiday dinner ... and her.

He could almost hear the laughter from days gone past. The delight of his children as they opened their presents. He could see the glow in her eyes, when all alone, thinking no one was watching, she would open her gift from him.

Damn, but it was funny. They could just be so mad at one another! Maybe fear had had something to do with it lately, but sometimes, even before the war, they'd gotten caught up in the work of living. They'd forgotten just how much they'd loved one another once upon a time. And right now, with the threat of death all but imminent, she was all that he wanted. *He could see her face.* Oh, God, yes, in his mind's eye, and all he wanted right now was one last chance to hold her, one last chance to say he loved her, a chance to say good-bye without the harsh words between them.

The prisoners were allowed to walk and stretch their legs in one of the paddocks right in front of the main house.

The captain liked to be out. He'd used this field for his horses. He'd bred damned good horses here.

All of them gone now. Gone to the Confederacy.

Gone to war.

Their guards weren't actually cruel taskmasters; some of the Union boys set to watch over them seemed downright unhappy about the duty. Southern boys had given over lots of tobacco. The Yanks had shared their good coffee with the Rebs on an equal footing. Still, six guards were set around the fence of the paddock where the Rebs walked, and the captain knew, through Darcy's fine hearing, that the Yanks had been given orders to shoot to kill if the Rebs made any attempt to escape. He'd ordered them not to do so. They were out-numbered and well-guarded. Their best chance would be to wait for reinforcements. Surely, Mosby himself might manage to come for them. Or some brigade, perhaps from Lee's Army of Northern Virginia. Lee was great at breaking up his troops and coming at the Yanks from different angles. They never knew what hit them half the time.

"Captain! Captain!" Some of the local folk had gathered along the road. They waved encouragement to him and his men, even as the Yanks moved forward to urge them onward. He saw tears in a young girl's eyes. He lifted his plumed slouch hat to her with a flourish. A sprig of holly grew along the fence, and he plucked it and threw it to her. A cheer went up, and another local woman cried out even as the Yanks urged her down the road at rifle's length. "The Lord bless you and your men, Captain! We're praying for you."

"God bless you all! Merry Christmas!" he cried in return.

The folks moved onward. Then the Yank unhappily in charge of him and his men entered the paddock.

Billy was suddenly at one side of him.

Darcy was at the other.

Lieutenant Jenkins, not long out of West Point, with barely a bit of stubble on his face, approached him, saluting. "Captain, I regret to inform you that upon direct orders from General Custer . . ."

Lieutenant Jenkins faltered. He wasn't up to this task of execution, and he darned near looked as if he were going to cry.

"It's fine now, Lieutenant, you go ahead. Say what you have to say," the captain said.

Jenkins rallied. "Five of you got to be hanged, sir. We're mighty sorry, the boys and I. But it's got to be five. Would have been ten, but then it's Christmas . . . Well, sir, you've got to draw straws. Every man of your company is to take a straw. The short straws . . . well, the short straws are the chosen ones." Two Yanks, nearly as pathetically green as their Confederate counterparts, carried the straws.

"Perhaps we should choose among ourselves," the captain suggested.

"It's got to be straws," Lieutenant Jenkins said firmly. He hated his duty. He apparently feared Custer's wrath more.

"Gentlemen?" the captain said politely to his soldiers.

And the soldiers, to a man—including the boy, Jimmy—drew their straws.

The captain gripped his in his hand. If it was a

long straw, he just might survive the war. The prison camps were hell, but he might be traded, he might survive. He was a healthy man, uninjured. He could withstand a great deal of hardship. Because he wanted to live. He wanted another Christmas, oh, God, just one more Christmas. . . .

If his straw was short, he would die. Hanged on his own property.

Thank God she wasn't here to see it.

If he could just touch her one more time, say he was sorry, say he loved her . . .

Say good-bye.

God, it was hard not to want to live. Especially when the sky was so beautifully clear a blue, when the sun was making diamond patterns upon the snow.

He looked at his straw. It was long.

Relief flooded him.

He was ashamed.

"Well, God's got some good sense," Billy said, and not without a certain dry humor. "I'm the oldest man here; I've lived the longest, and God sure does know, I'm the one the most ready to go."

Billy had a short straw. Pierce Roswell had another. "I've seen my fair share of things as well," Pierce said, clapping his hand upon Billy's shoulder. "Well, old-timer, old friend, think we can die well?"

"That we can," Billy assured him.

The captain stared at the two with admiration, then looked to see who had drawn the other three short straws. Harry Sams, outside with them in the clean, fresh air but lying on a litter since he'd been gut-shot in the skirmish in which they'd been taken, lifted his straw. Short. Harry was twenty-two.

"Oh, sweet Jesus, Harry—" the captain began.

"Hell, Captain! I'm dying anyway," Harry told him with a wry smile. He sobered. "And that's the truth of it, Captain. Those Yanks will save me some pain."

"Me, too!" called out Martin McCorkindale. Like Harry, he was in his early twenties. He wasn't shot up as bad as Harry, but his leg needed to be amputated. And fast. It was already putrefying. The poisons could well have spread throughout his body. The Yanks hadn't meant to leave their prisoners half-dead; their surgeon had been killed in the fighting and they were awaiting help for their own number as well as for the Rebs.

Martin cocked his head to the captain with a shrug. They both knew that his survival was one hell of a gamble.

"It's all right, Captain. In fact, it's damned fitting. Harry and I can die well, too."

Their logic was sound, if painful.

It seemed that God had been looking over them

for Christmas. Two men who might well be dying anyway had chosen the short straws, along with the two men who were the oldest in their company.

But there was still one more straw.

The Yanks were away from them, letting them make the discovery among themselves of who was to die.

"Where's the fifth straw?" the captain asked.

He heard a choked-back sob. Then little Jimmy Haley came walking toward him. His head was high. His shoulders were squared. "It's me, Captain, sir." Jimmy, with his tousled brown hair and huge brown eyes, looked up at him with a fine show of bravado. But then his eyes filled with tears he blinked back furiously and his fine-squared shoulders began to tremble. "I—I ain't afeered of dyin', sir. I—I know damned certain that I can die well, too. I won't holler or blubber or anything, Captain. I promise. I'll make you proud."

"Jimmy, you've always done us proud," the captain said softly.

The Yanks were coming back.

Oh, hell, oh, hell, oh, God, the captain thought.

He'd wanted to live so much. He'd wanted to live so damned badly. See her face just one more time again. Hear her whisper, touch her, kiss her, stroke the past and the pain away . . .

God, yes, he wanted to live.

"You're too young to die, son," the captain said curtly, and he snatched the straw from brave little Jimmy Haley, dropping his own long one in the snow.

The Yank, Lieutenant Jenkins, was back, and the captain turned to meet him.

"Wh—who—" Jenkins stuttered.

"Lieutenant, First Privates Sams, Roswell, McCorkindale, Larson—and I myself—have drawn the short straws," the captain said without blinking.

Tears filled Jimmy Haley's eyes in truth now. "Wait—" he started to protest.

But Darcy, behind him, clapped a hand over his mouth. He knew the captain would have none of it, the men letting Jimmy try to step in now when he had taken the boy's place.

"If you men will come with me . . ." the lieutenant said unhappily.

"I will gladly accompany you, Lieutenant, as will Privates Larson and Roswell. My other two friends, you will note, in truth all but cheat the hangman, and they will need your assistance."

Lieutenant Jenkins nodded. His Adam's apple jiggled.

"You've time with the chaplain, sir, if you'll accept the services of a Yank."

"Indeed, Lieutenant, my men and I will be glad of a man of God, since I'm quite certain in my heart God wears no uniform Himself. Both of our causes have claimed that God is on our side, yet I suspect that He is heartily disgusted with us all at this point."

The captain spun, gallantly saluted his men. Then, as ordered, he followed the lieutenant back to the house.

To prepare for his hanging.

At his own home, from his own tree.

If he closed his eyes and prayed hard enough, perhaps he could discover that he had slept. . . .

And he would awake.

And it would be Christmas.

Chapter One

Christmastime
South Florida
The Present

"It's not just a tedious, monotonous, wretched drive through tons of steel and horrifically rude people—it's an adventure!" Julie Radcliff muttered bitterly, stuck again in another traffic jam-up. Every day it got worse. She glanced at her watch again. She was going to be late. All she needed was ten minutes more each morning, but no matter how hard she tried, she never seemed able to get the household ready that simple little ten minutes earlier. Of course, it would help if once in a while—just once in a while—Jon's work wasn't more important than hers.

She realized that Ashley was staring at her. Ashley, just six, and in real school this year—first grade. Ashley seemed to have heard all the things that Julie had managed not to say—that she could be on time if only Daddy would handle his share of things. Julie tried to make her smile real as she reached over and squeezed her daughter's hand. "We rocketed down U.S. One, sped along Fifty-seventh, dodged that light at Eightieth . . . then plowed right into a wall of BMWs and Mercedes Benzes at your brother's school, huh, sweetie?"

"We're not that late, Mommy," Julie thought she heard Ashley say. Her defense of her father was as silent as Julie's earlier criticism of him had been. Ashley, this last of her brood of three, just would be her father's daughter. Ash had Jon's unique light green eyes, a color that must have been somehow touched with hazel so that it could actually change to gold at times. Her hair, too, was her father's, a thick, rich russet, though Jon seemed concerned these days that his wasn't as thick as it should be.

Good. She hoped he went cue-ball bald—and that the fashion didn't become him.

He would definitely deserve it.

"Honest, Mommy, it will be okay."

Her daughter's attempt to make her feel better meant much more to Julie than the ride to school and work that morning.

But then Ashley started complaining that her stomach hurt from being in the car. That was because her sister had insisted on sitting in the front before, and Ashley always complained about sitting in the back. The kids practically came to blows over who got to sit in the front seat. This morning, it just hadn't been Ashley's turn.

So she moaned. All through the traffic.

"Maybe I shouldn't take you to school," Julie muttered.

"If you stop driving, maybe my tummy won't hurt anymore," Ashley said.

"If I stop driving, maybe my head won't explode," Julie muttered.

And they were late. They were seven minutes late. If they'd been five minutes late, the first-grade door with Pooh Bear on it would have still been open, and Ashley could have slipped right in. But once that five-minute mark had been passed, Pooh Bear no longer faced the hall. Arriving with Ashley at the door, Julie found herself greeted by plain hardwood with a notice that stated: STUDENTS ARRIVING LATE MUST ACQUIRE A PASS FROM THE OFFICE.

"They're real nice in the office," Ashley offered. Her eyes were very grave on her mother's. "And Mommy, my tummy is all better. I'm sorry I made you mad."

Julie was suddenly very sorry, aware that she inflicted her emotions on her children.

But that, too, could be blamed on Jon.

She spurred herself to another smile. "I'm not mad, just aggravated. Traffic does that to people. And they *are* very nice in the office, and I'm so glad that you like the people at the school. You like your teachers; they're just great, right?"

Ashley nodded solemnly. "Don't forget to see if anybody wants to buy chocolates. You know what?"

"What?"

"Jillie sold over two hundred bars already. She's going to win a stuffed bear. I need to sell chocolates. I really want to win a prize, too, Mommy."

Julie gritted her teeth. She supposed that the school needed fund-raisers, but she was completely opposed in principle to anyone using bribery with first-graders. No parent with any sense was going to let a six-year-old sell candy door-to-door—not in their modern world. That meant that parents had to cajole friends and family into chocolate bars. Everybody loved chocolate bars, especially around the holidays—that was what the school said. They lied—and Julie knew it. Her friends winced at the very whiff of chocolate in the air, especially around the holidays. Even those who were usually especially generous with one-dollar bills could clam up in December.

Jillie's mom must be wallowing in chocolates.

But it seemed that other moms were always able to be up on the supermom scale. Jillie's mother was a damned saint. She read to the class two days a week, she was room mother, she ran the parent meetings—and looked down her nose big-time when a mom couldn't make sure to fit her young daughter's class meeting into her schedule.

"Chocolates," she murmured. "Sure, chocolates."

She just wasn't great at selling chocolates.

Actually, the time of the year didn't matter. Nor the fund-raiser, nor the child who was involved. She usually always wound up with a freezer full of chocolates herself, having bought them all just so that her child—whichever child—could receive his or her prize.

This year, it was a stupid bear. She wished to God she could just give the school a donation and buy her daughter a bear.

"Mom?" Ashley queried with her eyes huge. She squeezed Julie's hand. Julie looked at her daughter. Six. It was a wonderful age. Ashley was getting so very smart, so articulate, and so a part of the world. But she was still young enough to want to cuddle, to need help dressing now and then. It was a special age.

"I'll sell chocolates," Julie promised.

She and Julie walked to the office and received a pass from the secretary, who handed it over with pursed lips—apparently, Ashley Radcliff was arriving late at school far too often.

It was those damned ten minutes.

And Jon.

Five minutes later, she was back in the car, muttering dire warnings and a few obscenities at the people driving in front of her. Luckily—since people had been known to come to blows and actually fire shots off in Greater Miami traffic jams—her windows were closed and the air conditioner in the car was blasting. It should be cooling down. It was December, for God's sake. Nearly Christmas. The heat was just awful. She'd be happy as a lark to agree with Jon—that they needed to escape to nice, snowy, rural Virginia for a cool-down Christmas— if only she could bear her husband.

Which, at the moment, she couldn't.

But then, Jon was aware of that fact. And knew exactly why she felt the way she did.

"Why, you idiot! You had a mile, a *mile*!" she advised the driver in front of her. The little Chevy Corsica had dawdled coming up to the light at U.S. 1—and missed it. She was going to have to sit through another.

She closed her eyes. A minor problem. Completely minor. She'd be fifteen minutes late instead of ten. Which wouldn't matter all that terribly much, except that she was meeting the Pearsons. And the Pearsons were never late. And not just that—the Pearsons were interested in a very expensive house. Her commission from the sale of such a house would allow her to rub Jon's nose in the fact that her income was *not* inconsequential.

She leaned her head against the steering wheel, suddenly hating herself and wishing that she weren't so awfully bitter. Especially at Christmastime. That, too, she managed to blame on someone other than herself that morning. It was society. Christmas was purely commercial, and people were meaner and greedier than ever at Christmas. All in a bigger hurry to get to the malls, ruder than ever in traffic, downright nasty when stealing parking spaces.

When she found herself in a sorry-for-herself kind of mood, she usually remembered her father, his worn but handsome face serious as he would tell her, "Fish sticks may not be great, but lots of starving children in China would love to have them." They didn't have a whole, whole lot, he would say frequently, but they did have each other. They were alive and well and together. Look at the terrible things that could happen in life.

Well, a terrible thing had happened. Her father had died of cancer. Her mother still reminded her that her father had lived a good life, and that he had died before his children, the natural way. She shouldn't grieve so terribly, because he'd lived to see his grandchildren.

In honor of her father, she could usually tell

herself that everything was okay in her world—they were all alive and well and together for Christmas.

Right. The hell with that. She didn't want to be anywhere near Jon for Christmas. Unless, of course, she could watch him being crucified in lieu of Christ on a cross somewhere.

Blasphemy, her mother would say.

But her mom, bless her, had just remarried after five years alone, and she was on her honeymoon for Christmas. Just as well. Julie didn't want her mother with her for Christmas. She could never hide her feelings from her mother. She wasn't even able to hide them from her children.

The strident honking of a horn caused her to jump in her seat. The light had changed. She glanced in her rearview mirror. The driver behind her had a few choice blasphemies for her, she could tell. She couldn't hear him, of course, but his face was beet-red and his mouth was moving a mile a minute. She wasn't a great lip-reader, but she was pretty darn certain she could pick out "Asshole woman driver."

She gunned her way through the intersection, tempted to roll her window down first and tell him what he could do to himself. Except that she hadn't been paying attention to the traffic. Her own guilt in the matter made her feel all the more argumentative—and all the more like crying.

Coming into the curve off of Ponce, she was forced to slam on her brakes as the man she called Cruddy-Disgusting-Joe suddenly ambled out into the road. "Cruddy" and "disgusting" were certainly not part of the man's given name, nor was Joe, probably, but Julie had given him the name long ago, partly in fear, partly in disgust. He was actually a pathetic creature, a homeless misfit who lived in a halfway house near the South Miami area and spent his days walking back and forth, back and forth, around about a five-mile radius. His clothes were rags; he never shaved. He was dirty and thin. When she was walking, she gave him a wide berth. When she was with Ashley, she didn't even like her young daughter in the same basic cubicles of air. She kept trying to tell herself he was just sad; something about him still made her skin crawl.

Today, he just stared at her, unseeing, as the car behind her failed to stop as quickly as she had. It screeched, and bumped her.

Cruddy-Disgusting-Joe just ambled on across the street. The skinny young woman whose convertible had just crashed into the bumper of Julie's minivan leapt out of her car, hurling obscenities at Julie.

"Damn it, I couldn't hit the man!" Julie shouted back, leaping down from her own front seat.

The young woman, with her dark hair swirled in an attractive bun on top of her head, suddenly paused. "Maybe you should have hit him! Christmas present to the city!" she muttered.

She stared at the front of her car. "Hey, it was just the bumpers. No damage, right?"

Julie's left rear light had been smashed but what the hell. If she called the cops or her insurance company, her premiums would just go up anyway.

"No damage," she said dully.

The young woman grinned broadly and slipped back into her car. She gunned the motor and sped around Julie, nearly hitting the car that had started to go around the two of them.

Horns blared. Despite their mechanical nature, they sounded absolutely vicious.

Julie hurried back into her own car and drove away, unblocking the road.

By the time she walked into her office, her mood was supremely sour.

Still, she was determined not to inflict her personal woes on anyone at work.

Millie Garcia, Julie's broker and mentor and boss, short and bustling with iron-gray hair and a will to match, had paused by Jack Taylor—the retiree who had tired of fishing and come to work as secretary at the front desk in the small realty firm where Julie worked. They both looked at Julie as she entered.

Jack offered her a smile. "Julie, good morning, how's it going?"

"Fine, thanks," Julie lied, offering them a cheerful smile. Why was it that people so seldom answered that question honestly? *How's it going? It sucks!*

People seldom answered so honestly, she thought, because most of the time, those who asked the question didn't really want the real answer to it. It was polite conversation, nothing more.

"Oh, yeah!" Millie murmured. "Sweetie, you look just about as great as a legless heron!"

"Millie's having a bad day—just warning you," Jack said wryly.

"Julie's most obviously having a bad day as well," Millie said indignantly. "In my case, you'll never understand!"

"Hot flashes," Jack explained. He shrugged. "Women are not easy to work with. They go from PMS to hot flashes. Never a dull moment."

"Tell Julie what's going on," Millie said firmly.

Julie's smile faded. "I'm late. I'm assuming the Pearsons have been waiting?"

A grin curved Jack's lips and his dignified small white mustache twitched. He shook his head. "No, Julie, the Pearsons are not waiting. It's Christmas for you this morning. Dan Pearson's on the phone right now—and I saw you walking toward the door a split second before telling him you hadn't arrived yet. I told him that you'd just stepped outside to see if he and his missus were on the way. You can pick up on line five."

"You're worth your weight in gold, Jack," Julie told him.

"Maybe Pearson's had a heart attack or something," Millie mused.

Jack arched a brow, staring at Millie. "He sounded fit as a fiddle."

"Must be the wife," Millie said. "Women always do seem to suffer the most."

Jack arched his other brow. "Millie, you need to wear that BEWARE OF BITCH sign your realtors bought for your desk. Maybe," Jack suggested to Julie, "the Pearsons are just running late."

"I don't think so," Julie said warily. They could set time by Dan Pearson's schedule, so something must have come up. "But thank God for small mercies!" she added. She started around Jack's desk to reach her own small office. She paused long enough to shrug at Millie and plant a kiss on Jack's snow-white head before hurrying into her office to snatch up the phone receiver and hit the fifth button.

"Mr. Pearson, hi, it's Julie. Is something wrong?"

For a moment, her heart thudded painfully. What if nothing was wrong? What if he had just decided she wasn't a good enough realtor to handle his needs?

"Julie, I'm sorry, I know your mornings are busy, and I hate to ask for a postponement, but are you available right after lunch? Rita had a toothache last night and the dentist agreed to see her right away this morning."

Julie eased into the chair behind her desk. There was a God. "Mr. Pearson, just let me check . . . yes, yes, this afternoon will be fine. Say one o'clock?"

"Perfect. Again, my apologies."

"Think nothing of it, Mr. Pearson, nothing at all. Toothaches are absolutely terrible. And if this afternoon doesn't work out, I'll understand as well. I don't want Rita suffering through a showing if her mouth is killing her."

On the other end of the line, Pearson sighed. "I really wanted the perfect place by Christmas, you know?"

"And Mr. Pearson, the Trendmark property could be just perfect. But don't worry—I won't show it to anyone else until I've gotten you out there this afternoon."

Pearson thanked her. She set the receiver back into its cradle. She glanced up. Jack was standing in her office doorway, smiling. She grinned ruefully in return, shaking her head. Jack was a godsend himself. Seventy, tall, slender, extremely dignified, he was always like the Rock of Gibraltar. He'd been in banking, and was incredibly knowledgeable about real estate. Despite the fact that he was woefully overqualified for his job, he appeared to enjoy it very much. He'd bailed Julie out of problem situations a dozen times, and he'd constantly refused to accept the most minimal percentage on one of her properties.

"See, you do have some kind of a heavenly guardian looking over you," Jack said.

She lifted her hands. What the hell. Maybe sometimes people really cared. And wanted the truth.

"A guardian? Now that's amazing," she said. "Because so far, you can't imagine how badly this morning has sucked."

"Wow. And it's only nine-fifteen."

"And I've won a reprieve."

"Want coffee?"

"Sure. It should be de—"

"Mrs. Radcliff, I wouldn't think of offering you anything that wasn't completely decaffeinated."

Jack left her doorway. Julie glanced down at her desk. The advertisement her husband had been insisting she read was on top of a pile of stats on property values she'd drawn from the computer right before going home last night. She frowned, not remembering that she'd left it on top of everything else. She'd been arguing with him about going away; for the first time in all the ups and downs of her married life, she'd made an appointment with a divorce attorney. She hadn't exactly made the decision as to what she wanted to do, but she did want to know her legal options.

Going away for Christmas seemed like putting a Band-Aid on a gushing artery.

Still, Jon's one argument did make sense. "You can give the kids a last family Christmas. Surely, two more weeks won't matter in your plan to destroy everything."

Bitter. They were both so bitter. Blaming one another for every little thing that went wrong.

"Enjoy Tradition!" the ad in the historical magazine blazed boldly. Julie picked up the advertisement and eased back in her chair. "Worn out by the bustle of a modern, commercial Christmas? Come to Oak River Plantation for the most special family Christmas of a lifetime. Yuletide carols, chestnuts on an open fire. We guarantee snow, sleigh rides, and an absolutely unique holiday experience."

There was a picture of the house. *Oak River Plantation.* Small, as such places went, but very pretty, and certainly picturesque. Snow settled around a porch bordered by Greek pillars. Horses ambled about in a paddock in front of the house. A fire could be seen blazing behind the panes of a front room window. Its warmth seemed to radiate from the picture.

Naturally. It was an advertisement.

Jack came back into her office, setting her coffee on her desk.

"Husband Jon, line four," he said.

Julie stared down at her cup quickly, wincing. She nodded. Jack left her office; she picked up her phone line.

"Yes?" she said curtly.

He was silent so long she thought she'd picked up the wrong line.

"I take it you made it in close to on time, despite the fact that you were overburdened with our daughter?" Jon said at last.

"I'm not overburdened with my daughter. I'm overburdened by the fact that my husband somehow manages to avoid morning traffic on a daily basis."

"Julie, I had to be in court—"

"And yesterday, you had to be in a meeting with Tom. The day before, you had to be in a meeting with Harry—"

"Julie, it isn't the driving," Jon argued quietly.

"Right. Maybe it's the fact that you never fill out the chocolate sales sheets."

"We don't sell the chocolates. We buy them."

"I still have to make up a bunch of lies on those sheets. Then, what else? You never fill out the school forms, you come to Jordan's ball games when you're ready, not an hour before for practice. You—"

"Julie, I can drive the kids tomorrow."

Tears stung Julie's eyes. "Well, you won't need to take Christie. Her boyfriend is picking her up."

"You allow that? She's still a minor, and she may think she's an adult, but she's only seventeen, just barely seventeen at that, and he's—"

"He's from a broken home and lives in an apartment complex that should be condemned. Fine—you tell her she's not allowed to see him. I wanted her to date a kid already determined on a career in medicine rather than one who may still be innocent himself but lives between crack houses. But I've got news for you. One year is damned close to eighteen, and if you want to have any influence with your daughter when she is a legal adult—"

"What is my influence going to matter then if you've already killed her?"

Julie drew the phone from her ear, stunned. She hung up the receiver.

Half the buttons on her phone were lighting up. She laid her head on her arms.

Jack came back into the room.

"Jon again, three this time."

"Tell him—"

"Julie, I'm not a good liar," Jack said apologetically. "Talk to him. You kids will work it out."

"That's just it, Jack. We're not kids."

But she picked up her receiver again.

"Yes?"

"Julie, I'm sorry."

"Are you? I think you meant what you said. You think I'm too permissive, and I'm going to kill one of our kids."

"I said I'm sorry."

She was silent.

"I called to see what you'd decided about the Virginia vacation. It might be just what we need."

"Jon, we can't fix things by running away from them."

"But it would be nice to clear our heads just a little bit, don't you think?"

"I don't think that I can clear out what's in my head."

She heard him groan. "Julie, I can't pay for one mistake forever."

"One mistake. And years now in which we've been strangers."

"Look, when we get back, you can do what you want. Hell, I can't stop you anyway. But this close to Christmas, for the love of God, let's give it one shot—for the kids, even if that is a cliché. Let's take Christmas away from both our jobs, from killer traffic, from school fund-raisers, boxed lunches, faulty plumbing, and everything else."

Julie hesitated. "It's an historic mansion, right?"

"Right."

"So how do you know the plumbing won't be faulty?"

He was silent a minute, then he laughed. A pleasant sound, a laugh with no anger, guilt, or bitterness. "Okay, so I can't really guarantee the plumbing. We'll get away from the traffic—it's supposed to be really rural."

"What if it's too rural?"

"We won't be that far from D.C. We can see what the Capitol is like for Christmas."

She hesitated. "No phone calls, Jon. No clients with the phone number."

His turn to hesitate. "All right, then, here's the deal. I'm completely out of touch for the holiday, and the same with you. No Mr. Pearson in the middle of the night with something else to add to his list of requirements."

Julie hesitated. "I don't know, Jon."

"You can't give up Mr. Pearson?" he demanded.

"No, no, it's not that. . . ." She hesitated, shrugged, then said bluntly, "I just wonder if it's going to be worth my giving up Mr. Pearson."

"I see."

Julie winced. Maybe she was wrong. Just a little bit wrong, but she was angry, deeply angry; she'd been betrayed. And she couldn't give up the anger, even if he had said that he was sorry a million times, even if it had all happened in the past.

"I have the advertisement right in front of me. I'll think about it today, I promise. And if I think we can give it a shot, I'll make reservations."

"All right, I guess that's fair."

"Good."

"Julie?"

"Yes?"

"I—I—never mind. I'll see you tonight at dinner."

"Right."

She hung up. She picked up a pencil and tapped the eraser against the advertisement. It would be nice. Once upon a time, it would have been a dream vacation. Chestnuts roasting on an open fire . . . for a kid born and bred in the deep, deep, dead end of the South, the very concept was wonderfully romantic. Sleigh rides. Blanketed against the cold with someone you loved, feeling the wind, feeling the warmth . . .

The kids, of course, might be horrified. No video games, no long phone calls—for Christie, no Jamie Rodriguez. She'd want Jamie to come, of course. She'd try insisting they invite him—after all, they'd invited friends for her before, why not this friend? Hadn't they always taught her not to be prejudiced?

Why was it that everything good they tried to do backfired?

Maybe it just seemed that way. . . .

Jack was standing at her door again. She looked up at him.

"Well?"

"Well?" She stared at the coffee she hadn't touched. "Oh!" She took a sip of it. "It's great."

Jack laughed. "Not the coffee. The trip. Are you going?"

"Eavesdropper!" she accused him.

"Not on your life. I just know that you've been wrestling with this."

"So what'd ya decide, honey?" Millie asked, ducking beneath Jack's arm to enter Julie's office with a cup of fresh-brewed coffee herself, taking one of the handsome office chairs in front of Julie's desk. "Jack, take five, have a seat," Millie invited, patting the spousal or significant other seat next to her own.

Jack obliged. The two of them stared at her.

"If the two of you are in here, who's going to be answering the telephones?" she asked politely.

"Casey Edwards is in—she doesn't mind," Millie said. Her eyes were as gray as her hair, very stern at the moment. "Now, you should go on a Christmas holiday."

Julie wasn't certain whether she should be resentful of her employer's busybody and dictatorial attitude, or grateful that she did have such a warm and personable place to work.

She decided on the latter.

"Selling to the Pearsons is really, really important to me," she said. "Quite frankly, I'm afraid to leave."

"Jack, comment, please," Millie commanded. "God, I wish I still smoked."

"You don't wish you still smoked," Jack corrected her.

"The hell I don't. I could really use a cigarette now."

"Maybe you could really use a cigarette, but you're getting up there in years now, and you don't want ugly, disgusting black lungs to do you in early."

"Why did I hire you?"

"Because I'm cheap and brilliant."

"You need this holiday," Millie said to Julie.

"I need the Pearson sale," Julie said quietly.

Jack leaned forward. "You're a good realtor. You work a fairly light schedule, but you keep your family going. You're married to an attorney, Julie. You don't actually *need* the Pearson sale."

"Especially if you're planning a divorce. Community property state, you know," Millie said.

"Millie!" Jack admonished, appalled.

"The writing is on the wall," Millie said. "Take him for all he's worth!" she exclaimed.

"I thought you liked Jon," Julie said.

"She does. She's just a nasty old witch in the middle of menopause," Jack advised sagely.

"That's right, men-o-pause," Millie snapped. "And it's no fancy Latin name or the like; it means what it says—men make me pause. I hate them, and they give me lots and lots of desire to pause—before shooting the suckers all off the face of the earth and letting God sort them out."

Even Julie lifted a brow.

"Well, I didn't exactly mean that, but I am having a bad day," Millie acknowledged. "Now as to Jon—trust me, honey, men do come much worse. Not that he's perfect; who is? I don't even claim that for myself. But you go on that trip, honey. It could be really important for you right now. Go—and I mean it."

"But the Pearsons—"

"You can sell to the Pearsons today," Millie

advised. "You've got the perfect property for Dan and Rita; I can feel it in my bones."

"And I can do your follow-up work until you get back," Jack said.

"Jack, that's not fair. You won't take a percentage—"

"Julie, my wife died in '91, my son is an architect, and my daughter is a plastic surgeon. We've done all right. I've got grown-up kids—decent enough as kids go, but they've got their own lives. My financial status is just fine. I enjoy picking up some of the work—I like feeling alive and useful. Old and used up is no good, and with my wife gone, well, time hangs heavy. This sounds like a fun trip. Like a good time to take a damned good look at things before you take drastic steps, or set things into motion that you can never stop once started."

"He's right, honey. If you're going to take him for all he's worth, you've got to let him go down fighting first," Millie said.

Julie stared down at the advertisement. "Well, they might be booked already."

"Won't know till you give it a try," Jack advised. "I'll buy a chocolate bar if you give it a go."

"Ouch!" Millie protested as Jack elbowed her. "Oh, all right, all right. I'll buy a chocolate bar if you try, too. Hell, I'll buy a few of 'em."

Julie found herself smiling.

Millie stood, staring down at Jack. "Jeez, Jack, what am I paying you for? The phones are ringing off the hook." She lowered her voice. "That Casey is a downright flibbertigibbet. You just can't get good help these days!" She sighed.

Jack stood, groaning. "She doesn't need to wear that BITCH sign. She needs the words tattooed all over her body."

"That's sexist!" Millie snapped, prodding him out of Julie's office.

"I didn't say it ought to be tattooed on your breasts or fanny or anything," Jack protested.

Millie was out of the office first. Jack turned back, winking at Julie. "Her fanny's been dragged down a bit too much and too long by gravity for a decent tattoo anyway," he whispered.

Then the door to her office closed.

She sat in silence for a few minutes.

It just didn't feel like Christmas. She'd been going through most of the motions, of course. She had children. Christmas was definitely important to children.

But . . .

What was one more Christmas?

Especially, as Millie had said, if she was planning on a divorce.

She didn't know what she was planning. She only knew that she was tired. And hurt.

She sat another minute.

Then she picked up the phone and dialed the 800 number listed on the advertisement.

One more Christmas.

For the family.

Maybe the place would be completely booked. She was calling so very late. She'd hang up after another ring. . . .

But someone answered.

"Hello? Oak River Plantation."

The voice was feminine, soft, nicely modulated.

Just a bit impatient.

"Hello? Is anyone there?"

"I—yes!" Julie said quickly. "I'm calling about your Christmas holiday plan. I suppose I'm too late, but I thought I'd like to give you a try—"

"Actually, we had a cancellation just this morning," the woman said pleasantly. "Your timing is wonderful."

"Oh—oh, great. Except that . . . well, we're a family of five. Two adults, three children."

"Girls or boys?"

"My children?"

"Yes." The female voice sounded slightly amused. "Well, perhaps I'm being presumptuous in this day and age, but the way you said *family* . . . I imagined you meant your husband and yourself, and naturally I assumed your husband to be a boy. I'm sorry, a man." She sighed, struggling to get her meaning out right. "Male!"

"He is. Yes. Naturally," Julie said, and she found herself leaning back in her chair, smiling.

"I was referring to your children. Can two share a room?"

"Oh, yes, of course. I've one boy, two girls."

"You'll be perfect in the guest suite," the woman said. Her tone was lovely, her laugh captivating. The warm sound of her voice fit in perfectly with the look of the place in the advertisement. Julie felt her uncertainty slipping away.

"Good. That's—great," Julie said.

"It is a bit primitive out here," the woman warned her. "We're not difficult to find, but we are quite remote. Of course, that does add to the beauty of the place."

"That's the part we're looking forward to most," Julie assured her. No traffic. Oh, God.

One morning without traffic. That just might be a Christmas present in itself.

No Cruddy-Disgusting-Joe to walk across the road, no cars on the butt of her own to crash into her when she was forced to brake to avoid vehicular homicide—or roadkill, whichever you might want to consider Cruddy-Disgusting-Joe.

"Well, then, we'll be looking forward to seeing you. When do you expect to arrive?"

Julie thought out the distance. They'd fly into National, probably, on the same night the kids finished with their schools for the Christmas break. They'd spend a night in the D.C. area, rent a car, maybe spend some time in D.C., and drive out in the afternoon. How far could it be? She looked down at her calendar, trying to figure out the holidays. "We'll arrive . . . the night of the twenty-second?" she suggested.

"That's fine, Mrs. . . . ?"

"Julie. Sorry, Radcliff. Julie Radcliff. My—husband's name is Jon."

"Great. We'll see you for Christmas!" the woman said.

The line went dead. Julie hung it up. She brooded over her decision for a minute, then determined she needed to study her new multiple-listings book. She looked at the book, then realized she wasn't seeing anything.

Christmas. Wouldn't it have been better if she had just said No, it's falling apart, let's just end it now, cleanly?

Something inside of her rebelled against doing that. The vacation would be good. She'd have chestnuts before a roaring fire.

With a husband she couldn't forgive.

She snapped her multiple-listings book shut and tapped into her computer. She needed some busy work. She needed to sound intelligent and informed this afternoon when she attempted to sell property.

It was a half hour later, and she was in the middle of computer comparisons on Gables waterway houses, when she realized the woman hadn't asked her for a credit card number to hold the reservation.

She dialed the number back.

"Hello? Oak River Plantation."

"Hi, this is me again. Julie—"

"Radcliff. Yes, hello again! What can I do for you?"

"I just wanted to guarantee our reservation."

"I beg your pardon?"

"I need to give you a credit card number. To guarantee our reservation."

"That isn't necessary, Mrs. Radcliff."

"Really?" Julie stared at the phone. Every hotel, motel, and bed-and-breakfast in the country—from five-star establishment to broken-down flea joint— seemed to require a guarantee these days.

"I'm sure we'll see you as planned."

"Yes, but don't—"

The woman's musical laugh sounded. "Mrs. Radcliff, we only want our guests if they want to be here. If something comes up, do please call; that's all we ask. And we are looking forward to meeting you, of course. Till the twenty-second, then?"

"Till the twenty-second," Julie agreed.

She replaced the receiver slowly. The day was improving. Human nature did, at times, prevail, so it seemed.

She felt just a little bit better about her smashed rear light.

But later, when she came out of the office to drive down the street for a quick bite of lunch, Cruddy-Disgusting-Joe was sitting on her bumper. He was nibbling at a half-eaten burger he probably got from the Dumpster at the far side of the parking lot.

She slowed down, then tried not to shudder as she walked toward her car. He looked up from his burger.

He stared at her with his colorless eyes, the left lid slashed by a scar.

He certainly didn't appear to recognize her from that morning, but he did seem to know that he was sitting on her car and that she needed to drive it.

He stood, crumpled up the wrapper in his hand, looked to the ground, and ambled away.

Poor man! she tried to tell herself.

So pathetic. He needs help.

But her shudder continued on the inside.

Poor man, poor man, poor man.

She knew she was going to have to get her car washed when she got the rear light fixed.

Chapter Two

Christmas Eve
1862

She sat in a rocking chair on her cousin's front porch just outside Front Royal.

Rocking, sewing—Confederate wives were constantly sewing these days—and waiting.

He would come. He would come because it was Christmas Eve. He would come because he had a way of getting leave at just the right moments, because he could move so quickly. So damned quickly. He was the ultimate horseman, an extraordinary cavalry officer, and his field of war was the field of his home. He knew every inch of the terrain. Perhaps other men could not move so quickly, but he could. He could come, he would come. He would come, because he knew that she would be worried, so anxious about him, about their boy. He would come, because they had parted so badly. . . .

Maybe he wouldn't come.

He would! she assured herself.

If only . . .

She jabbed her needle angrily through the shirt

she was mending. She stuck her fingertip, drawing blood. A sharp yelp of dismay escaped her.

Oh, God! If only they hadn't fought with such anger.

But she was so weary of this war!

Oh, they'd all been such hotheads when it all began, the Southern men. Because they did know how to ride, and they did know how to hunt—though now they tracked men instead of game. They believed that they fought for states' rights—she believed they were fools. They saw themselves far too easily as romantic heroes—the direct descendants of their founding fathers. "We are just the same as our forebears!" the captain had told her angrily. "George Washington, our founding father, risked his neck daily to free the colonies from tyranny. Patrick Henry cried, 'Give me liberty, or give me death!' Thomas Jefferson wrote the Declaration of Independence, and I tell you, my love, these men weren't just our founding fathers—they were Virginians. If they were alive today, they would be heading up the very battle we fight now."

Perhaps a great number of the Southern men believed they fought for states' rights—but they were wrong. It was an economic war—even if a mere woman wasn't supposed to see such things. The South was dependent on slavery. She pointed out to the captain that Thomas Jefferson, who had written the Declaration of Independence, had been well aware that the issue of slavery would raise its ugly head soon enough. He—like *the* founding father, George Washington himself—had freed his slaves *at his death*. Neither Jefferson nor Washington had brought about the freedom issue while still being served in this life. The simple point was that slavery was wrong, and men who seemed to know that very fact somehow managed to ignore it.

She wished to God that Washington and Jefferson had somehow managed to take the bull by the horns and settle the matter *during* their lifetimes!

But men . . . men would be men.

Stubborn, determined. Narrow-sighted.

Like the captain. He had taken his boys and signed up with Mosby. They were the Gray Ghosts of the Confederacy and could ride circles around the Northern forces; they so often thought themselves invincible, even when they had seen so much death and carnage already. The beautiful hills and valleys, mountainside and coastline of Virginia all raged with battle, and few living there had been left untouched. She had left her own home time and time again, aware that Northern troops were advancing in the area. The Northern troops were frequently enough in and around Front Royal. The difference here was that she was not alone, and at Christmas she had determined not to be at her home alone with her daughter should the Yankees choose to seek a fine, warm Southern plantation for their December headquarters.

Her fingers moved deftly upon her sewing again. Pride, she mourned suddenly. She sat here mocking the captain for his pride, when it was really her pride that had brought her here. She'd been so angry with him. And he'd refused to see things her way. So she had left their home. The Yankees might indeed take her house—that was no idle fear. But they would come, and they would go. They would steal everything in sight, but it would be most unlikely that they would hurt her. She had left the house because she so desperately wanted her husband to follow her, to come to her.

And now, she just wanted to see him.

How easy it had been before the war to take advantage of one another! To lose patience with each other.

She was so sorry.

If she could just see his face . . . see him ride up to her now! So tall and handsome, so quick to smile. Not perfect in any way, but neither was she. He was just the man she loved, for his many valiant qualities, and even for his faults. The way he could make her laugh on those few occasions when he managed to say that he was wrong, and apologize.

His face . . . oh, God, just to see his face . . .

She jumped up suddenly, staring down the roadway. A horseman appeared on the road. He was dressed in a gray wool frock coat, she could see that much, slouch hat pulled low over his features.

For a moment, her heart soared.

He had come. He had ridden through the forest to keep himself hidden, and he had taken one of the narrow trails known only to the men who came from these parts. He had appeared on the roadway just in front of the house, coming with the greatest secrecy. The captain, her captain . . .

But it wasn't the captain. Even at a distance, far before she could realize she wasn't seeing his beloved features, she knew it wasn't her husband. This man rode differently. He didn't sit quite as tall, he didn't stare straight and hard ahead. He rode nervously, anxiously looking behind himself time and time again.

His horse suddenly broke into a canter, and he turned through the gateway of the picket fence leading to her cousin's house.

"Mrs. Captain!" She heard herself hailed in the way that his men had come to reverently address her.

It was young Lawrence Boulet, she saw, a sergeant from her husband's company. Beneath the Rebel-issue frock coat draped around his shoulders—probably taken from a fallen regular-army man—he wore dark trousers and shirt, and well-worn boots. He rode hard to the very steps of the porch, then drew his mount to a sudden halt.

And it was then that it seemed her heart ceased to beat. The captain hadn't come.

This boy had come.

No, something deep within her cried. If the captain had been killed, she would know, she would know deep down in her heart. He couldn't have been killed; they wouldn't be fighting major battles now in this kind of cold, in the winter, at Christmastime. . . .

But the captain was one of Mosby's Rangers. They fought skirmishes, they hounded the Yank army, they stole supplies, and they fought at any given time. But she would know! In her heart, she would know if he had been killed!

"The captain?" she whispered. "Lawrence, where is the captain? He is all right?"

"I've—I've come for you," Lawrence stuttered. "There was a skirmish. The captain and his group managed to steal nearly a hundred Federal horses and a good stock of medical supplies. But when they were trying to escape . . . a group of Custer's men came down on them. They were outnumbered ten to one. The boys have all told me that you can ride well and quickly—"

"Lawrence, how is the captain? Damn you!" she swore, shocking the boy, though she wondered how anything could shock anyone after the years of war. "Lawrence, you tell me now, does the captain live?"

Lawrence exhaled. "Yes, Mrs. Captain—" he began, and in her relief she stumbled to the porch post to hold on so that she wouldn't fall. "But—"

"Oh, my God, but what?"

Lawrence blinked back tears. "He's been sentenced to hang within the next few hours. He's—"

"Hang?" Oh, God, yes, she'd heard about Custer's ultimatums regarding Mosby's Men. But she'd never believed that the captain might be caught!

"Mrs. Captain, we've got to ride fast if you're to see him. I can only take you so far, then you'll be on your own," Lawrence whispered miserably. "Maybe—maybe you can find some way to stop them."

She stared at him for a split second, then ran down the steps. Lawrence offered her a hand and she leapt up on his mount behind him, her heart racing. "How far do we have to go?" she demanded, slipping her arms around him to hold on for the ride.

He hesitated again, then turned his head slightly,

angling his face toward her. "Oak River Plantation, Mrs. Captain. I've—I've just got to get you home."

She was twelve, nearly thirteen, nearly a woman. She heard her mother's voice, heard the soldier.

Heard what had happened.

Saw her mother ride away.

No!

She raced for the door.

Aunt Rachel came running down the stairs. "Wait, sweetheart, where are you going—"

"My mother has just ridden—"

"You must stay here."

She should fight Aunt Rachel. She never did such things, of course, but these were desperate circumstances. She knew it, deep in her heart. She had to follow her mother.

Or never see her father alive again. She knew.

Aunt Rachel wasn't that much bigger than she was.

Uncle Andrew was.

Hmm . . .

"Fine, Aunt Rachel," she said, subdued. She lowered her head. "I'll wait by the window."

"I'll find Uncle Andrew and he'll see to it that we find out just what's going on," Aunt Rachel promised.

She nodded, and pretended to be the perfect

lady, sitting with tremendous protocol on the love seat by the bay window.

She waited, with outward impatience.

Until Aunt Rachel was gone.

Then she fled from the house.

She was going to follow her mother.

She was going home.

Chapter Three

There were extra cars in front of Jon Radcliff's house when he finally made it home. He swore softly to himself. The last thing he wanted tonight was company, and surely Julie would know that.

But then, Julie didn't care a heck of a lot what he wanted anymore.

He irritably switched off the ignition of his car and sat staring at the house for a minute, hearing the echo of whatever tune had been playing on the radio.

Court had been horrible. The meeting with his fellow counselors afterward had been worse. After all his years of schooling and now more than fifteen years as a practicing attorney, he was still just learning to accept the fact that the law wasn't perfect, that there was often no way that justice was going to prevail. Deep in his heart he believed that, though the system wasn't perfect, it was still the best to be had in the modern world. Guilty men might walk, but the law tried very hard to see to it that innocent men didn't hang—or weren't electrocuted, executed by lethal injection, or cut down by a firing squad. Or even incarcerated unfairly. Still, it was damned hard to see it when a guilty man went free because of a technicality, which was stupid.

Until five years ago, he had worked in the D.A.'s office, and though he'd been exhausted and underpaid, he'd been happy.

Then he'd had a great job offer. And he'd gone from being a prosecutor to being a defense attorney for one of the most prestigious law firms in town.

And now he was defending Bobo Vinzetti. They called it the Vinzetti pizza case—the media had started it, now the people on the streets followed the media. It was a horrendous case. In Jon's opinion, Bobo Vinzetti—decked out in a ski mask to disguise himself—had willfully and with malicious intent attempted to smother his philandering wife with a cheese and pepperoni pizza. But Jon was obliged by the law to defend Vinzetti, and that very fact was making him crazy. His cocounselors thought he was insane. Defense attorneys defended the accused. That was life. It was unlikely Bobo Vinzetti would ever attempt to kill again, his cocounselors said. His wife intended to divorce him and move to Tahiti the minute the case was over.

Bobo should be no threat to society. Unless, of course, he were to marry a philandering blonde once again.

Jon's firm was trying hard to get a continuance on the case. They had agreed the best course of action would be for Vinzetti to admit his guilt and make a plea—since the pizza trail led straight to him despite the disguise he had worn.

Vinzetti, however, was certain that good attorneys could get him off.

And he might just be right.

The fact that the entire country—other than the city in which he lived and worked—was having a good laugh over the case didn't much help Jon's continual feeling of absolute frustration.

And his wife was certainly no help whatsoever.

Sometimes, he was desperate to talk.

She was never willing to listen.

If she wanted a divorce so damned badly, he should just give it to her. She was making his life a living hell as it was. If she didn't understand anything about him anymore, it was probably time that they did move on. Why the hell didn't he just give it up?

Because he loved his home. He loved Ashley throwing her arms around his neck when he came in the door. He was continually aggravated by the teenage Jordan and Christie, but sometimes they'd just walk across the room and he'd be proud. Christie was almost all grown up and beautiful, a carbon copy of Julie twenty years ago. Jordan was going to be tall. He wasn't a great athlete, but he loved sports, liked people, and was a great-looking kid with a pleasant manner to match. He had no interest in the law at all, but he loved biology, and if his mind could just maintain a semblance of direction . . .

He might be headed for med school.

Right. He loved his kids. His wife was torturing him, but he loved his kids.

He took a deep breath. He loved his wife as well. They had lost something, and what they had lost might have been his fault. Was his fault—in her eyes. But she wouldn't take an apology for what he had done, much less a suggestion that she just might have driven him to his actions. And still . . .

He did love Julie.

Even if right now she was . . .

"The worst bitch this side of heaven or hell!" he muttered, sliding out of his car at last, his briefcase in hand.

He had barely stepped out of his car when Sam, their neighbors' Saint Bernard, came loping around to the front of the house.

"No, Sam!" he shouted.

Too late. Sam came rocketing toward the car,

jumping up to slam Jon against it. With his massive, sticky tongue, he licked Jon's face from chin to forehead.

"Get down, you lunk!" Jon demanded, pushing at Sam's gigantic barrel chest. Sam had enough dog spit to drown a human with a single lick. "Sam!"

His voice was firm and hard and Sam fell to all fours, wagging his lethal tail a mile a minute.

"Sam, Sam!" Mari Twigs, the skinny little twelve-year-old from next door who considered herself Sam's master, came running into the yard. "Oh, Mr. Radcliff, I am so, so sorry!" she gasped.

He wanted to yell. He wanted to tell her to keep her moose-dog creature in her own yard, but somehow, he counted to ten. "Mari, get him home, huh?"

Mari nodded gravely. She clutched Sam's collar. The dog started to drag her home, but she was still looking at Jon, giggling.

"Um, there's just a bit of mud on your shirt, Mr. Radcliff," Mari said. "Sam's sorry though, really sorry."

"Yeah, Sam's sorry," Jon muttered, heading into the house.

He banged on the front door, but no one answered. He could hear an old Doors number blaring from his daughter's stereo system. He fumbled in his pockets for his keys, then realized the door wasn't locked. Swearing, he entered his front hallway.

He tripped over his son's Rollerblades, nearly falling himself, sending the Rollerblades sliding so that they knocked against the foyer table. The vase upon it crashed to the floor.

Still, no one appeared.

"Hello, I'm home!" he called out.

Right. As Christie would say, *Like anyone cared!*

Skirting the smashed vase, he made his way through the handsome sunken living room, the dining room, through the pantry, and into the kitchen. Julie was leaning against the refrigerator, sipping a glass of champagne. Millie Garcia— dragon woman—was seated at the kitchen table, and old Jack Taylor was at the sink, working at the cork of another champagne bottle. Ashley was cutting the napkins into tiny pieces with her new plastic scissors, and Jordan had his gerbils running around on the kitchen counter. No one seemed to notice Jon as of yet—the strains of "Light My Fire" weren't quite as loud here, but they were still more audible than the sound of footsteps.

Jon discovered that he was almost uncontrollably angry. Whatever the hell had happened to a home being a man's castle? Hell, he didn't need a damned castle, just a quiet refuge from the storm.

He strode into the kitchen, tossing his briefcase

on the table and loosening his tie. It probably didn't help that the temperature seemed to be holding at an all-time high for December. "Hello, darling," he told Julie, who looked startled and unhappy at his arrival. Julie would be thirty-eight on her next birthday; somehow, she still managed at times to look no more than a woman of twenty or so. She stayed very slim, and her face was a classic oval that never seemed to age. Her blue eyes had gone from an excited, exuberant bright shade to a dark and guarded one the second she had seen him. Her smile had faded. If there had not been others in the room, he was certain she would have moved away when he planted a quick kiss on her lips. As it was, he was certain that she'd cringed.

He could damned well guarantee she didn't pucker in return.

But he didn't care right then. He opened the refrigerator, drawing out a beer even as Millie offered him champagne.

"Naw, thanks, I'll stick to the classless stuff in the can," Jon told her. "What's the celebration?" he asked, taking a long swallow and staring at his wife. God, he was starving. He'd skipped lunch to get to his meeting faster. Now one swallow of beer and he felt a strange buzz in his head. No food. He'd better be careful. The kitchen might smell of champagne, but there wasn't the first scent of food within it.

Julie didn't answer; she was swallowing champagne, a big swallow of it.

"Jon, your wife made her first half-million-dollar sale today," Millie told him. "She sold the Pearsons the Trendmark house in the Gables."

He arched a brow to Julie, feeling the strangest sinking sensation. Well, hell. He didn't think that he was that much of a chauvinist. He wanted her to be a success, right? Or did he?

Honestly—no. So far, he'd thought that maybe she was holding on to him for the money. Not in a really greedy way—just holding on because his was the income that kept the home and the kids in good shape. His was the income that would send Christie—then Jordan and Ashley in good time—to college. *And admit it, old buddy!* he told himself. He had wanted her to need him for that income.

He lifted his beer can to Julie. "Here, here! Congratulations!"

He set his beer down. Not to kiss his wife again. One brush of cold lips was enough for the moment. He went to the table and slipped his arms around Ashley. She looked up from her industrious cutting at last. "Daddy!"

"Ash. Napkins aren't for cutting, huh?" He

kissed the top of her head. "Jordan—get the rodents out of the kitchen," he said firmly.

His son, tall for his age, a nice-looking combination of him and Julie, with his green eyes and Julie's light blond hair, looked up guiltily.

Jon glanced to Julie. His glance, he was certain, was condemning, and he just couldn't manage to care that he was going to aggravate her further. "Julie, what's he doing with the rats in the kitchen?" he grated.

She was going to hate him for that. She hated to be humiliated in any way in front of Millie. Millie was the next best thing to the Messiah in Julie's eyes. He didn't care. No matter what the celebration, the gerbils didn't belong in the damned kitchen.

"They're not rats, Daddy," Ashley corrected, "they're gerbils."

"One and the same, honey," Jon said.

"They weren't hurting anything," Jordan protested, eyeing him evilly.

Right. Jordan's mother was the good parent, willing to overlook the small things.

"I love the gerbils, Daddy," Ashley said.

"But you're going to get gerbil poopies in your peanut butter sandwiches if you're not careful!" Jack Taylor warned.

"Get them out of the kitchen, Jordan," Jon said firmly.

Jordan obeyed. Ashley started to laugh, pointing at Jon's shirt and jacket. "Daddy, you have marks all over you. Are those gerbil poopies?"

"No. It's mad-dog muck," Jon said.

"Mad-dog muck?" Ashley asked.

Even Jack Taylor was smiling then. "It does look like your latest client was a mountain lion out for blood," Jack said ruefully.

Jon tried to smile. "Yeah, right. My last client was that Saint Bernard. Julie, haven't you asked the neighbors to please keep that animal in their own yard?"

"I've asked them, Jon," she said. Her tone was abrasive.

"Daddy, I like Sam in our yard!" Ashley wailed. Her eyes welled with tears. She stared at him as if he were planning to send her best friend away. Jordan suddenly swore as he dropped a gerbil. Jon snapped at him quickly. Before Jordan could apologize, a door slammed from elsewhere in the house. Jon frowned and started back through to the living room in time to see his elder daughter chasing out after the dark-haired kid who was hurrying from her bedroom toward the front door.

"Christie!" he thundered.

She stopped. The dark-haired kid had already

gotten out. Christie looked fearfully from the door to her father as if he were the worst possible nuisance imaginable.

"What!" she snapped out.

"What the hell were you doing in your bedroom with a boy?"

"Playing the stereo. I've got to go, Dad, I've—"

"Get back in here."

"I can't. He's going to think—"

"Want to hear what the hell I'm thinking?" he demanded. His fists were clenched at his sides. He was about to blow a gasket. He had to get himself under control. "I think that I'd better not see a male coming out of that side of the house again, unless you want to find yourself grounded until your twenty-first birthday!" he raged at her.

Christie gasped. Good. He hoped that he was rattling her, damned hard. She had on too much makeup, and her little plaid skirt was too short. And she was too thin. She was dieting for her boyfriend, or so it seemed. All the fool girls wanted to be toothpicks.

"Mom knew I was in there with Jamie. We were just listening to music."

"Just listening to music."

"Mom knows enough to trust me."

"I don't want boys in your bedroom."

"Why, Dad?" she demanded belligerently, hands

on her hips. "Why can't you just trust me in my own house with my own family in it? You just hate Jamie, and you just hate him because he's different. What, Dad? You think I can't sleep with a guy in a car, a park, an alley, somewhere else, anywhere else?"

He froze. His temptation was to walk over to his daughter and give her a sharp slap across the face.

He didn't do it.

"Because this is my house, and you're my daughter, and I've told you that you won't have boys in your room, and that's that," he told her. "Because I damned well said so!" he added furiously.

His anger left him quickly. He felt weary, deflated. It wouldn't work, he thought. She was just going to ignore him and go racing after her boyfriend, and then what was he going to do?

They stared at one another. Damnation, but she was another Julie. Her mother's eyes seemed to stare at him as she defied him. She tossed back a length of her beautiful blond hair. Then she suddenly cried out, "I hate you, Dad. I hate you, hate you, hate you!"

Hate you . . .

God, did they all really hate him? What the hell had he done that was so very wrong? All he really wanted to do was love and provide for his family! He hadn't erred that far; it had been damned miserable and he'd only looked for someone else back then because . . .

Julie hadn't wanted him. Not then. At least, he hadn't thought that she wanted him.

And his ego had been at stake.

Christie ran past him. He heard her bedroom door slam.

Millie and Jack came into the living room, Julie following quietly behind them.

"You've been home five minutes," Julie said lightly, "and everybody's happy."

"I'm so damned sorry if I upset the gerbils," Jon snapped.

Julie's eyes were ice-blue with cool contempt.

"These kids can't just do whatever the hell they feel like doing while you're celebrating, Julie," he said.

"They weren't doing anything that terrible," she grated back.

"Well, well, busy day!" Jack said, brushing aside the darkening words between them. Jack offered Jon a kindly smile. "We're going to be getting out of your hair, Jon," Jack added. "Let you have your home back."

"It was a great sale," Millie said, smiling as she gave him a kiss on the cheek. "Your wife made a really, truly, great sale!"

"You're right, she did," Jon heard himself saying.

"So where are you two going? Such a great sale can't have been fully celebrated already."

Jack Taylor started to frown; Millie arched a brow. "Jon," Julie began uneasily, "Millie and Jack were just on their way out—"

"That's silly. Hey, we owe Julie a real celebration, right? We'll go out somewhere great to dinner. How does that sound?" Jon demanded.

"No, no!" Jack protested.

"You and Julie should celebrate," Millie said.

"Don't be silly—trust me, Julie would be crushed if you didn't come with us."

He didn't add that Julie would surely just as soon *not* celebrate with him.

As it was, Julie didn't look thrilled; again, it didn't matter. Jon walked around into the kitchen area, calling to his younger children. "Ash, Jordan, wash up, quick. We're going to take Mommy out to dinner. Oh—Jordan, go call Christie. Tell her we're taking Mom out."

Jordan, hands filled with gerbils, frowned. Ashley jumped up, giving him a hug and kiss at last. "Good, Daddy. Can we go to Chuck E. Cheese's?"

"Well, I'm not sure Chuck E. Cheese's would be Mommy's pick for a restaurant, and tonight is just for her. We'll get to Chuck E. Cheese's soon, though, I promise."

"Right. Mommy will get to take you." His wife's

dry voice sounded from directly behind him. He hadn't realized that she had followed him back to the kitchen.

She backed off somewhat when he spun around. The absolute dry and bitter edge left her voice when she spoke. "Jon, this isn't necessary. Jack and Millie bought me champagne. And I think that Christie will refuse to go. The rest of us aren't really dressed, and you're wearing paw prints."

"Two minutes and I'll have on a clean shirt and jacket," he said curtly.

Julie looked as if she were about to protest.

"Mommy, Mommy, we're going out special for *you*!" Ashley cried happily. "I'm so happy! It's like your birthday." She diverted Julie's cold gaze from Jon's eyes.

"Oh, yeah. Just like," Julie said.

"I'll just be a minute," Jon told them.

"But, Jon—" Julie protested.

"Is there anything to eat in the house?" he demanded bluntly.

She flushed. "I was—I was busy with Pearson late. Making his offer, negotiating . . . I mean, it all happened in one afternoon. I didn't get a chance to go to the store, and we were in sad shape to begin with. But I didn't see it as a problem; I'd figured we'd order pizza in."

"We'll go out."

"But it's rather late—"

"I haven't eaten all day. I don't want a damned pizza. Decide where you want to go."

He left her in the kitchen.

They went to an Outback Steakhouse, a mistake, because they had to wait almost an hour for a table. Even Ashley, who loved to hold the little buzzers that summoned each dining party when their table became ready, lost patience waiting for her little gray cube to jiggle.

Still, once they were seated and fed, dinner was decent enough. Or he was starving by then, one or the other. He wasn't in a mood to cut fat—he was in a meat mood. He-man canned beer and red meat mood. If he clogged a few arteries that night, so be it. His steak was delicious.

Millie was a barracuda—Jon had long since discovered that—but oddly enough, she seemed to be on Jon's side that night, though she was usually a bra-burning antimale militant. She was friendly throughout the meal—asking serious questions about the Bobo Vinzetti pizza case.

Maybe Millie was just trying to make sure that Jon and Julie didn't have much of a chance to talk.

Maybe that was damned fortunate.

Christie had come along meekly enough. She ordered a small steak and actually appeared to be eating it rather than shoving the little pieces around on her plate. She did argue with him throughout the meal about driving to school with Jamie. She did it well—she set forward her facts. Jamie Rodriguez had gotten straight A's in driver's education. He drove a beat-up old car, but it was a beat-up old Volvo wagon, and he was extremely careful. "If you only took some time, Dad, you'd like Jamie. He's a straight-A student all the way round."

"Thank God someone is. It's your last year, kid," he told his daughter. "If you don't get your grades up, you're going to be out of the colleges you want."

"I want to go to a state school," she said firmly.

"Christie, you're not looking at your opportunities."

Again his daughter stared at him with her mother's eyes. "That's interesting. You want your wife to stay at home and blow noses but you want your daughter to be superwoman, a Harvard grad."

"What's the matter with Harvard—other than the fact that Jamie Rodriguez won't be there?"

Christie stared at him—with her mother's condemning eyes, once again—and then excused herself in an icy tone to go to the bathroom.

Ashley knocked her silverware on the floor and spilled a Coke.

Jordan, who usually ate well, ordered a huge steak—and didn't touch it.

The restaurant was really busy. It had taken a long time to sit, a long time to eat, and even a long time to get coffee.

By the time it was all over, Jon had just one thought.

The meal had been exhausting.

It was almost eleven before they were home. Julie was saying they'd never get out of the house in the morning. Ashley was going to be cranky and miserable.

"I told you, I'll drive the kids in the morning," Jon said irritably.

"Right. Well, good. Then I'll only have them whining for the first hour of the day because they're so damned overtired," Julie said.

"They can't possibly whine more than you do," Jon muttered.

He braced himself, ready for her response. Amazingly, she didn't have one. Maybe she hadn't heard him.

They were in his car, and Ashley was sleeping on her lap. Christie and Jordan were bickering in the backseat.

He pulled up in front of their house. He started

quickly from his own seat to come around and lift Ashley from Julie's lap so that she could get out.

Julie was already out of the car, Ashley crushed to her breast. In quick, precisely whispered words, she told him what he could do to himself.

Apparently, she had heard him.

She hurried into the house.

The older kids muttered good night.

He stood by his car for a few minutes, staring up at the sky. A feeling of hopelessness suddenly invaded him. Where the hell had it gone so wrong? They should have had everything. He did have a great job—even if he'd liked the D.A.'s office better. They had a good home with a decent, payable mortgage. He and Julie had their own cars, and they'd planned on buying one for Christie when she graduated from high school as long as she kept up a B average or higher.

Their kids were healthy. Damned healthy. And they both knew they had to be thankful for that.

How the hell had they managed to have everything and yet be so miserable?

He walked into the house. It was already in darkness, only the night-lights on. He went into his own bedroom, shedding his jacket and shirt as he did so.

Julie was already in bed. All the way on her own side of it—in fact, it looked as if a sudden breeze would roll her onto the floor. Well, she didn't want to touch him. And she didn't want to be touched by him. It was surprising that she didn't throw a pillow and blanket out on the sofa.

But then the kids would have seen that. And somehow Julie was always the one who came out smelling like a rose to the kids.

He stripped down to his briefs and crawled into bed.

His side of it. No sense touching her.

"Congratulations on selling the house," he told her.

"Thanks," she said curtly. Then she made a point of yawning. Fine. He didn't have anything else to say anyway.

He was shocked, minutes later, when she spoke.

"I made that reservation."

"What?"

"I made the reservation for Christmas. For that place. Oak River Plantation."

Jon lay very still. He exhaled after a long moment, his feeling of absolute hopelessness fading. In fact, something close to warmth filled him.

He loved his wife.

He didn't even want to love her anymore, but he did.

He loved his wife.

"That's great," he heard himself say.

"That's just Christmas," she responded firmly.

He rolled over, touching her shoulder, trying to talk to something other than her back.

But she cringed. Cringed, just at his slightest touch.

He swore, loudly, angrily.

And he left his bed.

The hell with her, and the kids. The damned couch was starting to look mighty fine.

Chapter Four

Christmas Eve
1862

The greatest sin seemed to be that it was such a beautiful day.

A beautiful day in which to die.

The captain stood upon the hastily erected scaffold on the rise by one of the oaks in front of his own property. It was a good oak, a strong oak. The men would be taken along the scaffolding one by one, and hanged from that oak.

He listened while the chaplain droned on. He felt both the courage and the fear of the men lined up by his side, and when he opened his eyes, he could see the anguish in the faces arrayed before him, both the faces of friend and foe, for even their enemies were heartsick at their duty.

Not one of his men was blindfolded, nor as yet were they bound. No execution had ever been carried out with greater dignity, perhaps because the executioners were nearly as shaken as those about to die.

He could see the noose, hanging over a strong limb of the old oak tree. The rope didn't touch him; it was many feet away. And still, he could feel it as if it already chafed against his neck.

Life.

Just minutes now remaining . . .

Snow lay on the ground. A light snow, a new-fallen snow. Clean and clear and pure. A soft crystal blanket of ethereal beauty. The sun shone upon that snow, dazzling in its brightness. The sky was blue, breathtakingly blue. Not a cloud marred the perfection of it. The air was cool and crisp; the day not the kind of cold that was uncomfortable, just chilly enough to wake a man up with each breath, and let him know that he did breathe, that he was alive.

The sheer beauty of the day, the touch of sun and sky and snow upon his senses, told him that life itself was precious. And now that he was about to lose it, he wondered if he had ever thought to be thankful for it. Yet he could leave life behind, the blueness of the sky, the crystal beauty of the hills and valleys that rolled so gently in their winter blankets. He could close his eyes and say that he had seen the beauty, and he could let it go.

If he could just see her face one more time again.

Life was precious; love was the gift that made it worth living against all odds. He didn't hear the words that the chaplain was saying, but he thought in his heart that it was a sad time indeed to die, for Christmas had been the hope and the promise of life everlasting, the greatest gift of love. Oh, God, if he could just see her face . . .

Talk with her, laugh with her, one last time. Hold fast and tight, knowing then that the little things were just petty things, that love was strong, love was what mattered. If he could just see his son . . .

Stroke his daughter's cheek, see her eyes.

If only.

While the chaplain continued with his prayers, the company about the scaffolding, Yanks and Rebs alike heard the coming of the horsemen.

No cry of alarm was given by the Federal lookouts, nor was a cry necessary, for the men who rode toward them were a company of Yanks. Standing very still, the captain realized the company was being led by a brigadier general, and the brigadier general, in charge of the command, was now dismounting from a fine sorrel horse.

He started suddenly, realizing that he recognized the man in the Union army brigadier general's uniform.

The man was an old friend.

They'd gone to school together.

His name was Peter Tracey, and he hailed from a

township not far away. They'd ridden together, hunted together, drunk brandy together . . .

Shared dinner together. At this very house. And more. They'd entered into a special association together, the brotherhood of Freemasons.

Freemasonry was an ancient brotherhood. George Washington had been a member, but the founding of the Masonic organization went back further than the founding of the country; many historians theorized that the rites went back as far as the days of the ancient pyramids and Egyptians. Then, perhaps, it had stood for the work-related industries of man. Now, of course, it was far more a gentlemen's club, but one dedicated to the good of its members and the world around them. Being a Mason demanded certain secrecies of its members, and called upon them to help one another in times of need.

The brigadier general—whose rank equaled that of George Armstrong Custer, who had ordered the hangings—was staring at the captain. The captain could hear him demanding to know what was going on that Rebel prisoners should be executed on Christmas Eve. Young Yank Lieutenant Jenkins was explaining the situation.

And watching the brigadier general's eyes, the captain saw dismay. He would have little right to gainsay Custer's orders.

The captain was grateful that his hands were not bound, for his friend was staring at him now with horrified eyes. Rebs and Yanks lost friends frequently in battle. Brother had been called upon to fight brother; sons and fathers had taken different positions in this wretched war.

Yet to see a man, a friend, hanged for no greater crime than fighting for his own convictions was a hard sight.

A bitter one. The captain suddenly found himself praying. He wanted to live. He wanted to breathe the cool, fresh air, touch the icy smoothness of the snow.

He wanted to cherish the gift of love he had known, and forgotten to value. . . .

The captain offered the brigadier general a signal.

The ancient Masonic signal that he was in distress.

Any Freemason would have been obliged to help.

The brigadier general watched the captain.

The captain barely dared breathe.

He waited. . . .

Chapter Five

When she stepped into the living room the following morning, Julie was relieved to see that her husband had awakened early.

The sofa was clear of both pillow and blanket. Jon was already dressed for work, brewing coffee, popping toast, and on the phone in the kitchen when she emerged from the bedroom. He was in a suit and tie, his customary outfit, but this morning she was somewhat startled to realize how nice he looked in it. Jon was a nice height, and the shoulders of the suit emphasized the fact that he'd kept himself in good shape the last twenty years. He was brisk, businesslike, and competent on the phone, all appealing qualities. His auburn hair was freshly washed, smoothed back, his green eyes were sharp and aggressive as he spoke, and he moved about the kitchen with a strange domestic grace as he dictated a memo to the secretary who was apparently on the other end of the line.

He was good. When he chose to be. When he opted to give the family his time, he could do it with impressive agility. Not only was he managing, he was managing well. His focus and energy were high. What he didn't understand was that it was easy to be at a high level one morning every three weeks. When she was solely responsible for mornings every single day, day after day, was when it got tough. He was great at stepping in once in a while—then wondering why she complained when he was so damned perfect at the same tasks.

Was she just incompetent? Or was she simply worn out?

Or was she still simply so angry that nothing he could ever do would be right?

He was definitely on this morning. Not only was breakfast going, lunches had been made. And he was already in business mode, showered, dressed, immaculate, and disturbingly attractive.

Julie was, in contrast, in her threadbare corduroy bathrobe. She hadn't hopped into the shower yet; she'd been too concerned about waking him up before the kids could rise and find him on the sofa. Her hair was everywhere. Jon looked like a million bucks. She in turn looked as if she should be shot and put out of her misery.

Sometimes, a voice taunted her, *it might be easy to understand why your husband had had an affair.*

It wasn't an affair. No matter how angry she could get with him or herself, it couldn't actually be termed an affair. It had been a one-night stand. And if Jon's accounting of it was true, it had been a rather pathetic evening at that. Maybe what had hurt the worst was that he'd been with a woman who had claimed to be one of her best friends. And maybe what had hurt even worse than that was the fact that she'd only found out about it a few months ago because Jon had accidentally told her. The incident had occurred nearly seven years ago, when they'd separated for a few months. Jon couldn't begin to understand how she could be so angry with him now for what had happened then. She couldn't begin to make him understand that it all had to do with trust. Her trust in him had been shattered. She'd never know again when he was telling the truth. She'd never know if he had told her all the truth. And that wasn't their only problem, of course. *Life* was their problem. Yes, he made good money, but it didn't mean that she shouldn't have the right to pursue a career as well. They'd separated the first time because it seemed that they couldn't get out of debt, with him working in the D.A.'s office. But his work still kept Julie from managing to get to her own job—in a dental office, back then—with enough frequency to maintain employment. Jordan had been sick with a virus that had caused all kinds of complications; she had spent her time running ragged between the hospital, home, work, and school, and trying to keep things halfway normal for Christie while she was at it.

She'd lost her job, and she'd asked Jon to leave the house. Just until she could pull herself together. And she'd pulled herself together; he'd taken on his new high-paying job as a defense attorney, and she'd gone to real estate school.

Ashley had been born, possibly a result of the very first night that Jon had come home. They'd laughed a lot; they'd drunk champagne and made all kinds of promises for the future. He'd failed to mention that Jennie Scott, one of her best friends from way back when they'd all gone to school together—*who'd been trying to convince her that Jon was awful and the only way out was a divorce*—had, in the meantime, been consoling Jon for his wife's neglect.

Jon, still talking, the receiver wedged between his shoulder and ear, was buttering toast at the same time. Julie felt his eyes on her. There was no warmth in his green gaze this morning.

She wondered if she'd managed to destroy last night what was left of their marriage, and she wondered if she cared. But if she didn't care, she wondered why she felt a stirring of jealousy watching her husband. He was a handsome man. A successful man, an attorney. And this morning, he looked like Mr. Mom.

If only the help had come a little more often.

If only he hadn't slept with Jennie.

She didn't know where the real problem lay, but she suddenly decided she didn't like the way she looked in her ragtag robe.

She didn't say a word. She quickly escaped the kitchen to shower.

When she emerged and reentered the kitchen, dressed for the day herself, makeup and hair in place, the morning was no longer moving along quite so gracefully. All three of their children were in the kitchen, giving Jon a hard time.

Even Ashley was protesting.

"No T.V., Daddy? No videotapes, no stereo, no movies to go to, no Chuck E. Cheese's?"

"It's an adventure, Pumpkin," Jon was trying to tell Ashley. "We can bring some books, we can color—"

"She can color right here at home," Christie said.

"We can't go away for Christmas. I was going to spend the day with Trevor and Mike; we're all three getting new in-line skates," Jordan protested.

"Let Jordan and me stay home," Christie pleaded.

"I'm nearly eighteen, I'm an adult, I can watch out for myself and my brother—"

"Oh, right!" Jon snapped angrily. "You and Jamie Rodriguez—looking out for Jordan, is that it? Should I leave you my car as well?"

"Yeah, Dad, that would be nice," Christie snapped back angrily.

"Christie, we're going away for a *family* vacation."

"Count me out."

"Christie, you're coming."

"Why on earth are we going?" Jordan demanded. "You and Mom hate each other—"

"We don't hate each other," Jon and Julie protested simultaneously.

Yeah, sure.

Jordan didn't say it out loud; Julie could tell he was thinking the words. He didn't miss a beat, though, he just continued with, "Christie only tolerates any of us when she has Jamie around, and I can only stand Christie when Jamie has her locked up in the bedroom."

"Thanks, you little toad head!" Christie snapped at Jordan. Julie didn't think that Christie meant to do it, but she had been eating her low-fat cereal while talking to her brother, and her spoon was suddenly flying across the room.

Jordan ducked.

The spoon hit Ashley squarely on the nose.

Ashley was dead silent for a second, then with a shriek, she began to cry.

"Ashley, Ashley, I'm sorry!" Christie said, but by that time, Julie was on her way into the kitchen, scooping up her youngest child and giving her eldest a narrow-eyed look of fury. "I didn't mean to hit her, Mom. Jerk face ducked—but I didn't even mean to hit him, the spoon just flew. I didn't mean it, honestly—"

"You hit her in the head, Christie!" Jordan bellowed.

"Right, yeah, like you're so good to her!" Christie yelled back.

"Christie, can't you just run away from home, elope or something, and live on love and food stamps?" Jordan demanded.

"Jordan!" Jon barked.

"She's a witch when she's on the rag, Dad."

"Jordan!" Julie snapped. "That sounds just horrible! I won't have you saying things like that!"

"At least there's an excuse for my personality," Christie jumped in. "Jordan's just a jerk-faced dick head and—"

"I don't want to hear it!" Jon jumped in angrily.

The doorbell started to ring.

Christie let out a shriek. "It's Jamie; I'm going."

"I told you, Christie—" Jon began angrily, standing,

staring furiously at his daughter, then striding out to answer the bell.

"Dad, please!"

Christie stared at Julie, alarm in her wide blue eyes, then went tearing out after her father. Ashley was holding her nose and sobbing in big gasps.

Jordan had quit with the argument. Head down, he was diligently finishing his cereal.

Julie, with Ashley attached to her skirt, hobbled her way out to the living room. Jamie Rodriguez was in the foyer. He was a tall, lanky, attractive boy. His hair was very dark, his eyes deep-set and also dark brown. Julie was sure he set many a young female heart to fluttering. But there was a serious side to the boy, and despite her deep reservations about Christie getting so serious so young, if pushed, Julie would have to admit that she liked him. But her daughter's relationship with him was scary. Jamie spent time with his divorced mother, and with his little sister and brother. And there had been a shooting just down the street from his home a few weeks ago in which people had been killed and a child had been injured. He came from a very bad part of town where drug deals were a daily occurrence.

He and Jon were talking. It was a surprisingly civilized conversation. Jon was laying down the driving law. Jamie was listening politely.

"Daddy, Jamie is the best driver I know," Christie insisted. "You don't need to harangue him—"

"It's okay, Julie," Jamie said.

"Home straight after school," her father said.

"No Coke, no fries, do not pass go, do not pause to collect your books!" Christie muttered.

"Christina—" Jon began.

Julie stepped forward at last—Ashley still attached to her, still whimpering. "You'd better get going before you're late," she advised. "Jamie, drive carefully; I know you will."

"Bye, Mom." Christie gave her a kiss on the cheek. She waved in her father's general direction. She practically prodded Jamie out of the house.

The door closed to a moment of silence. "You let her do whatever she wants to do," Jon said.

"What was she doing that was so wrong?"

"That kid is scary."

"Jon, if you tell her she can't see him, she'll want to see him all the more. And he hasn't done anything wrong."

"People were shot by his place. Do you want that for Christie?" he demanded angrily.

Oddly enough, Jordan chose that moment to pipe up for his sister. "Bad things can happen anywhere, Dad."

"Bad things happen more frequently in certain places."

"Jamie would never let anything happen to Christie. Can we go? It's not that I've been late every day to school, but I do just make it."

Jon nodded, still watching his wife. The look he was giving her made Julie more uncomfortable than when he was angry. She didn't know what he was seeing. She had the feeling he was ceasing to care what he saw.

"Yeah, let's go, Jordan. Ashley."

"I want Mommy to take me," Ashley said.

"Well, Mommy doesn't want to take you," Jon said irritably.

"Jon!" She looked quickly to Ashley. "I just need to be a little earlier once in a while," she explained. But some kind of damage had been done, she thought. She looked at the way Ashley was staring at her. Six. It was such a delicate age. Precious, because kids were still so darned cute. Fun, because they spoke well and had all kinds of things to say. Difficult, because they weren't babies at all anymore, and they weren't really grown-up enough to understand that love and anger could reside side by side.

She flashed her husband a glance, hating him. And maybe hating herself just a little because what he had said was true. She didn't *want* to drive the kids. The drive was a hassle.

She didn't have to feel guilty about that! she told herself. Things that were a hassle should be shared.

She felt guilty anyway.

In a million years, though, Jon shouldn't have said such a thing.

"Come on, kid," Jon said, "Mommy needs to get in early today. Give her a big kiss now. Jordan will play I Spy with you on the way."

Ashley suddenly started acting like a toddler going off to school for the first time. She kissed her mother half a dozen times before actually heading out to her father's car. Jordan brushed her cheek with a good-bye peck.

Jon didn't kiss her at all. He didn't come near her. He kept looking at her in that very strange cold way.

Maybe he'd finally decided himself that the marriage was over. That he just didn't care enough to fight her anger and apathy any longer.

Driving to work, Julie just didn't know what she herself felt anymore. One minute, she was certain that she was right. When Jon pitched in, he was great at it. It was just that he pitched in when he felt like it, on his terms.

Maybe she was wrong, maybe she did whine too much, maybe she should get a grip, and get going. Lots of women maintained homes under much worse circumstances. Some husbands didn't lift a finger to help.

Sometimes she thought she was crazy to be so hurt and furious over something that had happened so long ago.

But that was just it. Something had been shattered, and it made all the little molehills turn into mountains. Sometimes she looked at him and hated him, and then there were times, like last night, if he'd just been a little more persistent, she would have wanted to be held and cherished and loved.

As she drove across U.S. 1, Cruddy-Disgusting-Joe was ambling along the sidewalk once again, his feet shuffling as he moved, his eyes downcast. He looked up at her. His colorless eyes were bleak. He paused so that she could turn into her workplace. She shivered.

She realized, entering her building, that Cruddy-Disgusting-Joe had looked at her in much the same way Jon had earlier that morning.

The Vinzetti case wasn't scheduled to be back in the courtroom until after the holidays. Jon had a lot of cleanup work to tend to in his office—he'd made a promise not to be available during their Christmas holiday and he meant to keep that promise.

Even if it all seemed incredibly futile now anyway.

It had looked like the perfect escape for all of them. Snow, snowmen, snowball fights, a roaring fire by night. Of course, a ski lodge would have provided that entertainment, but they would have all been off skiing by day, avoiding one another as they did every day of their lives.

Was this holiday going to matter?

Probably not. There had been something about the way Julie had cringed when he'd touched her last night. Damn, he'd been wrong, but it didn't seem right that he should spend the rest of his life feeling like a slug because of it. He was suddenly exhausted with trying to make things right again when it seemed he made his wife's skin crawl.

"Hey, Jon!"

Trent Ragnor stuck his head into Jon's office, grinned, and came on in.

"Hey, Trent," Jon responded.

Trent perched on the corner of Jon's desk, smiling. He arched a brow. "You coming for drinks this afternoon?" he asked. "It's getting closer to the holiday, you know. It's time to be merry, merry, merry, and you're walking around looking more and more like Uncle Scrooge."

"I'm just tired. Looking forward to some time off."

Trent looked surprised. "Oh, yeah? You're going to go off and do the family thing? Old man Bentley gave you the time?"

Old man Bentley was the senior partner in the firm. He frowned on anything that was a distraction from the firm, and a distraction from the firm's quest to acquire money and prestige. Jon had wanted the holiday with his family badly, and he'd put a lot at risk when he'd stood fast in asking for the time off.

Now he was wondering if he wasn't a massive fool. He'd risked his job and reputation to be with a woman who cringed when he touched her.

It was for his kids, he reminded himself.

For kids who didn't want to be with him either. Except maybe for Ashley. And maybe it was worth it just for Ashley's sake.

"Yeah, I'm doing the family thing."

"Great," Trent acknowledged, but he grimaced. Trent was about to turn forty-five. Despite the fact that he was smooth, blond/tanned/beachboy handsome, he was taking middle age badly. On his twenty-first birthday, he'd married into money, the daughter of a now retired senior partner from the firm. His wife played tennis, golf, scheduled plastic surgery, and planned social affairs. They had two children in out-of-state colleges. There would never be a divorce, and they'd never much notice what the other did.

Jon didn't want Trent's life.

But once in a while he envied Trent's freedom.

And his ability to not give a rat's ass about his wife's opinions.

"Since you're doing the family thing, come out for drinks tonight," Trent persisted.

"I'm kind of busy—"

"Ah. Hard time from the wife, huh?"

Trent's tone was unbelievably irritating. So was his inference.

"We're going out of town. I'm kind of busy."

Trent threw up his hands. "She's got you by the balls, my friend."

"I happen to love my wife," he heard himself say defensively.

"Right. So if she loves you, what's a few drinks with the guys after work before the holidays?"

Trent had a point there. The rhythm of his life should have been much better. Both of them waking up each morning, getting it all together without anger or recriminations. He should be able to call her and say he'd be an hour late, he was having a drink with the guys. Lots of men did it; hell, lots of women did it. But there was always a difference. It was okay for Julie to have lunch or dinner with a client. He should be shot if he ever assumed it was more. On the other hand, drinks with the guys sounded like an orgy.

Trent lifted his hands and squeezed, laughing at Jon. "By the balls, buddy, by the balls."

"Trent, you just wish somebody—anybody—had you by the balls, old pal," Jon got in.

And just then, before an annoyed Trent could reply, old man Bentley stuck his face into the room as well.

"Jon, we've got the possibility of picking up a new client." His voice was excited. "No real meetings until after the holidays, but she's going to be down at our watering hole in the Grove this evening. I'd like you there."

Trent grinned at him. "Sanctioned drinks," he said cheerfully.

"Who's the client?" Jon asked.

The excitement in Bentley's voice grew. "The model, Trish Deva. She's suing her ex. It's a great case, Jon. A great case. Megapublicity. Sex, drugs, and rock and roll. If we win this one, we'll set a precedent."

Bentley left. Trent chuckled softly. "It's work, Jon. Be a man. Put her in her place." He hopped off Jon's desk, ready to follow Bentley out.

"Go to hell, asshole," Jon said pleasantly. He didn't know why he was letting Trent get under his skin so badly. He stood. "You're living in a different place. When my wife plays tennis, she narrows her concentration to focus on the balls that bounce back and forth over the net. I like to keep the play fair."

"What the hell's that supposed to mean?" Trent demanded.

"You know damned well what it means. We have different marriages."

Trent came striding back into the room. Jon was startled to see that he had unnerved his friend. "Are you so certain about that, buddy, huh? That's a nice-looking piece you've got at home."

"Julie is my wife, not a piece."

"A pretty, delicate little blonde who's kept a great body through three kids. How the hell do you know what she's doing all the time?"

"Trust. It's called trust," Jon told him. His words were solid. He felt a chafing at his collar.

That was it. Trust. Julie didn't trust him anymore. She'd never trust him again.

She'd thrown him out of the house at the time.

But that hadn't been supposed to matter. They weren't supposed to sleep with each other during the separation, but he should have known they weren't supposed to sleep with other people either.

The hell with her.

"Trust? Trust? Yeah, oh, yeah!" Trent laughed. This time, he walked out of Jon's office. Still laughing. He paused in the hallway. "See you at the old watering hole, buddy. And I'm sure Julie will trust you with Trish. One of the most beautiful women in the world. With insatiable appetites, so the tabloids say."

His laughter rang down the hall.

Jon rubbed his temples. He picked up his telephone receiver and had his secretary call Julie at work.

"Julie."

"Yes?" Always that guarded note in her voice now.

"I have to work late."

A very long hesitation.

"Why? Jon, you know this is extremely bad for me. I needed you home today. Jack is going to do a lot of work for me so that I can go away for Christmas, but—"

"Julie, I more or less got hit with this because I'm going away."

She was quiet a long time again. "We're always at a stalemate these days, aren't we?"

"Most couples have these problems."

"Most couples deal with them."

"Most couples care," he said dully.

"Maybe we shouldn't go for Christmas—"

"I'll get home as fast as I can. Ashley will be in after-school care; Jordan can get home on his bus." He hesitated. "Our daughter is probably off somewhere sleeping with her delinquent lover—"

"You don't have the right to make that kind of judgment."

"On whether he's a delinquent, or on whether they're off sleeping together?"

"Either."

"The problem is going to be getting Ashley home. I wish your mother—"

"Well, my mother is gone, and she can't help us. And Ashley is a little young to take a cab home from day care."

Jon exhaled on a long breath.

"Julie, I can't afford to get fired."

"Jon, I just made some really good money on this house. I can't afford to blow it, or my reputation."

"Damn it, Julie, I hate my job, but it is our main income!" he exploded.

"I have an idea. I'll call you right back," she told him.

She did get right back to him. He had set down the receiver, stared at the wall, and drummed his fingers on the desk, that was all, before she returned the call.

"Christie and Jamie were at the house. They'll pick up Ashley with Jordan, then stop at a fast-food restaurant for dinner."

The blood seemed to rush into his head, and explode there.

"Damn it, Julie, you know how I feel about Christie and that Jamie—"

"He isn't a 'that.' And I know that I can't get out early, and you're telling me that you can't get out early."

"I don't like that boy."

"You don't like his last name."

"That's not true—"

"He's polite, intelligent, and responsible."

Breathe.

He'd taken a business course once where they'd taught the class to breathe rather than speak in explosive situations.

Breathe. And count.

"Julie, you know where he comes from—"

"Jon, this is America."

"Julie—"

"You're going to judge him by his address?"

There was something in her voice that hit home. That was exactly it, and he knew it.

The kid did seem to be all right. He responded when spoken to—not just in full syllables or full words, but in full sentences.

It was true that Jon hated the kid's neighborhood. He hated the fact that drug deals went down there, and most of all, he hated the fact that shots had been fired near the kid's house.

That wasn't a crime, he told himself. Being afraid for his daughter wasn't a crime.

He expelled a long breath and realized that he'd just flunked Breathing 101. Didn't matter. He was feeling just a little bit more rational.

Jamie Rodriguez was in Jon's own "safe" neighborhood.

"All right. Your solution will work."

Now it was Julie's turn to be silent for a long moment. "How amazing. You can be compromised."

It wasn't a compliment. She wasn't saying that he was willing to compromise.

She was telling him that his work meant more to him than his concern for Christie.

Again, he fought to hold his temper. Their quarrels were degenerating into awful mudslinging matches where they both tried to make each other out as callous, selfish, self-centered parents. He didn't mean to do it.

He knew Julie loved the kids as much as he did.

He just didn't know what was happening to the two of them, and if it wasn't too late to stop it.

"Julie, I'm afraid of the kid's house. I'm afraid of his neighborhood. Hell, it's not even his folks; I don't know them—they might be great people. It isn't race, religion, or nationality that concerns me; it's the violence. And Julie, I really do hate my job. I mean I really hate it. I do this work for the money. I know that you just made a lot of money, but realty can be a more tricky business than the law. Julie—"

He broke off.

Julie wasn't there, and she hadn't been there since she had told him he could be compromised.

He stared at the receiver for a long time.

"The hell with you!" he whispered angrily to the phone. "The hell with you!"

He hung up.

And he realized that he wasn't as angry as he was depressed.

Christmas. The holiday season. Mistletoe, holly, and good cheer.

Bah, humbug.

Where was the spirit?

Two hours later, Jon found the Christmas spirit. Laria's was an Italian restaurant/bar in the Grove with an upscale, business clientele. It was inhabited by the locals, a bit off the beaten track for the tourists. There were no shorts, cutoffs, bathing suit tops, T-shirts or the like in the place.

It did boast a number of old Roman god and goddess statues in handsome marble; they were usually quite dignified looking. Tonight, they were all decked out in red and green Christmas lights. The soft Italian music was replaced by an endless stream of Christmas carols.

Holly lined the windows.

Mistletoe hung strategically from various parts of the ceiling, bound to give every male boss the chance to kiss the female employee he'd been lusting after all year.

Jon chided himself for his cynicism and prayed that at thirty-nine he wasn't about to catapult into a midlife crisis.

Is that what would happen if Julie left him?

He pushed the thought from his mind, because Bentley was there already, along with Trent and a number of the other fellows from the office. Felina Hines, Bentley's longtime secretary and sometimes companion, was at the bar. He joined her, ordering a beer on tap. "To the holidays!" he told her, clinking his glass to hers.

"To the holidays!" she replied, then lowered her handsome, coiffured salt-and-pepper head to his. "And to fame, fortune, and tabloid bitches," she added acidly. He turned around. Bentley was seated with Trish Deva. Trent was now on Bentley's other side, leaning forward, talking away with their potential new client.

Trish, however, was turned toward Bentley. Her knee was against his. She was pencil-thin, except for enormous breasts that seemed to spill from her tight, sequined bodice. Her hair was platinum— bleached blond, but bleached damned well, right to the roots. She possessed a stunning face. She had Bentley enraptured already.

Jon knew why he was sitting at the bar with Felina. For all his reputation and dignity, Bentley might be just about to make a fool of himself over Trish Deva.

"He's a good forty years older than she is," Jon said.

Felina arched a weary brow at him. "Remember Anna Nicole Smith? Wasn't she a good *sixty* years younger than that rich, decaying bastard she married?"

Jon had to smile. But then he heard Bentley calling his name.

"Better go," Felina warned him.

"He doesn't scare me."

"Honey, you've got a future with a fortune in it if you just keep your nose to the grindstone."

"To the grindstone, or up somebody's tail section?" Jon muttered. Felina smiled. "You know, you're all right, Radcliff."

"I wish my wife agreed with that," he muttered out of earshot, walking toward the table where Bentley, Trent, and Trish Deva sat.

Bentley introduced him to Trish Deva as one of the brightest and most imaginative attorneys in the firm. Trish Deva assessed him, and seemed to like what she saw.

"Sit down, hon. Let's get acquainted." Her long fingers curled around his hand, dragging him down.

He sat. She wanted to know about him. Her huge blue eyes were wide on him. He started sweating a little bit under the collar. He talked about Christmas, telling her how he was anxious to get away with his wife and kids. She seemed amused that he had to bring up his wife, as if in defense against her. "I definitely prefer married men," she told him.

And he didn't know if she meant that they didn't hassle her, or that it wasn't a hassle to get involved with them.

Her hand fell lightly on his knee.

She was talking, he wasn't listening, when he happened to look up and see that Julie had just entered the establishment with the Pearsons and Jack Taylor. She looked great in a white business suit that adhered to the body, padded shoulders, tapered waist. Her hair was half up, half falling down. She was speaking earnestly to Rita Pearson, and she hadn't seen him.

Yet.

Then she saw him. And Trish Deva.

Her eyes widened. She just stood there. He stared back. He stood then, awkwardly. He needed to introduce her to Trish Deva.

Damn, why was he feeling like an embarrassed

schoolboy? He was working; this was work. Just as it was for her.

He squared his shoulders, ready to excuse himself, walk toward his wife, bring her over.

But he hadn't realized that Trent had already risen and walked to Julie. He happened to reach her beneath one of the strategically placed sprigs of mistletoe.

"Julie—the chance of a lifetime with a married woman!" Trent boomed with loud Christmas humor.

He kissed her. Kissed her long enough to draw a few stares. Long enough for Trish Deva to say, "Julie? I'm confused. Didn't you say that your wife's name was Julie?"

"Yes."

"Oh, then . . . is that your wife? Or Trent's?"

"Mine," he said flatly. "Excuse me."

He walked over to Trent and Julie. He knew his expression was probably childishly furious. Not that Trent had kissed her under the mistletoe. But that she had been so willing to respond. At his expense.

Well, she did think that he deserved to pay. He knew that much.

Damn it. He'd never humiliated her in public.

"Julie, meet Trish Deva," he said coldly. He made

no attempt to kiss his own wife beneath the mistletoe.

Julie was perfectly polite to Trish Deva. She smiled; she was gracious.

Charming.

She refused to join them, explaining that she was with clients.

Jon waved to the Pearsons. They waved back.

"The kids okay?" Jon asked Julie.

"I assume."

"I won't be here late," he said.

She smiled. "I might be," she said, and started to leave.

He stood quickly, catching her hand. "I'll wait and follow you home."

"It's not necessary—" Julie began.

"Christmastime," Trish Deva said cheerfully. "Let him follow you home!" She shivered. "Every idiot robber, rapist, and burglar comes out for the season, you know."

"I'll follow you," Jon repeated.

"Fine," Julie said.

She walked away.

Great. What a victory, Jon told himself. They could leave this place together.

Drive home.

And have the rest of the evening to rip one another to shreds.

Mel Tormé began to sing about chestnuts roasting on an open fire.

It was too bad Mel Tormé wasn't really singing right there, in the room with them.

Jon wanted to tell him what he could do with his chestnuts.

Chapter Six

Christmas Eve
1862

Brigadier General Peter Tracey dismounted from his horse and made his way through the crowd of local citizens and soldiers to the steps leading to the makeshift scaffold. "Lieutenant!" he barked, addressing Jenkins, who stood—green as grass—at the chaplain's side. "What in God's name is going on here?" he demanded.

"Orders, sir!" Jenkins reached into his jacket pocket, producing his command from Custer. "General Custer, sir. He—well, sir, his orders that Mosby's Men are to be hanged are fairly well known, sir."

Tracey studied the paper in his hand, then looked from Jenkins to the captain.

"Not this man," he said after a moment.

"Pardon me, sir?"

Tracey turned, angry. "Not this man, Lieutenant. Not this man!"

"But five must be hanged," Jenkins explained.

"Then hang five, but not this man."

The captain—who had touched the sweetness of life once again so fleetingly—felt his heart sink.

"Thanks, Pete," he said softly. "Thanks, but no thanks. I can't let another man die in my place."

Pete, a fierce soldier, a fine man with a flourishing head of red hair and a fine mustache to match, came to face him directly, his voice low. "Damn you, my friend, I'm trying to save your fool hide!"

"I know, and I thank you, I thank you sincerely. But I cannot be spared at the expense of another. Sweet Jesus, Pete, you know that in my position you couldn't exchange the noose for the blood of another!"

Pete squared his broad shoulders and straightened his back, keeping his face from the stare of the audience that had gathered to see the hanging.

A chant had gone up. "Free the captain! Free the captain! Free the captain!"

The locals were shouting. The crowd was growing more unruly by the moment. Even a few of the townsfolk the captain had always known to be Northern sympathizers were crying out that his life should be spared.

He closed his eyes. The sounds of their cries were sweet. Life could be a struggle. Little heartaches, pain, big disappointments. But life could be sweet as well.

And he could taste that sweetness now.

Brigadier General Peter Tracey remained before him. "Damn you, friend! Custer will have my balls on bread for this one!" he growled.

Then he turned to face young Lieutenant Jenkins. "Jenkins!"

"Sir!"

"This man will not hang. 'Tis Christmas Eve! He is both young and uninjured. And he will not hang."

"Sir, you don't understand. We'll have to take another soldier then, and the captain won't have no part of that—"

"Four will hang, and the captain will take the pain of that to his grave, for eternity, I promise you," Peter Tracey said firmly. His voice grew loud as he spoke to the crowd. "A gift—from Mr. Lincoln. The captain receives his very life for Christmastide!"

A roar of approval went up. Yet voices broke out above that roar. They suddenly heard the sound of hoofbeats, pounding hard against the earth through the snow.

"It's an attack!" someone shouted.

"Rebs!" someone else shrieked.

"Yanks!" came another cry.

"To your weapons, gentlemen!" Lieutenant Jenkins commanded his men.

His young voice carried a disturbing note of panic.

Hoofbeats, someone coming . . .

Someone coming to rescue the condemned men.

The captain suddenly felt something like a chilly trickle of winter's ice running down his nape, encompassing his back.

"Take heed—" he warned.

"Rebs!" someone yelled again.

"Yanks!"

"There will be a battle!"

"Down!"

"Draw your weapons!"

Shouts were coming fast and furious. Confusion rose like an evil wind.

A cry rose against the falling dusk. A woman's cry, high, firm, ripping through the cool blue air of the winter's afternoon.

"Wait! Wait!"

The captain saw her then. She was on a cavalry horse that had been one of their own—once upon a time.

She was racing pell-mell along the dirt road that led to the fences surrounding their home.

No! he thought. No, no, no. They would think her the enemy, they would think . . .

She raced down the path to the property, wild as Satan's fury.

The captain looked to his left. More Union troops were indeed arriving. A party of perhaps five or six men in Federal cavalry uniforms were bearing down on the crowd.

God, no, he thought.

God, no.

She was coming closer and closer.

Long black hair flowed behind her as she leaned into the animal she rode with such grace, speed, and expertise.

He saw her face.

Blue-green eyes dazzling with tears. High, handsome cheekbones, lean, yet the classical perfection of her features not marred by her thinness, but rather accentuated by it.

"Stop. Wait!" she shrieked again, scattering the crowd as she rode through it in her fear and fury.

"Stop!" she cried once more.

With a sudden, rising unease, the captain saw that she carried a weapon. A Colt six-shooter, one of his own guns. He had given it to her because of its rapid-fire ability to deliver six sound shots, and because of its accuracy. It was a good gun, one he had wished he'd had on him upon occasion.

But he'd eventually have the opportunity to take

one off a fallen enemy. Hopefully she'd never have such an opportunity.

And yet . . .

Pray God, why did she wield it now? Now, when these men were so on edge.

So unnerved.

So ready to fire . . .

Her face, oh, God, her face. He had prayed to see her face just one more time again.

"Stop! Good God, no, stop!"

He was the one crying out now.

For she raced toward disaster.

Chapter Seven

Heavy metal was spewing from his stereo, but Jordan Radcliff was still aware and alert to the sounds of doors slamming in front of his house.

He'd been lying on his bed, inhaling, right when he heard the slams.

He reached over and flicked off the stereo in a second flat.

Then he leapt up, flying out of his bed, running into his bathroom to flush down the toilet the joint he'd been smoking. The room was still filled with the smoky-sweet aroma of good Colombian reefer, but Jordan dashed about, opening windows, waving the air madly, and spraying pine-scented room deodorizer all about. He had an incense burner on his desk which definitely helped explain the smoke that remained in his room no matter how wildly he waved his arms around. His mother, bless her, did tend to be naive. His father—always the attorney—was more suspicious. If his dad came into the room now, he still might find himself up a creek.

His door burst open. Christie stood there, adjusting the buttons on her blouse.

"You son of a bitch! You pothead. You dope fiend!" she cried to him. "You're going to get us both fried!"

"Me!" he yelled back. "What the hell are you doing in here, dictating to me—tramp!"

"They aren't stupid—they can smell pot!" Christie told him.

"Yeah? Well, there are other things they can probably smell as well," he informed his sister.

She hit him. Slapped him right across the face. He went falling back on his bed. Man, he was dizzy. Couldn't function. Maybe he'd gotten a little bit carried away. Maybe he'd popped just a few too many pills along with the pot.

They both heard the front door open.

Christie stared at Jordan in a panic. He stared back with his eyes wide as well.

"Ashley?" Jordan whispered.

"Sleeping," Christie responded. She spun out of his room, closing his door as she left. He heard her flying into her own room next door.

He inched back on his bed, bracing himself. They were going to come in on him any minute. His father would probably have him arrested, sent straight to jail. If his old man freaked out over gerbils, he was going to have a hell of a time over this.

Jordan waited, tense, nervous.

He was certain that Jamie Rodriguez had been sent flying out the back door, and that he'd be running around the block now to his own car.

If he got out okay, of course.

Despite his dizziness and the fog that seemed to pervade even his panic, he was somewhat sorry about what he'd said to his sister. Jamie really was an all-right guy, and he cared a lot about Christie. Christie did her homework a lot of the time because Jamie was doing his. Christie got home on time frequently because Jamie made sure that she did so. Jamie was the first guy Christie had fallen for like this, and what their folks didn't seem to grasp was that they were damned lucky. Lots of guys—guys from good neighborhoods, guys with rich fathers—wouldn't care about Christie the way that Jamie did, and wouldn't be responsible with her the way that Jamie was. Lots of guys who had everything had access to booze and drugs, and just liked to have a good time, 'cause hey—what could really happen to them?

Their fathers could come home and lose it and beat the pulp out of them. Or call the cops on their own kids. Fathers didn't do that very often, though. Mothers wouldn't let them.

Still . . .

He felt himself tensing. Winding up, like a pitcher getting ready for a throw. Any minute now, any minute now . . . They had come into the house. His door was going to burst open and . . .

Footsteps, moving through the house. Heavy footsteps. People stamping around. His folks, stomping. His folks, angry to begin with.

Oh, man, if they caught him at something now, they'd shred him. Into little tiny pieces. They'd kill him, just kill him. He'd be in juvenile hall for sure.

Maybe they'd go to Christie's room first.

Kill her.

The blood lust might abate by the time they got to him.

"Business? Oh, right!" he heard his mother saying. Her footsteps were taking her toward the kitchen.

"Oh, damn it, Julie, yes, what the hell do I need? A note from my boss? Trish Deva is about to sue her ex-husband, and Bentley thinks the case is worth millions. What the hell am I explaining this to you for? This is incredible! You were in the same damned place as I was!"

"Right. I just wasn't as close as Trish Deva."

"Damn it, Julie, you've got to trust me—"

"Oh, right! I should trust you!"

"Julie, you're being absurd! One time—and you'd thrown me out of the house!"

"I never threw you out of the house."

"You asked me to leave."

"I didn't ask you to go sleep with my friends."

"Yeah, and you sure as hell didn't ask me to sleep with you!"

Jordan heard his mother slam her way into the kitchen. His father followed.

He lay back on his pillow, the dizziness that had seized him receding.

All he felt was a surprisingly deep and bleak misery.

They'd calm down in a minute. They'd grow quiet, both accusing the other of making a show and dragging the kids into their problems.

A few minutes later, his door opened.

"Jordan?" His father's voice.

"Yeah, Dad?"

"Did I wake you?"

"I've been half-asleep."

"Everything okay?"

"Fine, Dad."

"Jordan?" His mother's voice now.

"Yeah?" He made the sound as sleepy as possible.

"Did everything go all right?"

"Yeah, it was great. We all had hamburgers and

fries, and Christie made us eat grapes when we got home."

"Good," his mother said, sounding relieved. "And everything's all right—"

"Everything's fine, Mom."

"Good night, son," his father said.

His mother tiptoed into the room, kissing his forehead. His father followed.

Whatever essence of illegal substance that might have remained in the room was apparently overlooked. They had other things on their minds.

"Night, Jordan, love you," his mother said, and hurried out. His father tousled his hair, and followed his mother. He heard them entering Christie's room. He heard his sister innocently murmuring that they had awakened her.

They entered Ashley's room.

Jordan wished fervently that Ashley had been sleeping. Ashley was a royal pain in the rear end, but he hated to see how hurt she got when their folks went to war with one another. Poor Ashley. She was hanging onto something that just wasn't there.

Ashley was either really sleeping or pretending to sleep. Her parents very quietly closed her door as they exited her room before moving across the living area of the house to their own bedroom on the other side.

The fight would continue, Jordan thought. It would just do so more quietly now.

They'd stab each other in silence, he thought bitterly.

He leaned back against his pillow. Well, maybe the dopey trip to a dead-end place in Virginia for the holidays would be called off. That would be like a small miracle, one big Christmas present. Maybe they'd start getting their divorce tomorrow—that could actually be kind of cool because then they both might try to outdo one another being nice to their kids. He had friends with divorced parents, and all of them had told him one of the main benefits of divorce was that the parents usually hit some kind of point at first where they tried to outdo each other in the present department.

Jordan closed his eyes.

Tears ran silently down his cheeks. He tried to wipe them away. Pills and pot didn't mix. It was like a bad trip.

He couldn't think of any presents he really wanted. He just wanted . . .

He reached out into the darkness of his room.

He just wanted . . .

He didn't know what it was. It couldn't be touched. But he wanted it.

And whatever it was that he tried to reach for was just about as far away as the moon.

* * *

Christie told herself that she should have just been glad that her parents were so busy arguing that they hadn't noticed anything at all amiss at home.

Not that anything had really been amiss. Ashley had been well taken care of, Jordan—well, Jordan was being Jordan. Nothing new about that. He'd been getting into the drugs for a while now, hanging around with older guys easily because he was so tall and mature-looking when most guys his age—nearly fourteen, trying to go to forty—were squirty little dipsticks with squeaky voices. She and Jordan were ready to strangle one another most of the time, but she never squealed on him about the drugs and he never squealed on her about Jamie. The only problem was . . . well, she knew what she was doing with Jamie, her folks just hadn't gotten it yet. Admittedly, she was ready to get into just about anything with Jamie, she was just wildly in love with him, but Jamie was grounded. Jamie had given her a lot. They fooled around, sure, but they were careful and responsible. And Jamie didn't do drugs and he didn't drink. He worked hard, because he had to work hard. No one was going to pay for him to go to college, and he was going to go to college—not because he felt he had to be rich or famous or anything, but because he felt that knowledge was the greatest gift in the world. He wanted to be a teacher. He especially wanted to be an inner-city teacher. He thought that lots of kids had dreams, but that too many of them found that no one ever gave a damn about their dreams or believed in their dreams. If he could be a teacher—sure, he'd get his tires slashed in the school parking lots a few times—he might be able to touch a few kids who just might be teetering on a rope. If those kids were scoffed at, they'd wind up scoring on the streets. But if someone just believed in them . . . well, then, they could fly.

Jamie didn't know too much about Jordan and his drugs. The one day he'd found out about Jordan just smoking pot, he'd told her that—whatever Jordan might have to say about the two of them—she had to tell her folks. Christie hadn't quite gotten to that point yet. For one thing, she was hoping that Jordan would just grow out of the phase he was in. For another, her parents were like kegs of dynamite. She didn't know what they might do to Jordan. Or to her. Or to one another.

Like last night.

They hadn't noticed a damned thing.

And when they'd needed Jamie to pick up Ashley for them, well, suddenly Jamie had been all right.

He was driving her to school this morning, and her father had better not say a damned word.

Jordan had his face in his Cheerios when Christie came into the kitchen—dressed and ready to go the minute the doorbell rang. She didn't see her parents anywhere. She quickly sat across the table from her brother.

"They say anything to you?"

He looked up, shaking his head.

"To you?"

She shook her head.

"They didn't realize the Latin lover had just run out?"

"They didn't smell the 'eau de illegal substance' in your room?"

Jordan scowled at her. He leaned closer to her.

"No. They were fighting about some woman," he whispered.

Christie frowned. Funny. She was mad at her dad half the time. He was totally unreasonable. But she'd been around him all her life. Of course. And he wasn't a flirt.

"She just doesn't trust him."

"She's worn out. He doesn't pick up much of the slack."

"You think she's right?"

Jordan shook his head. "Right? Who the hell can be right or wrong? All I know is that all they do is yell. The only bright spot in it is that we get out of that sick Christmas trip."

Julie came clipping quickly into the kitchen then on her high heels. She paused, a hand on Jordan's chin, lifting it so that he faced her. She frowned. "Jordan, you look really tired. Your eyes are all red."

Jordan pulled away quickly. Too quickly, Christie thought. Her brother didn't look good. How serious was this getting? Should she say something to her parents?

Their father came into the kitchen then, adjusting his tie in front of the coffeepot. "Julie, did you make flight reservations yet?"

"Flight reservations?" she repeated.

"For Virginia. Or D.C., I suppose. Have you rented a car?"

Christie saw, looking at her face, that her mother had a stricken look in her eyes. She'd forgotten to make the reservations.

"No, not yet," she said.

"Not yet?" Jon thundered.

Chill, Dad. Chill! Christie thought unhappily.

"No, damn it, not yet. Did *you* make the flight reservations, did *you* rent a car? After all, this hare-brained scheme is your damned idea!"

"We'll never get reservations now," Jordan said with a sigh. "Looks as if we'll just have to forget the whole thing!" he added cheerfully.

"It was a stupid damned idea anyway," Christie was surprised to hear her father say.

He looked worn. Tired. As if he just didn't care anymore. Oddly, she felt a sense of panic. The fighting was one thing. This just not caring was another.

"I can cancel the room reservation much more easily than I can get a car rental and airline tickets now, I'm quite sure," Julie said icily.

"Good. Then it's all forgotten," Jon agreed, pouring himself a cup of coffee and staring at his wife.

But that announcement was followed by a sudden howl that drew all their eyes to the kitchen doorway. Ashley stood there, huge tears rolling down her cheeks, her teddy bear held tightly to her slim little chest, her green eyes bright and damp.

Her lower lip trembled.

"You promised we'd go and build a snowman, Daddy. You said there'd be horses."

Jon, startled, set his coffee cup down. "Sweetheart, I—I can find a horse somewhere, I'm sure. . . ."

Christie frowned, watching her baby sister. Ashley's little lip doubled its tremble tempo and her eyes grew bigger as another wave of tears fell down her cheeks.

"Mommy, you said we'd go away. All of us.

We'd have snow. And the people at the old house dress up, you told me that, Daddy, that they'd dress up like old-time people, and that it would be like Christmas more than a hundred years ago." She inhaled on a remarkably pathetic sob, then let out a shuddering, "You promised!"

Christie watched as her parents' gazes met. They both started for Ashley at the same time, crashing into one another in their haste to reach their youngest child. "Baby, baby, it's okay . . ." Jon tried.

"Maybe I can still book us a flight. And find a car," Julie said.

"And maybe we can all get packed by tomorrow night to get on the flight," Jon said slowly.

"Please, please, please!" Ashley cried softly.

"I'll try, I'll try, I promise—first thing," Julie said. "First thing when I get into work."

"All right, all right," Jon said. "I'll drive the kids so that you can get in earlier."

"Jamie is coming for me," Christie said.

Jon hesitated, only a fraction of a second. "Yeah, all right. Jordan, Ashley—I'll be right back."

"I'll just grab my purse," Julie said.

Christie watched as both her parents went running out of the room. She stared at Jordan, and Jordan stared at Ashley.

"Now look what you've done!" Jordan exclaimed to her.

Ashley very calmly dried her eyes. Her lip no longer trembled. She stared at her brother with a gaze that was almost frighteningly mature.

"You don't care," she accused Jordan, "but I do! And I don't want Mommy and Daddy to get a divorce!"

Ashley spun around, leaving her older brother and sister in the kitchen.

Jordan and Christie just stared at one another in surprise.

"I wonder what else she knows," Jordan said glumly.

"Scary, huh?" Christie asked him. The doorbell rang and she leapt up.

She forgot about her parents and her family. Jamie! She couldn't leave Jamie for the holidays!

Maybe her mother wouldn't be able to get them a flight after all.

Chapter Eight

Christmas Eve
1862

The captain pushed past Pete and started running down the scaffold stairs just as she leapt from her cavalry mount, firing into the air.

"My God, what's happening, what's happening?" Lieutenant Jenkins demanded.

Suddenly, shots were being fired from all over. The half-dozen Union cavalrymen who'd been racing toward Oak River Plantation had leaned into their mounts, galloping wildly now in their hurry to reach what was quickly becoming a melee. More townsfolk were arriving on horseback and on foot, and it seemed that everyone had a gun, and everyone was firing.

She was firing. Oh, God, his wife was still firing, trying to get someone to pay her heed, trying to stop the hanging that had already been stopped!

"Stop this, now. I demand that you stop this now!" she shouted, and she fired another warning shot into the air.

She was a Virginian. Born and bred. She could shoot a squirrel in the tooth a hundred yards away.

Her shot whizzed right through Jenkins's very proper hat.

The captain shouted out her name.

She saw him.

Saw him racing toward her.

For a moment, she was dead-still. Then her features came alight with joy.

"My love!"

She barely breathed the words. She started running again, running toward him, as quickly as her feet would carry her. She forgot the Colt in her hand, forgot it completely and dropped it as she threw herself into his waiting arms.

The Colt struck the ground without its safety on. As the captain molded her into his arms, he heard shots explode once again.

Cries arose. . . .

He looked into her face.

Her face . . .

So precious. He touched it. She caught his palm. Kissed it.

Her beautiful face, her warmth, the touch of the dusk falling hard now upon them. Stars beginning to blink out in the heavens.

A winter's night. Crisp, cool, tender, in her arms.

Snow beneath his feet . . .

Her face.

Shots began to explode from everywhere. Shouts and cries arose, and he *knew*, oh, God, he *knew* . . .

Her face . . .

He raised his head as if seeing what was happening to change things.

All he saw was that it was his son leading the racing Federals toward their home. He saw his boy's eyes, and the look in them. And if the situation had not been so explosively damning, he would have smiled.

His boy had come to save him. He wished suddenly and fervently that his son had not grown to be such a brave and determined man.

And there . . .

Oh, God, there, coming, riding toward inevitable tragedy now, his daughter.

Pray God, watch over her!

He looked back into his wife's eyes. She hadn't seen. Didn't know yet, wouldn't know . . .

Her beautiful, beautiful face.

Bullets pierced flesh, ripped and tore, broke and mangled. Blood flowed, so warm . . .

Firing, everywhere.

The Yanks panicked, thinking they were under attack. The townspeople were firing in every direction.

Oh, God.

The pain.
The numbness.
Her eyes.
The blood.
So red against the purity of the snow . . .
Six o'clock.
Dusk.
Christmas Eve.
1862.

Chapter Nine

Miraculously, Julie was able, with the help of a friend who worked for the airlines, to get them tickets on an American flight that left Miami International just after 6:00 P.M.

In the last two days before their family vacation, Julie wondered more and more what they were doing. Not just she and Jon were at odds—though they had actually managed to cease fighting; they simply didn't bother talking at all—the children couldn't seem to get along with one another in any way, shape, or form.

Jamie's car went into the shop, and on what Christie was calling her last crucial days with the man she loved, she wasn't able to ride to school with Jamie.

She sat in Julie's car, along with her younger siblings.

"Stop it, brat!" Christie snapped at Ashley, elbowing her in the shoulder.

Naturally, Ashley started to cry.

"Damn it, Christie—"

"She was spitting."

"I wasn't spitting!"

"Fine, fine, she was rolling water on her tongue and squeezed it out her lips."

Jordan, in the front, turned around. "Christie, did you just let out a big one?"

"What?"

"Christie farted, Christie farted, I can't wait to tell lover boy that Christie farted—"

Christie was halfway out of the backseat, reaching for her brother's neck. She elbowed Ashley again in her efforts, this time accidentally.

"Christie, get back into your seat belt!" Julie roared. "You're going to kill us all."

"Small loss!" Christie muttered.

Julie felt a chill. Not that Christie had said such a thing. Kids talked like that all the time.

What gave her the shivers was the tone of her daughter's voice. She seemed to mean it.

She found herself driving off the road and onto the embankment two blocks from Christie's school.

"Stop that, damn you! It's Christmas! Don't you see the frigging lights hanging everywhere; can't you hear the damned music? It's Christmas. And we're going to have a good time and act like human beings. Have you got it?"

They all stared at her blankly for several long moments. Jordan lowered his eyes first, then raised them to her again. "Yeah, sure, Mom, I've got it. Do you?"

She wanted to backhand him. Somehow, she managed to refrain.

She jerked back into the traffic.

Christie fought the prospect of leaving until the very last minute. She sobbed to Jamie on the phone. She threatened to have a fit once she was seated on the plane, which would force her parents to take her off it.

Jordan had remained sullen while the rest of them packed.

So sullen that Julie found herself in his room, demanding to know what was going on with him. She looked from the heavy-metal posters around his room to all his little incense-burning pots and she felt a real fear developing within her. Had she been blind?

"Jordan," she told him. "Drugs kill."

"There you go accusing me of things when you haven't the first bit of proof about anything."

She shook her head. "I don't run around making accusations, Jordan."

"Yeah, well, Dad does."

Julie hesitated. She had heard once that kids lived up to—or down to—their parents' expectations of them. She'd spent her life trying to make sure that she always believed the best of her children. Jon told her she was like some combination Mary Poppins/ Eliza Doolittle and that she needed to wake up and see the world. She did see the world, more so than he realized, and she just wanted her children to know that she'd always side with them against that world when it got rough.

"Dad wants the best for you, Jordan."

He stared at her, arching a brow. "Well, hallelujah, you just said something kind of nice about him."

"Jordan, you're an intelligent young man. Drugs do kill. I'll leave you with that." She started out of the room.

"Right. 'Cause living in this household makes the value of life so evident, huh?"

She walked back into his room in a fury. "You ungrateful brat! Whatever our problems are, we've done our best to give you everything you need."

"Yeah, well, you're missing something."

She slapped him. Hard.

Then she wanted to die. To crawl under the rug and disappear.

She walked out of his room instead and went quickly into her own.

Jon wasn't home yet. He was going into work in the morning, but getting out by noon so that they could both collect the children and get to the airport.

She felt the tears streaming down her cheeks. Were her children just spoiled and ungrateful? Had she really ruined their lives? Was this Christmas worth it all, or was she just torturing everyone further by making a futile effort to reach out and grab a last happy memory for a young child?

She got up, walked into her bathroom, and reached for a bottle of P.M. painkillers. She took three instead of the recommended dosage of two. She set the container back and started to cry again.

Hadn't she just told her son that drugs kill?

Despite the fact that they had all been like a pack of wild dogs snapping at each other's feet since the trip had been planned, they flew out of Miami International on the night of December twenty-first.

They were only able to get three seats together, and even that was incredible luck, so Ashley, Jordan, and Christie were in those seats.

Jon was toward the front of the plane.

Julie was toward the rear.

And that, Julie determined, was best. There had

already been terrible delays at the airport along with the incredible tension of the spirit of the season—people determined to get where they were going at all costs. It was probably good that she and Jon were separated, because their nerves were frayed and frazzled, and if they were apart, they wouldn't be able to start arguing again until they hit solid ground.

Their plane had to circle over National for forty-five minutes. Julie found herself more tense, wondering if they would run out of fuel.

Finally, they landed, only to have to wait for their baggage.

Ashley was so tired that she was nearly dead to the world. She wasn't a particularly small six-year-old, so between passing her around and trying to get the baggage, she, Jon, Jordan, and Christie were all miserable.

It took another hour to get the pathetic little rental car they had managed to reserve.

They checked into their hotel in Crystal City just outside the airport at 3:30 A.M. At least they wouldn't have to check out the next day until four, since Jon's business travel allowed him to belong to the hotel chain's frequent-stayer program.

And they did sleep. Christie, Ashley, and Julie shared a room, as did Jon and Jordan. When Julie awoke, she found that Ashley was staring into her eyes, patiently waiting for her to awaken. Ashley offered her a beautiful smile. Julie had to smile in return, and pull her daughter close.

Julie had wanted to bring the kids to the Smithsonian, but there was a threat of snow, and by the time they were all up and had eaten, it was three in the afternoon.

"They should get something educational out of the trip," Julie offered.

"We're going to an inn where costumed staff recreate an entire era; that should be educational enough," Jon argued. "Besides, the museum will be closing by the time we get there, and I'm not comfortable with that car if it snows, Julie."

She didn't argue with him. She didn't like the car herself.

It turned out to be good that they left when they did. Darkness came incredibly quickly on the lonely country roads they followed. They passed no restaurants, but as it grew later, Jon saw a small country store, so they bought microwave hotdogs and chips as a poor excuse for dinner, and moved on again. The driving remained long and monotonous. By seven that evening, they were all at one another's throats again.

"Julie, you're not reading that damned map right!" Jon swore in frustration.

"I have to go to the bathroom," Ashley said.

"Mother, I must have something to drink, I am dehydrating here by the second," Christie complained.

"It must be a hundred degrees in this car, Dad. Can we turn the heat down? Christie, will you get the hell off me?" Jordan snapped.

"I'm not on you!"

"Mommy, I have to pee!"

"Quit wiggling!" Christie cried to her sister.

"Stop, Jon, I'm going to have to let Ashley go in the trees."

"In the trees?"

Ashley thought that was fun. They pulled off the road and crunched through the snow to reach the trees. Ashley even laughed that her bum froze when she squatted. Christie came running over with a container of wipes—not so that her sister would be comfortably clean, but because Ashley just might touch her with dirty hands.

Jordan had gotten out and gone to another tree. "Mom!" he cried somewhat excitedly.

"What?"

"Pee melts snow!"

She arched a brow. He had said the words with a kid's excitement. She suddenly found herself smiling. They were Florida kids. Seeing something new. Maybe the trip was going to be all right.

When they returned to the car, Jon was pointing forward, smiling. He was excited as well.

"Look!"

She peered into the darkness ahead of them.

"I've found it—see, see the light just ahead? That has to be it."

She nodded. "Let's hope."

Five minutes later, they followed a winding path along a gorgeous drive. The snow shimmered and reflected the moonlight. The house was charming, a two-storied, columned antebellum mansion that was straight out of *Gone With the Wind.*

Jon parked in front. As they exited the car, they could hear the whinny of horses from the nearby stables.

"Horses!" Ashley cried happily.

"Yeah, cool," Jordan admitted.

"Dumb animals," Christie muttered.

"It might have been hot in the car, but it's cold out here," Jon said. "Let's get in."

He opened the trunk. They all struggled to get their bags out; even Ashley was helping. She groaned her way up the steps to the grand porch with Julie warning her to be careful, it might be slippery, all the way.

Julie was the first to reach the door. There was a bell pull, and she tugged it. She heard the bell ringing inside the house.

No one came.

She rang the bell again.

Jon stepped up and rapped firmly on the door.

"No one is answering," Julie said, shivering. She set down the bag she carried and rubbed her hands together.

"Perhaps we should just open the door and go in—it is a bed-and-breakfast, right?" Jordan said hopefully. "Like, there's public dining or something, isn't there?"

"Yes! It's open to the public, isn't it?" Christie asked. She was huddled into her coat, shivering.

"Cold, honey?" Jon asked her. It looked as if he wanted to put an arm around her, pull her close.

He didn't.

"No, I'm not cold!" Christie snapped, staring at her father with exasperation. "I'm merely about to congeal. No, we couldn't just spend Christmas at home where it's beach weather! We had to come to the middle of nowhere to turn into icicles!"

"Don't talk to your dad like that, Christie," Julie heard herself saying.

To her surprise, Christie didn't answer her back. She flushed. "Sorry, Dad. Yes, I'm cold!"

The door opened suddenly.

Julie, Jon, Christie, and Jordan stared at one another. It seemed the six-year-old had been the only one with sense. Ashley had listened to her sister's suggestion and opened the door—assuming it was a public place.

"Okay, Daddy?" Ashley asked.

"Hey, sweetheart, looks okay to me. Let's get inside."

Ashley pushed the door open, and they all stepped in, Jon closing the door tightly behind them.

They stood in a large, graceful foyer with a handsome staircase to their right, a balcony open to the foyer above them, and four doors opening to other rooms arranged symmetrically on either side of them. Ashley instinctively veered toward the door to their left. It was opened wide, and the sounds of a crackling fire could be heard from within.

Like a huddled mass of sheep, they all walked into the room with Ashley.

There was something of a hotellike desk against the wall nearest the door, but otherwise they were in a parlor. A fire was blazing away, its warmth and crackle cheerful and inviting. Handsome, thick area rugs in shades of deep cobalt blue and softer rose lay scattered atop gleaming hardwood floors. Victorian chairs and sofas were gathered about the fire, while a small table and a couple of high-backed brocade-upholstered chairs sat in a charming little window nook toward the front of the house. The ceilings were elegantly corniced; the wallpaper was a pretty rose pattern that picked up on the soft

shades in the area rugs that lay upon the floor.
Beautiful oils, portraying hunting scenes and handsome men and beautiful women, lined the walls.
All in all the room was perfect—historical, comfortable, and entirely warm and inviting.

"Hello?" Jon called, setting down the luggage he
carried.

"There's a bell on the counter," Julie said, hurrying toward it. She rang the bell as the others at
last broke from their sheep formation and moved
about the room.

Ashley especially liked the room. She didn't
mind at all that they had come here—but then,
Christie had told her, that was just because she was
a little squirt and didn't realize that their parents
were destroying their lives as of yet. But Jordan
hadn't really fought coming here either. He had
liked the idea of making a snowman, maybe having
a few snowball fights, and he really liked horses. It
might be a little boring sharing all that with his
sisters, but then, once he got into it, Jordan would
be okay.

Ashley especially liked the pictures on the walls.
She moved about the room, looking at them. There
was a really pretty picture of a sunset blazing over a
rolling field with plenty of horses in it. That was her
favorite. Then there were a bunch of people on
horses riding with a bunch of dogs that looked like

beagles running around and barking all around them. There was a picture of a dour-looking man, and there was a picture of a man and a woman. It was a really beautiful picture. The man was dressed in some kind of a gray uniform with a plumed hat on his head. He had light, wavy hair that came all the way to the top of his shoulders, and a very nice-looking face. The woman at his side was very pretty as well. Her head was tilted—Ashley was going to have to get closer to see her face—but she had very long hair that was black and shiny and nice.

"Ash?" her mommy called a little worriedly. Ashley knew she was the youngest. Jordan said that was why Mommy was always worried about her, calling her name anytime she didn't see Ashley standing right in front of her. But Ashley was getting big. First grade. That was certainly no baby.

"I'm right here, Mommy," she said, coming back around one of the sofas so that her mother could see her.

"I wonder where—" her mother began.

But just then, a lady came into the room at last.

"Hello, welcome, I'm Clarissa Wainscott. I'm so very sorry to be late!" she said.

She was beautiful, and she certainly belonged in the house. She was wearing a long, full dress with some kind of a sweeping petticoat beneath it. It was a beautiful deep green color, and it moved with her with every step she took. It fell a little bit off her shoulders, and it made her neck and face look especially pretty and slim. Her hair was dark, and swept up in a knot at the back of her head.

Ashley's family was still for a moment—everybody was staring at the beautiful lady. Ashley hoped that Mommy didn't mind the way that Daddy was staring at her, but then Mommy was staring as well.

"Uh—uh—" Daddy began.

Mommy jabbed him in the ribs with her elbow, but then she stepped forward herself, offering the woman a hand. "Hello, I'm—"

"Julie Radcliff," the woman said, taking Mommy's hand, smiling. "Welcome to Oak River Plantation."

"Thank you. This is my husband, Jon."

"Jon, how do you do, welcome," the woman said, taking Daddy's hand as well.

"These are our children, Christie, Jordan, and Ashley," Mommy said.

"Christie, Jordan, Ashley," Clarissa Wainscott repeated. She smiled, her eyes lighting on Christie, Jordan, and then Ashley herself. Her smile was a really beautiful smile. "Welcome to all of you. I suppose it's a bit different here from the usual vacation resort, but I hope you'll have fun."

"Can we ride the horses in the stables?" Jordan asked anxiously.

"Jordan, we're not even officially checked in yet!" Mommy said.

"The horses were the lure to get him here," Daddy admitted.

"It's quite all right," the lady said. "And of course you can ride the horses. Tomorrow," she added, looking toward the windows. "When the sun has come up." Her smile faded for a minute, but then she looked brightly at Jordan once again. "My husband isn't here right now and he attends to the horses. Well, let's see, shall we get you up to your rooms?"

"That would be lovely," Mommy said. She still looked cold, and tired.

"Supper is a bit early here," the lady said apologetically, leading the way out of the room. "Six precisely, but then you must help yourselves in the kitchen if you wish something later, and we're well-stocked with drinks and the like in the library opposite this room. Again, help yourselves at any time. You must feel that it's your home the entire time you're here."

"Thank you," Mommy and Daddy both said.

"Come and settle in," the lady said.

"Ash, come on!" Mommy called.

Hugging her teddy bear, Ashley started to follow

them all out of the parlor. She was the last to leave the room, and she paused, looking around again as she did so.

She liked the room. It was warm in a very special way. It was kind of like coming home. She didn't just feel as if the fire had chased away the chill from outside, she felt as if the warmth had something that made everything inside all right as well.

But then . . .

Something was different in the room. She wasn't sure what, but something was different from when she had first come into it.

Then she saw what it was.

The picture had changed.

Changed! As if . . .

She opened her mouth to call out to her mother, but then she fell silent.

It just looked like an ordinary picture now. If she tried to explain . . .

No one would believe her.

They would think that she was making it up. She was little—she had imaginary friends and had imaginary tea parties. Nobody ever believed her when she was just telling the truth.

She walked back toward the picture. Well, she was right.

She wondered if she should be afraid, but then

she decided that she wasn't. The picture hadn't done anything to her. She was just a little bit . . .

A little bit scared.

"Ash, Ashley, where are you?" Mommy called.

"I'm here; I'm coming!" she called back. She looked up at the picture. "I'm not going to be afraid, and I'm not going to tell on you. You're going to be my special secret!" she said to the picture. She winked at it.

It winked back.

Now she was afraid. Just a little bit afraid. She turned and ran out of the room, and Mommy didn't have to call her again.

Chapter Ten

They were alone in their guest suite. Ashley still felt a little unnerved by what she'd seen in the painting. She knew now, of course, that she wasn't going to say anything about it at all.

Not to anyone in her family.

"Well, guys, what do you think?" Daddy asked excitedly now that Mrs. Wainscott had left them and they were alone with just each other.

"I think we're in the boonies," Jordan said.

"But they do have horses," Ashley reminded her big brother hopefully.

"You're too little for those horses," Jordan told her impatiently.

"Am not!" Ashley protested.

"There's nothing to do here, nothing," Christie complained.

"You'd be happy with nothing if lover boy were here," Jordan told her.

"Leave her alone, Jordan," Mommy said.

Christie was staring hard at Jordan. "Well, not all of us have a way of making life all right no matter what!" she snapped.

"What does that mean?" Daddy demanded.

"Yeah, Christie, what does that mean?" Jordan repeated. Ashley thought he sounded just a little scared.

"It means everyone is overtired," Mommy said. "We need to get some sleep."

"Kids, find your places," Daddy said.

Then Ashley knew that the two of them were going to go at it again.

Over their rooms.

"We can do this the way we did last night," Mommy insisted. "Me with the girls—"

"We have three rooms," Daddy cut in.

"It doesn't matter," Mommy said.

"Christ, there's a damned couch in here!" Daddy muttered beneath his breath.

"It does so matter," Jordan said. "You dragged me here; at least I can have my own room."

"Ashley and I—" Mommy began.

Ashley quickly stepped up next to Christie, slipping her hand into her sister's. "I want to be with Christie," she said firmly. "I want to be with my sister."

Mommy seemed stunned. Hurt. Good, Ashley

thought, then immediately was ashamed of herself. But Mommy never seemed to mind hurting Daddy these days, and even if Daddy had done something that hurt Mommy, he'd tried really, really hard to make up for it.

"The rooms all connect," Jordan said, picking up his duffel bag. They were standing in the first bedroom—the master room, as the lady had called it. "And they're just right. The middle has that thin little daybed—for me. The last room has the two beds, and it's all frilly—for girls. This has got the fireplace, the little breakfast table, the brandy decanter, and all that stuff adults like. A parents' room, a girls' room, a maturing young male's room. All right?"

Mommy and Daddy just stared at Jordan. Christie nudged Ashley. "Grab your stuff. Let's go."

Ashley grabbed her Cinderella backpack and sped after Christie.

The room was cute. It was a little bit frilly.

"Christie, look, both beds have sheets for roofs."

"Canopies," Christie told her.

"Canopies," Ashley repeated. She dropped her stuff and lay down on the bed closest to the wall.

Christie didn't say anything more. She had slunk down on her own bed. Ashley suddenly heard her sobbing softly. She waited a few minutes, then she leapt out of bed and came running around to her sister. Christie could be mean sometimes. Not wanting to have anything to do with Ashley. And sometimes Ashley thought she was better off not to say anything. But right now she wanted to hug Christie and somehow make it better.

Christie didn't push her little sister away. When she felt the small hand coming around her shoulder, she found that she smiled a little, sniffed, and felt better. Half laughing, she stared into Ashley's green eyes.

"It's going to be okay, Christie," Ashley told her.

"There's not even a phone up here."

"I know. We can ride the horses into town and find a phone and I'll keep watch for you."

Christie laughed.

"I don't think we'll find a town."

"We're not far from D.C., Daddy says. There are lots and lots of towns around D.C. It's our nation's capital."

Christie smiled again. Ashley was parroting what their father had been saying that day. Dad got all caught up in the patriotism thing every time the family came near Washington, D.C. He loved the monuments, the museums, everything about the capital. He tried to impart his enthusiasm to them— and admittedly, it was like casting seeds on rocks half the time.

She missed Jamie.

If Jamie were just with them, she could listen to whatever Dad had to say.

She choked back another sob.

"What if he forgets me?" she heard herself ask. It was pathetic. She was asking romantic advice from a six-year-old.

"How can he forget you?" Ashley asked, truly puzzled. "He knows you really well."

"I'm not there. All kinds of other girls are there. What if he's lonely and someone consoles him? Mom and Dad don't understand just how great Jamie is, that there are dozens of girls out there just waiting for me to make a mistake."

"What kind of a mistake?"

"Going away and leaving him alone."

Ashley thought about that a minute. "I don't think that matters."

"How can you say that?"

Ashley shrugged. "Daddy goes away on business sometimes. I love him just the same. And I can't wait for him to come home. Remember how special that used to be? Mommy would make cakes and things."

"Yeah, I remember. Vaguely," Christie agreed. *But Mommy doesn't love Daddy anymore*, she thought—but she'd never say such a thing to Ashley. Yet, still, something about what her baby sister had said was true. She really did love Jamie

Rodriguez. It wasn't a crush; it wasn't puppy love. And Jamie loved her, too. If the way they felt was as good as she believed it was, then Ashley was right.

He wouldn't forget her. He would miss her. And it would be very special when they saw one another again.

"Go get your nightie on, Ash," she told her sister. "It's late."

Ashley obediently got off the bed and went to change. "Christie?" she asked her older sister.

"Yes?"

"They will let me ride a horse, won't they?"

"I'm sure they will," Christie said.

While her sister changed, Christie washed up.

The bathroom was strange, Christie thought. This magnificent old mansion was all fixed up, restored as good as new, but the bathrooms . . . well, they were small. The tubs were ancient, claw-footed things, the toilets seemed even older, the shower heads were all but archaic, and to get water into the sink, it was like working a pump.

Nothing was perfect, she reminded herself.

As if anything at all could be even halfway decent about this holiday!

When she came back into the bedroom, she told Ashley to brush her teeth. She lay down on her bed, dozing.

A few minutes later, she woke up to find that

Ashley, her little face a bit white, was standing at her side, teddy bear in her arms.

"Christie?"

"What is it?"

"Can I crawl in with you?"

Christie smiled. "What, Ash, you think it's a haunted house because it's so old?"

"It is a haunted house," Ashley told her gravely.

Christie opened her mouth to tell her sister that haunted houses and ghosts didn't really exist. Ah, well.

She could still remember what it was like to be so young.

"I don't want to go to Mommy," Ashley said in a very scared little voice.

Christie hid a wry smile. It would probably be just fine if Ashley did go in to Mom. It was unlikely she'd be interrupting anything these days.

But Ashley had come to her.

"Crawl in, Ash."

Her sister crawled in. Christie slipped an arm around Ashley and lay awake and listened to the wind groaning.

Jordan, somewhat alone with both connecting doors closed, sat on the daybed. Sheets and pillows were piled neatly for his use at his side, but though he was tired, he didn't make the bed as yet. He wasn't tired enough.

Words of a song kept filtering through his head. A song from his folks' generation, really. When Grace Slick's group had been called Jefferson Airplane. *One pill makes you larger, one pill makes you small . . .*

All he wanted a pill to do tonight was make him sleep.

He opened up his knapsack and the little tin that should have held breath mints.

He admitted, for a moment, that he was needing the pills more. Some to sleep.

Some to wake up.

He picked up the kind that made him sleep.

Swallowed one down.

And lay back.

The bathrooms were god-awful, Julie thought, especially since she'd determined to undress in there. Although it was difficult, she didn't exit the tiny niche until she was covered to the neck in flannel.

If Jon noticed, he didn't say anything. He stood at the window with a brandy snifter, staring out at the snow.

"It's really beautiful," he said.

"Yes, it's that."

"Did we make a mistake coming here?" he asked.

She shrugged. "I don't know. So far, it doesn't look as if the kids are having a great time."

"Are you?" He stared at her pointedly.

She shrugged again, wondering why she was suddenly so uncomfortable. "It's all right. The place is pretty; the woman is charming. I'm sure that tomorrow the girls will get all excited about the authenticity of her clothing and the house—and Jordan can't wait to ride. I—"

"What?"

Julie hesitated, wondering why it was so hard to admit that she might enjoy or anticipate anything. "I think I'd like a ride around the countryside as well."

"Yeah, that would be nice."

"Well, I'm going to sleep. I'm exhausted."

Julie crawled into the bed, staying far to one side. She heard Jon sit on the sofa with his brandy. After a few minutes, she sat up. "You can have the other half of the bed, you know."

"I'm growing fond of sofas."

"Suit yourself."

Julie wondered why she felt so wounded.

First Ashley. She felt like crying. Her baby daughter found greater comfort in her grumpy older sister than her mother.

Now Jon.

Well, Jon had been sleeping on the sofa at home.

It was all over but—the paperwork.

She heard him moving around the room, going into the small bathroom, coming out. Standing at the window again.

Then he did lie down on the bed.

Keeping to his own side as she kept to hers.

"You don't need to be ridiculously uncomfortable," she told him.

"Right. The distance is there, no matter how close I get, isn't it, Julie?"

She was quiet, wondering why everything they did just seemed to make her more miserable.

"You betrayed me," she told him.

"Julie, we weren't living together."

"We never made any agreement to see other people."

"I never meant—"

"But you did."

He sighed.

"So that's just it. You can never forgive me—no matter how long I grovel."

"That's not the point."

"It's not?"

Her fingers curled into her pillow. "I could never trust you again. Never. Damn it, Jon, you hurt me, you destroyed something that had been special and unique between us."

He was quiet for a very long time.

"Julie, no matter how much I wish I could, I can't go back and undo the past."

"The future looks no better," she reminded him bleakly.

She waited for an answer.

He was quiet for a minute, then he curled away from her, turning his back to her.

The wind rose. Tree limbs tapped against the windows. The fire crackled in the hearth. Julie held her eyes half-open, watching the play of the firelight. Through the moisture of her silent tears, the colors danced in a radiant display.

She woke up to the sound of shrieking.

In a panic, she leapt up from the bed. She stared at it, looking for Jon, but she'd been sleeping alone. Jon was gone.

She heard the shrieking again.

She rushed to the window and looked out.

They were down there in the early morning sunshine. All of them. Her family. Jon had taken the kids out to build a snowman. For a Floridian, he was doing a fair job. The snow creature stood a good five feet or so tall; it was much heavier at the bottom, still round in the middle—and the head was just a wee bit too small for the frame.

Building a snowman had led to a snow fight. Christie and Jordan against Jon and Ashley.

Julie found herself longing to join them.

She hurriedly brushed her teeth, washed up, dressed, and ran out of the room and down the stairs.

She hesitated, wanting to tell Clarissa Wainscott that they would all be outside, but she didn't see anyone in the house.

Something did, however, smell divine. Somewhere breakfast was cooking.

She'd given up bacon. It was one of her favorite foods in the entire world, but she knew of course that what was so delicious about it was the crispy fat. Artery-clogging stuff.

Bacon had never, ever smelled so good.

Maybe, when she came back in . . .

"Mrs. Wainscott?" she called.

There was no answer, so she went on outside, running around to the side of the house.

The snowman was there. Topped off with an old clay pipe, button eyes, a scarf, and an ancient, all but decaying hat. Still, Julie stood back, smiling.

The snowman was good. Damned good for kids who didn't have the least idea what they were doing with snow.

Julie let out a startled gasp when a figure suddenly

rose from behind the very round bottom of the snowman.

"Good morning. Sorry to have startled you, though I admit you gave me something of a surprise, standing there so silently as well!" the man said. He smiled.

He was a handsome fellow. Quite handsome, sandy-haired, with warm, mahogany-shaded eyes. He was wearing an old hat that angled over his left eye and a long overcoat that had to be an absolutely perfect re-creation of those worn well over a hundred years ago.

Jon must be loving this, she thought briefly.

Just as he loved the Smithsonian, the monuments, and all that went on in Washington, D.C., he loved the history of America, from the Revolution on down. She could remember him pointing out a similar coat to her once in the Museum of the American People.

"I haven't scared you speechless, have I?" the man queried politely.

"No, no, I'm sorry, I—I was admiring your coat." Julie stepped forward, offering her hand. "How do you do? I'm Julie Radcliff."

"Yes, of course you are," he said politely.

"You're . . . Mr. Wainscott?"

He nodded. "Jesse Wainscott, ma'am, at your service."

"The house is magnificent."

"Thank you. We think so."

"You've turned time back ... so completely," she said.

He cocked his head slightly. "Do you think so?"

"Yes, it's ... remarkable."

"So you think you'll enjoy your stay?"

She hesitated just slightly, wondering why it seemed that he was asking more than a completely innocent and natural question.

"It's a beautiful place."

"Remote."

"Yes, that—"

"Eventually, it forces you to think," he told her with a wink. Then, with a slight nod, he started by her.

"Mr. Wainscott—"

He turned back to her. "Just 'Jesse' will be fine. We don't cotton to much formality around here these days," he told her.

She smiled. "Jesse, then. Have you seen my husband and children?"

"They were going for a walk, and then on over to the stables. They want to go riding today. Will you be joining them?"

"Yes, please, I'd like to very much."

He nodded. "You might want to have some

breakfast. I've suggested to your husband and children that they do so. If we start out, you'll be surprised to find how pretty the terrain is, and we might not be back for a while."

"Breakfast smelled wonderful."

"A plantation breakfast always is."

"I didn't see your wife—"

"My wife," he repeated softly. Almost reverently. His eyes softened with both tenderness and a strange pain, and Julie was startled by the look in them, almost as if she were viewing something very intimate, and she should turn away. But he quickly collected his thoughts. "My wife . . ." he said again, and smiled wistfully. "You did—you did see her last night?"

"Oh, yes, she welcomed us here." Julie didn't know why, but she felt compelled to go on. "She's charming. We were very tired; we'd been very lost. Her costume was wonderful; she was just as lovely as she could be."

"Ah, yes, she lights up the night, doesn't she?" he queried with such tenderness that Julie again felt strangely that she'd intruded. "Ah, well, rest assured, she is about," he said cheerfully. "And breakfast is on a casual basis; it's buffet in the dining room. Just go help yourselves whenever you choose, and amble on back to the stables when you're ready. That suit you?"

"Sounds great," she said.

He smiled again, tipped his hat to her, and started on off through the snow.

Julie watched him go, startled by the very strange feelings of envy and something like nostalgia that had filled her.

He was a very handsome man. Charming, very charming. Very good-looking, and with such an easy, confident manner. He was arresting, compelling. But that wasn't it. She wasn't longing to flirt with him, or anything of the sort. She didn't wish that she could have such a man for herself.

Then what was it? she asked herself.

She tried to be honest with herself, tried to think. In the greatest heat of her anger against Jon, she had never really wanted to sleep with anyone else to get even with him. What had hurt so badly was that she'd always liked what she'd had—it wasn't a lack of attraction to her husband that had caused their problems. It was life. It was traffic. It was the Miami Dade Water and Sewer bills, it was trying to get ahead, and trying to be on time. Petty little things, but zillions of them fused together.

So what was it that she wanted?

Fingers seemed to close around her heart and squeezed just a little bit, and she knew what it was she wanted.

Someone who loved her enough to have that look in his eyes when he spoke of her.

My wife . . .

My wife.

What she wanted was incredibly simple, and simply impossible. Now.

Between her and Jon.

All that she wanted was . . .

That much love.

Chapter Eleven

Jon was breathless when he ran up the last of the porch steps behind Ashley.

He'd thought he kept in something that resembled decent shape on his treadmill. Maybe not. And maybe he'd given less and less time to the treadmill lately, just as he'd given less and less time to his children.

And his wife.

Almost ex-wife, he thought. She was dying to be an *ex-wife*. How was that going to be? He'd have the kids every other weekend and holidays. No, it would never be that bad. Julie wasn't vengeful—they'd just hit a dead-end together. Still, it was going to hurt like hell. Like having limbs amputated. It wouldn't be bad with Christie and Jordan—they had their own lives. Lives they preferred to be private—apart from their parents now.

But Ashley . . .

He stopped on the porch, inhaling deeply. The kids had run on in ahead of him.

Ashley was still young enough to live in wonder. In fantasy, in belief.

Ashley still believed that everything was going to be okay.

God bless her.

Ashley. Not seeing her every morning, with her optimism that belonged only to a child, was going to be anguish.

But wasn't this constant bickering in front of the kids just as bad?

It was. And he knew it. And he wasn't a child, and he couldn't keep on believing in fantasy. Something had died, and that was that.

"Daddy, come on!"

Ashley was back at the door, her eyes wide on his.

"Coming, Pumpkin."

"Daddy, you wouldn't believe!"

"What?"

"There's so much to eat. So much! Bacon and ham and, ugh, fish things! Pancakes and syrup and eggs. Sausages, potatoes—big chunky potatoes, not like B.K. hash browns."

Ashley loved Burger King's hash browns.

"They going to be okay?" he asked her.

She giggled. "Don't be silly, Daddy. I'm having pancakes with syrup."

She spun around again. He followed her to the door, then he paused, stamping his feet to knock all the snow off them. At that moment he was glad that they had come, no matter what followed.

Christie had laughed this morning. Almost like a real little kid again, his little girl. Jordan had joined in, telling Ashley that he was defending an invisible fort, and that she'd better watch out when his snowballs came flying. They'd had a good time.

No fighting.

He'd been away from Julie, he suddenly remembered with a wince.

"Daddy!"

Ashley was back at the door.

"I'm here, I'm here."

He left his coat on the tree in the foyer and came into the dining room. He was starving, he realized.

Julie, sipping coffee, was staring out the window that faced their snowman. She was dressed in denims, boots, and a sweater. Julie loved horses. She always had. They'd talked about buying one now and then to board out in west Dade, but they'd never gotten around to doing it. Too busy.

She turned around when he entered the room. "Hey," she told him. "Good snowman."

"Thanks."

"The snowman's eyes are crooked," Christie said critically.

"Watch that," Julie said. "Your father hasn't seen much more snow in his life than you have. That's a damned good snowman for a beachboy."

Jon, startled by the compliment, didn't reply.

"You should have seen the snowball fight," Jordan told his mother. "In fact, you should have been in it. Dad and Ashley might have had a chance."

"Oh, yeah?" Jon inquired indignantly. "Ashley, I thought we beat the pants off of them."

"We did."

"Sounds like I'd be a fifth wheel," Julie said.

"No, Mom, you'd just be the deciding factor," Christie said. She was making herself a breakfast plate. To Jon's astonishment, his granola-and-yogurt daughter was indulging in every vice on the buffet. She caught him watching her.

"Dad, it's all right to eat bad things once in a while, just so long as you don't make a habit out of it. Mom already ate half the bacon."

Jon looked from his daughter to his wife with surprise, a grin tugging at his lips.

Julie shrugged. "It's all right to eat bad things once in a while," she echoed her wise daughter.

"It's not actually 'bad' food, you know," Jordan said, piling up his own plate. "It's very good food. In fact, Mrs. Wainscott is a wonderful cook. Food is only bad when you overindulge in one particular food group."

Christie was staring at her brother. "Well, you are the fast-food king," she reminded him.

He shrugged. "I'm a growing teenage boy. I can take more abuse. I'll change my habits when age wears me down. Like Dad."

Jon's brows shot up.

Julie laughed.

The kids didn't miss a beat.

Jon turned around to make his own plate of food. Playing in the snow had made him ravenous. He piled on sausages, bacon, and hotcakes, added eggs and potatoes. Jesse Wainscott had warned him earlier that they might be out late—and he was quite certain there was no B.K. or Mickey D's in the near vicinity.

Then he hesitated as he was about to take a bite of food. Julie was watching him.

She turned quickly away when his eyes met hers. He set his fork down for a minute, thinking about the morning. He'd had a great time with his kids.

Maybe he should give her the same. He wasn't as all fired up about horses as she was; he should let her take the kids riding on her own.

He started to eat again, slowly.

"Hey, Dad, hurry it along. Jesse—Mr. Wainscott—says that it's just about pitch-dark by five o'clock."

"It's only about noon now," Jon said. "Trust me, you haven't been riding in a long time, son. A few hours out, and you're going to be sore. There's plenty of time. But listen, you go on ahead. I think I'm going to pass on the horses this morning."

Ashley frowned. "Why, Daddy?"

"I'm a Florida boy, remember? All snowed out for the time being. Mommy is the horsewoman. You'll have a good time with her."

"And Jesse Wainscott," Jordan said. He looked at his father. "Remember, he said it would be all right if we went riding alone once we'd been out with him at least once, but the first time out, he wanted to make sure we were comfortable with the horses and the trails."

Jon felt the slightest twinge of unease.

"Yeah. Well, it is important that you go out with Mr. Wainscott."

Julie was watching him.

Again, she turned away.

Christie got up. "Let's go riding, then. It's better than just sitting around."

She stood, then paused. "What about these dishes, Mom?"

"I wonder," Julie said. "I still haven't seen Mrs. Wainscott this morning."

"It's like a restaurant, isn't it?" Jordan asked hopefully. "We just leave our messes, right?"

"No, dope, it isn't a restaurant, it's someone's home," Christie said.

"Still, I wonder," Julie mused.

"Leave everything; I'll at least get things into the kitchen," Jon said. "Go—I'll pick up."

"I'll take a few things into the kitchen, Dad," Christie said.

"I'll help," Ashley said.

"No!" Christie snapped. "Short stuff, this is good china; I'll take care of it. Will you run up and get my gloves for me? I left them lying on the windowsill in our room."

Ashley nodded and ran out.

"I guess I should carry out my plates," Jordan said grudgingly.

He picked up his milk glass and plate. Julie picked up her own plate and followed her son.

Alone in the dining room, Jon sat back in his chair. He could see their snowman just outside the windows.

The eyes were crooked.

It was okay.

It was still a good snowman.

Julie came back into the room.

"It's cold out there, guys. Don't forget your coats," Jon called, still looking out the window.

He stood to get himself some coffee. He felt Julie's eyes on him again. He poured coffee.

"Just make sure that Ashley is on an animal safe enough for her to be riding, huh?"

"I'm sure that Wainscott knows his horses."

"But you know Ashley. Make sure she's okay."

"If you don't trust me, why aren't you coming?"

He sighed, setting down the coffeepot. "It's not a matter of me not trusting you with Ashley."

"What is it a matter of, then?"

He hesitated. "I was just trying to give you a little time alone with the kids. This morning was really kind of nice for me, and I—"

He broke off when he saw the way she was staring at him.

"Because I wasn't around," Julie said.

"Because we weren't fighting."

Julie nodded her head with a jerk. "I see. Well, thanks. Thanks a lot."

Christie came back out of the kitchen. "Mom, you've got to see the kitchen! There's an old pump at the sink and everything. It's great. I mean, that pump stuff kind of sucks in the bathroom, but the kitchen is adorable. There's a window seat in there, all kinds of herbs and things hanging from the ceiling—it's really charming."

"Charming?" Jon queried. "So, er, it's kind of nice, then, huh?"

"Oh, Dad," Christie said impatiently, "you act as if I don't appreciate anything at all."

To Jon's surprise, he and Julie glanced at one another at the same time, smiling wryly.

But Julie's smile faded. "Christie, I'll be right outside. Get your brother and sister, and we'll head for the stables."

She turned quickly and walked away and Jon wondered how he managed to blunder so badly just trying to be nice.

She was irresistibly drawn to the parlor.

Coming back down the stairs with her sister's gloves, Ashley paused. Instead of going into the dining room, she entered the room off the hallway where they had come last night.

The room with all the paintings. Daddy had told her that they were *paintings*, not just pictures.

She loved the paintings. They were so pretty, and there were so many of them.

But as she walked through the room, staring at them, she felt a sense of unease.

She came to the painting that had so unnerved her last night.

For a moment she just stared, gaping.

The painting had changed again.

She started to back away, and found herself staring at another of the paintings.

It, too, had changed.

Her imagination, her teacher would say. Miss

Bancroft had told both of her parents that she was very imaginative. Miss Bancroft didn't think that it was a bad thing to be imaginative. She just thought that children who were very imaginative needed to be very careful. Because they could easily mix up what was real and what was imagined.

The pictures changed.

They did.

She knew that it wasn't her imagination.

But no one else would believe that. They wouldn't be mad or mean, and they wouldn't think that being imaginative was a bad thing.

They just wouldn't believe her.

How could paintings change?

She didn't want to be afraid, but she was suddenly so terrified she wanted to run out of the room. A scream welled in her throat, and she started to back out of the room.

She backed into something.

She didn't scream; she gasped, and she spun around.

Mr. Wainscott was there. Jesse, as he had told her to call him. Jesse, tall and solid with his bright, handsome eyes and quick, easy smile.

He winked at her, and brought a finger to his lips. He knew that what she saw wasn't her imagination.

It was a secret they would share.

"No one would believe me if I told them," she said solemnly to Jesse.

"Probably not. But it's all right," he assured her. He reached out a hand to her. She smiled and slipped her hand into his, and they started out together.

Christie didn't go absolutely nuts over horses, not the way Jordan and Ashley did.

Still, there was something very special about the horses here at Oak River Plantation.

To begin with, they were simply beautiful animals. They were bred from Arabians and larger, more powerful European breeds to create smooth-gaited, long-winded riding horses with great stamina. They were groomed to perfection. They didn't even smell bad, and to Christie, that was the greatest feat of all.

Jordan was on a beautiful black gelding called Mico; their mother was riding a roan mare called Strawberry. Christie herself was riding a buckskin gelding named Shenandoah, and Ashley was in seventh heaven on a small horse—horse, not pony—called, most fittingly, Midget. With Jesse Wainscott ahead, leading them on his large bay, they moved quickly from the beautiful sloping pasturelands directly in front of the house into the wooded trails beyond—that same area they had driven around and around last night.

This afternoon, though, it was beautiful.

There were deer in the forest, wild turkey roamed here and there, squirrels raced over the snow, and as they followed a narrow feeder of the river, a pair of otters appeared to play haphazard games before them, racing madly about.

Christie wasn't much for speed; she was content to walk along and feel the cool air, watch the animals—and wish that Jamie was with her. She could imagine how wonderful it would be to come here with him. Jamie found so much pleasure in the little things. He loved deer; he thought they were such beautiful creatures. Jamie never hung around at the malls. He liked to go places and do things. He loved to go to the zoo, to the park, out on a boat. Jamie loved any place that was private, close to nature, down to earth. If her parents would only give themselves a chance to get to know Jamie, they'd like him.

If they'd liked him, they'd have invited him.

But, of course, that wouldn't matter after this year. They could accept Jamie or she'd be out of the house. The hell with them and their money and all the things they could do for her because they did make money.

She glanced ahead at her mother and felt a little bit

guilty about her train of thought. Still, she couldn't help feeling bitter toward the two of them. She loved them, of course. They were her parents. She had even spent part of her life liking them, which was difficult to do with parents, loving and liking not being the same thing at all.

But now . . .

"Want to hop down and walk around for a few minutes?" Jesse Wainscott asked, looking back to her and Jordan. He had been riding ahead with her mother and Ashley, keeping a good eye on Ashley all the while.

"Sure," Christie agreed. She was beginning to feel kind of like a wishbone two fairly strong people had been trying to break.

"Off to the left," Jesse said. "There's a stream just yonder."

The little copse he brought them into was exceptionally pretty. The ground was clear of the snow because it was so shaded by evergreens. The winter's sun was weak, and the very air seemed to be a haunting shade of green. Jesse helped Ashley down. Julie slipped off her mount easily enough, and Christie discovered that, despite her sore legs, she could still mount and dismount without assistance.

"What a pretty place!" Julie said.

"I've always liked it. Family cemetery's just there,

in the midst of the trees with the water winding by," Jesse said.

"It's wonderful!" Julie said excitedly. "I love old cemeteries with their funerary art!"

"Come explore it anytime," Jesse told her.

Christie held Shenandoah by the reins and turned to look where her mother was staring. The cemetery was just about twenty feet from them. In the uncanny green light, the sight was eerie indeed. Angels prayed, looking heavenward; crosses rose from the ground at odd angles. Some of the stones appeared very old, with death's-heads upon them, skeletons, and figures of grim reapers with their sickles held high in warning to the living.

"I'll definitely come back," Julie said.

"Hey!" Christie cried suddenly as Shenandoah sent his nose flying up and down as he protested her hold upon him.

"He wants a drink!" Jesse called to her, and laughed. He had a nice laugh. Very charming. As easy as his casual manner.

"Is it all right?"

"Loop the reins over his neck. He'll be fine. He'll get his drink, and he won't go anywhere."

Christie did as she was told. The others did the same. The horses ambled to the water.

Jesse went down on his knees at the riverbank himself, splashing his face with the cold, clear water, then drinking from the cup he formed of his hands.

There was no way in hell, Christie told herself, that she was going to drink from a stream where horses had their snouts in the water.

Ashley was quickly at Jesse's side, imitating his movements.

"Ash . . ." Christie murmured weakly, looking toward her mother.

Jordan elbowed her and hissed, "Don't be rude, sis!"

"Horses are drinking here!"

"Yeah, and in Dade County you drink two tons of chemicals."

"I never drink anything but bottled water."

"They probably bottled it here—when the horses were finished," Jordan said. Stepping forward, he too cupped his hands into the stream.

Christie sat down on a bed of pine needles, her back against a tree.

"Jordan!" she called quietly. Jesse Wainscott was now standing again, talking with Julie, teasing Ashley.

"What?"

"Oooh . . . didn't you see it? You just drank a big pile of horse snot! Listen, ooh, there! Shenandoah just sneezed all over the water again. It's big, slimy, disgusting yellow-green-looking . . . I think—I think that it's Shenandoah's horse snot. Oh, no! Oh, no, it's not Shenandoah's horse snot! It's—it's—oh, no, it's Midget and it's—it's—horse poop!"

Jordan spun around, looking as if he were going to fly at her.

"Mount up. Let's move on out!" Jesse called to them.

Jordan walked by Christie, kicking up pine needles as he did so. They covered her new mohair sweater.

"Little prick!" she called to him.

Standing up, she carefully pulled all the needles from her sweater. Muttering vicious threats, she went after her horse.

Her horse wanted nothing to do with her. Each time she tried to mount up, Shenandoah shied away. They circled one another.

"Jordan!" she called.

"Eat shit, Christie!" he yelled back.

"Jordan, I need help!"

But her brother was up ahead of her. He couldn't hear her any longer.

Or he was ignoring her.

"Jordan, you are a worthless pile of snot yourself!" she muttered to herself, then stared firmly at the horse. "I'm getting on your back, whether you like it or not. I'm the human; you're the horse."

She tried to calmly mount Shenandoah one more

time, mentally reminding herself over and over again that she had to let the horse know who was boss.

The horse knew.

Oh, yeah.

The horse was boss.

No matter how quickly, how firmly, or with what determination she moved, the horse moved as well.

"Fine! Fine, you stupid creature! We'll just stand here and stare at one another!" she snapped.

A breeze whispered around her.

The others were so far gone that she couldn't even see them anymore. The trail was well-marked, of course.

And it was daylight.

Kind of.

It was green daylight.

She was alone.

No, no . . . they were just ahead of her.

She turned around. The breeze was growing colder. The afternoon was growing later.

Darker.

Fog was beginning to rise from the ground. The wind stirred, swirling around. It was very cold on her neck. Sending chills down her spine.

It was the breeze. . . .

Or was it the cemetery?

The cemetery she all but stood in now.

Going in circles with the horse, she had come

closer and closer to the scattered tombstones, angels, death's-heads, and grim reapers.

"Please, horse, please . . ." she whispered.

Then she suddenly stood stock-still.

She couldn't breathe.

She couldn't scream.

She couldn't even gasp out a sound.

The air had been swept cleanly and completely from her lungs.

For within the green mist of the graveyard, a man suddenly rose.

Rose from the ground, straight out of the mist, standing directly in front of one of the tombstones.

Rose . . .

Rose out of the ground.

Dusted himself off . . .

And turned to her.

Chapter Twelve

Christie never screamed. She passed out cold—a fact that later worried her. Screaming in the face of danger would be a far better thing than simply succumbing to it.

When she opened her eyes, he was leaning over her, and she might well have screamed then, for he was so startling a figure. He wore a Union slouch hat—she knew what it was right away, having been dragged through at least a dozen Civil War museums by her father. He was perhaps twenty at most, extremely good-looking with deep, very dark eyes and collar-length tawny hair.

His voice, when he spoke, was low and husky.

"Hey, are you all right? I'm so sorry; I didn't mean to startle you."

"You didn't startle me; you scared me half to death."

He was real, flesh and blood, dressed in a dark

blue wool uniform, with a wonderfully handsome navy cloak around his shoulders. He helped her sit up, and she swallowed down her last impulse to scream.

"But are you all right?"

"Fine, fine!" Christie croaked. "Fine," she said again, finding a firm voice at last. She shook her head, staring at him. "It just looked as if—"

"Ah!" he said, smiling as he looked back toward the angels and headstones just feet from them.

"It looked as if you crawled right out of that grave."

"I was just resting," he told her. He flashed her a quick smile.

"Where—where did you come from?"

He pointed toward a large bay horse she hadn't noticed before. It was ambling around the stones, plucking up the tufts of grass that grew around a number of them in defiance of winter.

"You rode here?"

He smiled. "Mmm. I take it you're staying at Oak River Plantation?"

She nodded.

"Enjoying yourself?"

"It's beautiful."

"But are you enjoying yourself?"

She laughed and admitted, "Well, yes. So far."

"It's quite remote," he commented.

She smiled shyly, and nodded again. "Very remote."

He rose suddenly, abruptly, realizing that she was still sitting on the cold ground and he had been leaning over her—preventing her from rising. He helped her to her feet, brushing pine needles from her hair and clothing. Then he stepped back, not at all awkwardly. He looked her over from head to toe, dark eyes alight with a mischief that brought a smile to her lips. Oh, God, she was flirting. She didn't mean to be flirting. This guy was very good-looking, and she was glad to find a friend near her own age here—okay, so he was probably more of an adult, but . . .

"What's your name?" he asked her.

"Christie. Christie Radcliff."

He swept his hat from his head and bowed deeply. "How do you do, Christie. Christie Radcliff. I'm Aaron Wainscott. And now that I know your name, let's see what else I can tell you. Umm . . . you're here with your folks. You're not terribly pleased to be here with your folks because it's Christmastime and you should be with your friends. Ah . . . a special friend. Are you engaged to be married?"

Christie laughed. "You must be joking. I can't even get my folks to acknowledge him."

"Ah, but to you, he's very important. It's quite serious."

"And I'll be eighteen before too long."

"And you think that will solve everything?"

Christie frowned. "It will give me my independence."

He crossed his arms over his chest, and his look was just a bit superior then.

He couldn't possibly have been more than three or four years older than she was, and she resented his air of patronizing maturity, no matter how cute and charming he might be.

"The heart is never really independent," he said.

"No, but when the heart and the mind have made the right choice, being an independent age is important," she assured him with firm dignity.

His lashes lowered over his eyes, then he looked toward the gravestones once again. "Well, Christie, I can tell you that even being right doesn't always mean you're going to feel good about your choices." He looked at her again.

Christie arched a brow to him. "You've got great parents, Aaron. I can't imagine fighting with either of them."

"That's because they're not your parents. But trust me, turning your back on people you love isn't the answer. Compromise is the better way. Understanding is best."

"Oh?" she queried. "And what dire mistake did you make? I mean, you and your folks must get along, since you're here. I take it that you grew up at your parents' own Oak River Plantation?"

He smiled. "I did. But I left Oak River Plantation. And the circumstances weren't good. And now . . . well, sometimes you don't have the time to make things up the way you'd like to."

Christie was puzzled by the depth of emotion that seemed to dwell beneath the lightness of his speech.

"It's Christmastime, and you're here," she told him softly. "With your folks."

"It's Christmastime, and I'm here," he agreed. "I'm always home for Christmas. Hey, I guess you'd better get going. I hear them calling you," he said.

"I don't hear—" she began, but then she did. She heard her mother's voice.

Concerned.

"Mothers!" she sighed.

He laughed, and whistled. To Christie's chagrin, Shenandoah meekly trotted over. "Let me give you a hand," Aaron Wainscott said, and smiling again, he helped her up. "Go on, catch up," he told her.

Seated atop Shenandoah, she looked down at him. "Why don't you come ride with us?" she asked.

He shook his head. "Can't right now."

"Will you be around?"

He offered her a crooked grin. "Well, I'll be in this general vicinity tomorrow. And I'm always at the Christmas Eve dance."

"The dance?"

He nodded gravely. "We have a huge ball every Christmas Eve, and everyone comes. You'll enjoy it. But if you want to talk . . . ride out tomorrow," he invited.

Christie nodded. She heard her mother calling again, and started Shenandoah moving along the trail.

Julie, her face drawn with concern, was riding toward her. "Christie, sweetheart, are you all right?"

"Of course!" Christie said. She felt slightly embarrassed; Jesse Wainscott was riding right behind her mother. She felt like a small child. She forced a smile for their host, thinking all the while that she should have recognized his son right away—they looked incredibly alike. "I just met Aaron, Mr. Wainscott."

"Ah!" Jesse said.

"Aaron?" Julie queried.

"My son," Jesse told her.

"Oh," Julie murmured. "How nice. How old is he?"

"Twenty," Jesse said.

"I tried to get him to join us," Christie said.

"But he couldn't," Jesse told her.

"Right."

"Well, we should get on," Jesse said.

"Perhaps we should look for your son—" Julie began.

"He'll be around," Jesse said firmly. "We need to be getting on back. Darkness comes quickly here."

They started riding again. Julie fell back next to Christie. She glanced at her daughter speculatively.

"Is he attractive?" she whispered to Christie.

"Very," Christie assured her.

Christie could almost see the wheels turning in her mother's mind. *Get Christie interested in another boy. Let her see that the sun doesn't rise and fall on Jamie Rodriguez.*

"Nowhere near as attractive as Jamie," Christie said pleasantly; then she couldn't help but smile at her mother, "Still, I did enjoy meeting him."

Julie smiled ruefully. "Good. Too bad he wouldn't come with us. And how strange. I wonder . . ." Her voice trailed away.

Christie leaned toward her. "You wonder if maybe the Wainscotts may not be somewhat dysfunctional, just as it seems we are?"

"All families have their problems, Christie."

"Yeah, but . . ."

"But what?"

Christie shrugged. "But even when the Wainscotts aren't together, it seems . . ."

"What?"

Christie shrugged, remembering what Aaron had been telling her. Understanding was best, he had said. Not just independence.

When she turned eighteen, she'd have the legal right to tell her parents to go to hell. But was it something that she really wanted to do?

Sometimes, yes.

When they were so pigheaded.

"Even when the Wainscotts aren't together, what?" Julie repeated.

"I think they love one another," she said. Then she felt awkward. She hadn't meant that she didn't love her mother. It was just that the obstacles in her family all seemed immense. No one understood anyone else. They all just lived separate lives.

And waited.

For what?

Time. Time to take care of all the ills among them.

"Ashley's up there kind of alone," she muttered, feeling her mother's eyes on hers. She couldn't express anything that she was feeling.

She nudged Shenandoah and moved on ahead.

As she did so, she had to smile. Ashley. That little rascal. She was laughing at something Jesse

Wainscott had said. Her laughter was fresh and light and real.

It sounded like silver bells and almost made it feel like Christmas.

It was a different kind of vacation, because they didn't just dismount from their horses and go running back to the house for cocktail hour or hot cocoa.

Jesse showed them all around the stables, pointing out where saddles, blankets, and bridles went, and where brushes and grooming equipment were kept.

He gave Julie a hand, showing her how to brush down her horse, then went on to Christie and Ashley.

Julie had to admit to being a little bit surprised by the task—it was a bed-and-breakfast, but she'd rather assumed there might be more help about—but after five minutes of brushing her horse, she discovered that she was talking to the animal. Soothingly.

And the grooming movements, repetitious, physical, slow, were somehow as soothing as the ridiculous sound of her own voice. In her own little stable with her own fairly large horse, she realized that she was happy. No distant sound of traffic could be heard; she could hear her kids—each with his or her mount—apparently enjoying the task as much as she was.

Ashley and little Midget were having one hell of a conversation. Ashley, who carried on with her dolls frequently enough, had no difficulty at all carrying on quite a dialogue with a creature that at least snorted in reply now and then.

Julie smiled, listening, and finished brushing Strawberry. The roan tossed her head and gazed at Julie with her big brown eyes, as if contemplating her with curious concern.

Julie patted her neck and came out of the stall. Darkness had fallen; she didn't see Jesse Wainscott anywhere, but she could hear the children still busy in the different stalls.

"Ashley?" she called.

"She's with me, Mom," Christie replied.

Ashley giggled.

"We're braiding Midget's mane," Ashley told her.

"I don't know if Mr. Wainscott would appreciate that," Julie warned.

"He said it was okay," Jordan said, sticking his head out from the last stall, where the kids were together now with Midget. Jordan wasn't braiding; he'd doled out grain, and now he was just sitting in the hay in the corner, watching his sisters.

"Well, I'm going up to the house to take a bath," Julie said.

"Sure, Mom," Christie said.

"Come back soon; you'll need to wash up for dinner."

"Right," Christie said.

"Don't forget and leave Ashley out here alone," Julie said.

Christie eyed her. "Mom, I won't."

"I'll be with them both," Jordan informed her.

Julie nodded and turned to leave them at last.

She was glad to see her offspring getting along so well together.

Yet it was strange to feel . . .

As if they didn't need her at all. As if they could be complete with just themselves.

"Much better than them fighting like cats and dogs," she muttered aloud as she headed back for the house.

And still . . .

A heaviness weighed her down. A guilt.

They had banded together with one another because their parents were so miserable they had no other choice.

She shook off the thought.

The night could be incredibly dark way out here.

The light from the house beckoned with a warm glow and she hurried for it, moving faster with every step. When she reached the porch, she ran up the stairs, feeling just a little bit like a fool for spooking herself.

She opened the front door and stepped into the foyer, stamping her feet on the rug and slipping from her jacket and gloves, stuffing her gloves into the jacket pocket. "Hello?" she called, coming into the house.

There was no response, but when she moved into the parlor, a fire was burning away in bright, cheerful yellows, gold, and oranges. A pleasant smell pervaded the room, and Julie smiled. In a pot cast over the fire by an iron arm and hook, wine was mulling. The scent of cinnamon in the air was incredibly inviting. Stoneware mugs were set upon a little covered stool right by the fireplace, along with a dipper and tray.

It appeared she was welcome to help herself to the wine. She did so, thinking it would be delightful to sip the brew while sinking into a hot tub.

Mug in hand, she called out another Hello, but no one seemed to be about, so she took her wine upstairs, laid out some clean clothes, and fixed the hot bath she'd been contemplating. She set the mug of wine next to her, sank into the water, and luxuriated.

Hands in his pockets, Jon ambled back along the path to the house. He looked up at the sky, observing the various constellations. It was a very pretty night sky, the heavens like a backdrop of black satin, the stars twinkling against it like so many diamonds. The snow, too, remained crystalline and beautiful, having piled and drifted in various areas and cleared completely in others, without becoming muddy or dirty as it did in the cities.

He passed by an old oak at the front of the property and was surprised to see two men standing beneath it. They were in heavy winter coats and their hats were pulled low. One was lighting a worn-looking clay pipe.

"Evening," the gray-bearded elder of the two greeted him.

"Good evening," Jon replied. The two looked at him somewhat expectantly, so he paused. "Nice night."

"Fine night, yessir," the younger said. "Getting closer to Christmas. Closer and closer. It's going to be a perfect one."

"I agree," Jon said. "A little powder-white snow on the ground, crisp and cool without being killer-cold."

"Yep," the older man said.

"You men from hereabouts?" Jon asked.

The older man arched a brow to the younger. "Well," he said to Jon, "not originally, but then, it feels as if I've been here quite some time now."

"Where are you from, friend?" the younger man asked.

"Miami area," Jon said. To his surprise, they both stared at him blankly.

Surely with its recent reputation for things both bad and good, everyone had heard of Miami.

"South Florida," Jon said.

"Southern boy," the older man said to the younger.

The younger nodded.

"Well, if you can consider South Florida *Southern*," Jon said dryly. The men just stared at him, not seeming to comprehend his comment in the least. "Well, you know, we've a great percentage of Latin Americans in the area, and so many snowbirds you wouldn't believe it."

"Snowbirds?" the older man queried.

Jon had to smile. Okay, so they were out in the sticks. "Snowbirds—northerners transplanted to the South," he explained.

"Oh." The men looked at one another with sudden understanding.

They were definitely a little weird, but he found them entertaining after his solitary day.

He hadn't imagined he'd be quite so alone. He'd assumed that Clarissa Wainscott would eventually appear. Or a housemaid.

A gardener.

Anyone.

But the early afternoon had come and gone, and finally, he'd started out walking. He'd walked a very long way, and it had been great; it had felt wonderful just to walk outside and keep on going and going. He thought once about encountering a car or a mugger—which he didn't have to worry about in the gym, but then, there was no fresh air in the gym, either. And it wasn't that he didn't love his home; he did. Except that, of course, it seemed they never had time for the things they loved. He wanted a boat in the worst way, his own. And if he didn't get his own, he'd like to at least get out on the water more often. Play in the sun. Sun, of course, being among the millions of things that were bad for you these days. But that was all right; he didn't mind bathing in lotion first. It just seemed that he never did the things he wanted to do at home, never took the time.

Yes, walking was great. Seeing his breath before his face.

But walking hadn't been everything that he'd hoped. Plenty of time to think, but the same thoughts just kept revolving around and around. It seemed that he was a fool, just trying to hold on, when he and Julie were at an impasse. Still, he'd been right about Christmas, right about this time for the kids. They hadn't even been here twenty-four hours, but this morning, just this morning, had been special. Making a snowman with his kids. Such a simple thing.

Lots of guys living in the North would have that opportunity all the time. And they wouldn't take it, he reflected. They'd be like him at home. Caught up in the rat race, a rat like all the others. So it was good to be here. Even if, walking in the snow, as glad as he was of the air and the trees and just moving and being alive, he realized it didn't always mean so much to have quiet, and peace. Talking would be nice. Having someone to listen to him.

And since he hadn't seen another living soul all damned day, meeting the two somewhat strange fellows by the oak tree was at least contact with other human beings.

But maybe somebody was back at the house by now. He had a sudden craving to see someone he knew a little better.

His kids.

Julie.

Maybe Julie'd had a great time with the kids as well. And maybe she'd be even colder to him, more convinced than ever that it was over.

It wouldn't be so bad, he told himself. If they both took a big step backward, maybe all the anger and bitterness could fade away.

"Well, it was nice meeting you—" Jon began, even if they hadn't actually met.

"You staying at Oak River Plantation?" the older man asked.

"Yeah."

"Then we'll see you again. Christmas Eve."

"Really?"

"The Wainscotts throw a great party. Every Christmas Eve. We all get together," the younger man said.

"And let bygones be bygones," the older agreed.

"Well . . . great," Jon said. "See you then."

He dug his hands into his pockets and started on down the last of the trail toward the house.

Her bath was great.

The water was very hot.

The tub was a huge, old, deep thing.

No one was yelling.

No music blared.

She was very tired and sore, but in a wonderful way. The hot water worked over weary muscles. The wine seemed to ease into her blood. It was heaven. It was peace.

Yet as the water cooled at last, it was suddenly a bit too lonely.

How strange. She craved time alone so often. Now she had it. In complete comfort. And she wanted people. Her family.

She emerged from the tub, dressed, brushed her hair, and still heard no activity upstairs. Freshly clad in a denim jumper, she came down the stairs, knowing she'd feel just a bit spooked if the house was still empty.

But it wasn't empty. She could hear Jon's voice.

Along with Clarissa Wainscott's soft tones.

"You do enjoy the law?" Clarissa inquired.

"I love the law," Jon said.

"But you're not happy with what you're doing now?" Clarissa asked.

Jon's laugh brought Julie up short. It had a rueful and more than slight note of bitterness to it.

"I hate what I'm doing now."

"But every man is entitled to the best defense—"

"That money can buy," Jon finished for her, and Julie found herself standing very still on the stairway, listening.

Eavesdropping, not really meaning to do so, yet somehow thinking it was important to hear what Jon had to say.

"The law is beautiful when the law works," Jon said. "It's even beautiful when you're fighting to make it work. But it's true, I don't like what I'm doing now at all."

Halfway down the stairs, Julie could just see her husband, leaning forward slightly, hands prayer-fashion as he tapped his chin with his fingers and watched the fire. "I loved the D.A.'s office. It wasn't perfect. It was far, far from perfect, actually. My desk was always a mess, piled high. But ..." He shrugged, smiling a little. "I was good. I was really good at what I did. Cops are always taking a bad rap, but I worked with some good cops. And every once in a while, everything fell into place. The cops were right on the money, the evidence was sound and we managed to present it in the clearest way possible, and the law was good. God, I just hate it when I'm racking my brain to get a sleazebag off!" Jon shook his head, lifting his hands, letting them fall back again. "Every man is entitled to a defense, and God knows, innocent men and women do wind up in court, but hell, I never seem to be asked to defend the innocent ones. I get Bobo Vinzetti and his attempted pizza murder."

"Why did you change jobs?" Clarissa asked him.

Julie wished she couldn't see her husband's face quite so clearly. In the firelight, the planes and angles were clearly defined; there was a look both somehow hard and somehow a little hopeless about his features.

"Money," he said softly after a moment. He shrugged. "Money. Three kids to get through college. Clothes. Food. House payments, you know."

"But you and your wife both work, don't you?" Clarissa asked. "Surely your incomes ..." Her voice trailed away. "I'm sorry, it's truly none of my business."

"No, no, I started this conversation. I suppose we could get along. Julie's a realtor. She loves houses, and I don't think she even knows how good she is at her job. People don't have to ask many questions about her properties twice; she investigates it all to the hilt. We'd probably be all right, but no matter how good Julie is, real estate is chancy. Of course, one good sale can put us pretty far ahead. It just seems that everything has gotten so expensive lately. I don't remember it being so bad when I was a kid."

"Times do change," Clarissa murmured. "Maybe you and Julie need to change a little, too."

"It's sad sometimes, frustrating. I mean, life on paper looks just about perfect for us, and it should be. We've got three healthy kids, and God knows, with all the terrible diseases and accidents that can hurt children, I think sometimes that I should be a happy, grateful man just for the kids alone. And I am. I do know enough to be grateful for what I have, which makes it more frustrating—" He broke off, then laughed ruefully. "It makes it all the more frustrating to be miserable when I have a job, a roof over my head, food, great kids, and a paid electric bill. It's just that . . . well, you know, sometimes you get caught up in the rat race and then just lost within it."

"That's true," Clarissa agreed. "It's quite easy to get caught up in the events around you. But then again, maybe if you took some time . . . a step back, a step away, you'd see your way through. Naturally, you and your wife both need to take a good look at things."

"Naturally," Jon said.

Julie wondered if Clarissa Wainscott heard the way in which Jon said the single word.

Naturally.

He didn't say a word against her; only she could possibly hear and understand the edge to his voice.

He didn't say that life was expensive because his wife liked her house and car and intended to send all three of their children to the best colleges.

Oh, God, was she that selfish?

No, no, she had never wanted things; she had never craved or desired objects just for the sake of having them. What he had said had been the truth; they had both gotten caught up in a lifestyle. It had never seemed so bad.

Well, not to her.

Because she was happy in real estate.

She liked what she did. She liked the people she worked with; they were wonderful. And in all honesty, especially lately, she'd been so bitter toward Jon that it would never have occurred to her to wonder if he was happy with what he did or not.

He never talked to her about his work.

He was talking to Clarissa Wainscott. Spilling his heart to a stranger who ran a guest house. A woman he'd met only yesterday.

Right. Well, wasn't she so bitter because he'd done more than talk with another woman before? Because she'd lost something that she'd taken completely for granted? Trust.

Yes.

But . . .

She should have asked him about work. Now and then. She had wanted so desperately to make a major sale. Not because she had to make a sale. Because she wanted to make a sale. To show him that she could, to show him what she was worth. Well, she had made her big sale and nothing had changed. Besides, it had been the security offered by his job that had given her the luxury to develop her real estate career.

And now she was finally seeing what he was really thinking and feeling.

Because he was talking to another woman.

What did you expect when you've been all but throwing the man away? she asked herself.

Because, because, because . . . what was left when trust was gone?

Did she really have the right to be so furious? Maybe his logic made some sense.

Maybe her pride was just so wounded she couldn't stand it.

And he wasn't paying for his sins.

He was paying for her pride.

No, she had a right to be angry, she told herself. Yet standing there on the stairway, she was suddenly so miserable that she wanted to crawl beneath something.

She didn't have to crawl beneath anything. All she had to do was slink on back upstairs. She could pretend to fall asleep, and they'd all leave her alone. And the kids would come in, and dinner would be served. And the night would be pleasant, filled with delicious things to eat and the tantalizing, sweet smell of the mulled wine in the air.

Clarissa Wainscott's soft, pleasant laughter . . .

Her children, talking, laughing as well.

All the warmth.

Without her.

It didn't matter. She needed to be alone. She suddenly felt as if she were going to cry, and she didn't even know what she was going to cry about.

She turned to head back up the stairs. But she'd

barely taken a step before she heard her name called.

"Julie!"

Julie spun around.

Clarissa was at the foot of the stairs, smiling up at her with genuine enthusiasm.

"Julie!"

Clarissa had a way of saying a name that made it sound as if she were absolutely delighted to see you.

"I was beginning to think that my husband had lost you all in the forest! How was the ride? Beautiful, I hope. Not too cold?"

"No, no, the day was great."

Jon was up now, too, a mug of the wine in his hands as he stood at the foot of the staircase, looking up at her. He looked nice, she thought. Handsome in a crimson sweater and jeans. Hair half brushed back, half falling over his forehead.

"The kids?" he inquired just a bit anxiously.

"They did great."

"Ashley?"

"Ashley rode Midget. She did very well."

"Where is she?"

"At the stables."

"Ashley is still out—"

"With her brother and sister." Julie glanced at Clarissa. "They were braiding Midget's mane. Your husband told them it would be fine."

"My husband is an excellent horseman," Clarissa said. Her tone was proud. Her smile was just a bit tremulous. "You had a nice ride, I imagine? Jesse knows these woods like the back of his hand."

"He was wonderful with the children, Clarissa."

Clarissa Wainscott nodded. "He would be," she murmured softly.

Oddly, Julie found herself clearing her throat. "I assume the kids will be back to the house soon."

"You needn't worry about them. They're perfectly fine on the property," Clarissa assured her. "Well, excuse me for a moment, will you? I've got a few things to see to in the kitchen. Julie, come down; the wine is my specialty."

"I've tried it; it's delicious."

"Try more," Clarissa said, her smile curling as if with some inner secret. "It gets better and better with each sip. Jon, draw your wife another mug, enjoy the fire. I'll be right back with you."

She left them, heading off to the kitchen.

And for the first time in years and years, Julie found herself feeling just a bit unsettled.

She was alone with the man she'd been married to for almost all of her adult life. The man she lived with day after day. And he was, in a way, a stranger who had just shared a more personal conversation with the mistress of Oak River Plantation than he had shared with her for a very long time. She was surprised to realize that she was a little breathless. And that she wanted to hear him talking to her as he had been talking to Clarissa. She wanted him to talk, and she wanted to listen.

She wanted something back that she had lost, but that might still be there. She wanted to touch him, and be touched in turn.

Anger was a very cold emotion, she realized. She had lived in the chill of it for a very long time. She knew suddenly what she wanted for Christmas.

She wanted to be warm.

Chapter Thirteen

"So ..." Jon murmured, lifting his hands just slightly, awkwardly. "You really did enjoy the ride."

Julie came down the stairs to the parlor area. "I really did enjoy the ride. How about you? How was your day?"

"Uneventful," Jon said. "I walked. There's a beautiful little pond nearby, completely frozen over. I walked all the way around it and back."

"Nice," Julie murmured.

She had brought her empty wine mug down with her. Jon took it from her. "I'm supposed to be refilling this, I think." He walked toward the fireplace and the kettle. "You do want more?"

"Please."

He refilled her mug. Julie felt oddly as if she were conversing politely with a stranger, looking for casual things to say. "The wine is very good."

"Very," he agreed. "Everything here is good."

"Yes, it is. It was a good idea, coming here. The children are having a really good time. I heard them laughing this morning and . . ." She shrugged. "The ride was wonderful. The horses were beautiful; the landscape here is out of this world."

"And Jesse Wainscott must be far better company than that which you're accustomed to."

"What does that mean?" she asked.

He shook his head. "Nothing more than exactly what I said. They're both wonderful people."

"Jesse—and his wife, of course."

"Right," Jon said.

"She seems to be very easy to talk to," Julie said.

"Yeah, she is," Jon admitted. But then, it seemed that he was determined to avoid a quarrel. He smiled. "But we were just talking about life in general, and it seems you can get bogged down in that discussion easily. Tell me more about the ride. It must have been more interesting."

"Oh . . . well, like I said, it was really wonderful. The trails are beautiful; the air is perfect. We met the Wainscotts' son today—or at least Christie did."

"Oh?"

"In the cemetery."

"The cemetery?"

"There's an old family graveyard in the most marvelous green copse."

"And he was just hanging around in this cemetery?"

Julie smiled. "I think he'd been riding, too, and he'd happened to stop there."

"So did he join you for the rest of your ride?"

"No, but I think he made something of an impression on Christie."

Jon arched a brow. "Really? I wonder if he'll be at the Christmas Eve party."

"The party?"

Jon nodded. "There's a big party here. Everyone comes. I met a couple of oddball neighbors outside. They assured me that they came every Christmas Eve."

"Well, that should be fun."

"A very traditional costume ball, so it seems."

Julie smiled. "Wouldn't a traditional costume ball be Halloween?"

"Not here. This is an old-fashioned Christmas, remember."

Suddenly, they heard the sound of the front door banging.

"Ashley?" Christie called.

"Mom, Dad!"

"It was your fault!" Christie told Jordan.

"Mine? You're the one who yelled at her and told her that she did braids like a retard!"

Julie stared at Jon, then raced for the foyer where

Jordan and Christie, red-faced and frightened, were staring at one another, hurling accusations.

"Both of you stop it and tell me what happened!" Julie demanded.

They whirled around and stared at her. They glanced at one another.

The color drained from their faces.

"Ashley . . . is gone," Christie said.

"Gone!" Julie gasped in panic.

Jon set a hand on her shoulder. "She can't have gone far."

Tears welled in her eyes and Julie shrugged off his touch. "Gone—what do you mean, gone? For how long? When did you last see her?"

"Christie yelled at her," Jordan said.

"You called her a pest," Christie told him.

"Yeah, but you're the one who made her cry."

"She cries at anything!"

"How long has she been gone?" Jon demanded.

Jordan stared at his father, flushing uncomfortably again. "Just a few minutes, tops, Dad. We thought that maybe she'd come in the house."

"We didn't see her, but it's not impossible," Jon said.

"There's a pond on the property!" Julie said. She heard the panic rising in her voice.

"Frozen over," Jon assured her.

"It's dark away from the house. It's horribly dark,

and cold. There are thick woods. She could fall, hurt herself, start to freeze to dea—"

"Julie, she's only been missing a few minutes," Jon reminded her. "Come on, Jordan—you and I will search outside. Christie, take your mother, go through the house."

Julie was about to protest; she didn't need anyone to tell her what to do. She would search from now until forever for her daughter.

Oh, God! she thought. Please don't let Ashley's disappearance be a punishment for us being awful people.

Jon and Jordan left the house. Julie whirled around, so panicked she was ready to scream.

Clarissa Wainscott, calm and dignified as always in her voluminous period dress, was there. Julie hadn't heard her come back into the room.

"I'm sure that she's fine," Clarissa said, her beautiful eyes very soft, filled with understanding. Apparently, she had heard what was going on.

But Julie wasn't so sure she wanted understanding. She was even a little bit irritated at the moment with the oh-so-perfect Clarissa Wainscott. "You don't know, you don't . . ." Julie choked out in a whisper.

Clarissa didn't know what? Julie taunted herself. *That she was a bad mother and she deserved to lose her daughter? Oh, God, she'd sell chocolate from here to eternity with a smile if she could just see Ashley's face again.*

"I know that we'll find her," Clarissa said with assurance. "And I'm equally certain that no one is at fault in her disappearance; children can be very stubborn at times, and they certainly do have their own minds. We'll search the house."

She turned around, heading for the stairs. Julie followed her, her heart sinking.

Her sister and brother were monsters, Ashley had determined. For a few minutes, everything had been nice. They'd been having a good time together—even Christie had loved the horses.

Then suddenly Christie and Jordan had started fighting, and she'd tried to say something that would stop them, and they'd both lashed out at her instead.

"Stinks, stinks!" she said aloud. She sniffed loudly, trying to stop her sobs. Wouldn't matter, not up here. She had found her way up another flight of stairs to a dark, musty little room lit up only by the moonlight. She was far above them all, wondering just what she should do.

Run away.

Make them all sorry for being so mean to her!

She sniffed again.

"Are you all right?"

She gasped, and almost ruined it all by screaming at the top of her lungs in sheer terror. She had thought that she was all alone with the old trunks and dressmaker's dummies, boxes, papers, and spiderwebs.

But she wasn't. Yet she managed not to scream because it wasn't anybody scary or threatening who was talking to her; it was a young girl.

She was older than Ashley, younger than Christie.

And like everyone else around here, she was dressed up in an old-fashioned long gown. It was dark blue, with a very fine lace collar. Her hair was dark and had been braided, and then her braids had been pinned to the back of her head. It was a very pretty hairdo.

"I'm—I'm—" Ashley began.

"Big brother, eh?" the girl asked wisely.

"Big brother and big sister," Ashley said. She drew her knees up beneath her, resting her hands on her knees and her chin on her hands. "They're just so—mean!"

"They can be," the girl agreed. "But most of the time, I don't think they mean it." She sighed. "They get old so fast, and they forget what it's like to have fun. They start to take themselves so very seriously!"

Ashley nodded in agreement, sniffing, looking at the girl again.

"You're kind of old."

"A little old, but not that old. Young enough for this to still be my favorite place in the house."

"Where are we, anyway?"

The girl laughed. "What do you mean, where are we? We're in the attic."

"The attic?"

"You've never been in an attic?" the girl demanded incredulously.

"We don't have them where I live," Ashley said indignantly. "At least, I don't think we do. Well, anyway, my house doesn't have an attic."

"Well, then, you're in for a treat!" the girl said. "An attic is a playground. An attic is where everything old is kept: your mother's clothes, and her mother's clothes, and old clocks, and trunks—and see, there's my old wooden rocking horse from when I was just about your age."

Ashley saw the old horse; it was great. She looked at the girl eagerly. "May I use your horse?"

"Of course. And you have to go through the trunks. You have to dress up for Christmas Eve, you know."

"Dress up?"

"Sure."

"You mean, not just you people who live here, but everyone gets to dress up?"

"Sure," the girl said. She seemed amused, but nicely so. She wasn't making fun of Ashley or anything.

Ashley went running over to the rocking horse. She carefully climbed atop it, thinking how pretty it was, how beautifully painted. The girl walked around the attic, opening trunks.

"Here are some of my things from when I was about your size," the girl said. "Find yourself something in here. Then, of course, you could bring your family up here to find something special to wear, too."

"Yeah," Ashley said. She smiled. "But I'm going to find my dress first and make Christie ask me *nicely* where I found it!"

"That sounds only fair," the girl agreed.

"What's your name?" Ashley asked.

"Mary."

"I'm Ashley."

"I know."

"How?"

"I've heard people talking to you," Mary explained.

She was older, and smart. And she smiled a lot at Ashley, but not in a bad way. Ashley liked her.

"Ashley!"

She heard her mother's voice then, calling to her. And she sounded really upset, as if she'd been crying.

Ashley wasn't so sure that she wanted to run away anymore. Her brother and sister might be monsters sometimes, but it hurt way deep inside to hear her mother's voice sound the way it did now.

"Mommy!" she called. Regretfully, she crawled off the rocking horse. "I guess I have to go down."

"Come back up when you need to."

"Are you always here?"

"I play here a lot."

"Will you be coming down to dinner?"

Mary brought a finger to her lips. "I'm not really supposed to be here. But I'll see you at the party on Christmas Eve, if not before!"

Ashley nodded vigorously. She heard her mother's voice again, calling her name. And Ashley could hear in her mother's voice that she was about to cry. A feeling of shame overwhelmed her and she rushed to the attic door and opened it, then hurried down the narrow wooden staircase to the second-floor landing below.

"Mommy? Mommy?" she cried.

Julie came rushing along the hallway, falling to her knees in front of Ashley and encompassing her in a tight hug. "Ashley! Ashley, where did you go? I was worried sick; Daddy is worried sick! I was so afraid that you'd gotten lost someplace outside."

"I'm sorry, Mommy, honest, I'm sorry," Ashley said, hugging her mother back, shaken by the emotion in her mother's words and touch. Julie drew away at last, looking at Ashley. "Where did you go, honey? Even if Christie and Jordan make you mad, sweetheart, you can't just go running off!"

"I was just up in the attic. I didn't mean to scare you, really."

Ashley realized that Clarissa Wainscott was standing behind her mother, watching her. She caught Mrs. Wainscott's eye. Mrs. Wainscott smiled at her, then said, "I'll go down and tell Christie to call your husband and son in, Julie." She walked by Ashley, placing a hand lightly on her head and tousling her hair. There was a nice, warm feel to Mrs. Wainscott's touch. Ashley liked her very much. Mommy didn't even seem to notice her. She was still staring at Ashley, and she was holding her tight, as if she was afraid she'd disappear again if she let her go.

"Ashley, promise me you'll never just walk away like that again."

"I promise."

"I can't believe that you ran up to a spooky old attic."

"It isn't spooky. It's neat. There's an old rocking

horse and all kinds of old trunks and things. I'll take you there if you want."

Her mother smoothed back her hair. "I'm not so sure we should just go prowling around in someone else's attic. Attics can be kind of private places. They hold a family's memories. The things that hold a family together."

Ashley frowned, staring at her. "Is that why we can't hold our family together? Because we don't have an attic?"

"What? No, no, of course not, that's not what I meant. I just meant that the attic holds things that are personal to Mr. and Mrs. Wainscott and we should at least be invited to go there."

"I was invited."

Julie frowned. "Mrs. Wainscott told you that you could go up to the attic tonight?"

"No, no, I found a friend—"

"Honey, secret imaginary friends can't really ask you into the attic," Julie said, smiling.

Ashley didn't get a chance to explain that her friend wasn't imaginary because by then Daddy had come. Christie and Jordan were behind him.

"Ashley!"

Daddy picked her up and whirled her around before setting her down, kissing her on both cheeks, and crushing her into a hug. Then Jordan was on his knees at her side, hugging her, too. "Squirt!" he called her, but he said it nicely, with just a little bit of accusation in his tone.

"Don't you ever do that again!" Christie told her, but Christie, too, was down on her knees, pulling her into her arms from Jordan's. It was really nice. And weird. Nobody had wanted to pay any attention to her. And now they were all about to squeeze the breath from her.

"You called me names," Ashley reminded her sister.

"I call Jordan names all the time," Christie said dryly, "and I can't get *him* to go away!"

"She's just plain old mean, you have to remember that," Jordan told Ashley.

"You two stop it right now," Daddy said. "That's how this whole thing got started. No name-calling by anyone. And Ashley, young lady, no disappearing again, do you understand?"

Ashley nodded. Jordan and Christie were actually quiet.

"Hello, up there!" Mrs. Wainscott called from the foyer. "Dinner is ready for you, if you're ready for dinner."

"Let's go down," Daddy said. He offered a hand to Mommy, who was still kneeling in the hallway, right where she'd been when it had just been her hugging Ashley.

She slowly took his hand.

"What's the matter?"

She made a funny face. "It's a little unsettling. We've had this family fracas right in front of Mrs. Wainscott."

"We didn't do anything that terrible," Daddy assured her. "It's all right."

Mommy shook her head. "It's like—it's like she sees everything that's going on."

"Julie, our dinner must be getting cold. Ashley slipped by her sister and brother, and hid in the attic to brood a few minutes, and—" he gave Ashley a stern look, "scared us all half to death." He looked at Julie again. "Things like that happen. To all people."

She accepted his hand at last and stood. "You all go down. I'll take Ashley to wash her face and hands. She's all smudged with dust."

Ashley sneezed. "Are attics supposed to have dust?"

"Most do," Daddy assured her. "Jordan, Christie, let's go on down."

"Right," Jordan murmured, starting down the stairs. Christie, still silent, followed him. Julie set her hands on Ashley's shoulders, spinning her toward the double doors to their guest suite.

"Start washing up, sweetie."

Ashley nodded, quickly moving to do as she had been told. If it had been someplace else, she might have been scared being alone. But not here.

Because she was never really alone.

"Julie, it wasn't that big a thing, really," Jon told her. "Hey, we found Ashley safe and sound."

"I know. And I'm grateful." Something still seemed to be twisting in Julie's stomach. She was embarrassed. "The Wainscotts just seem so damned perfect themselves," she murmured.

"You're embarrassed," Jon said.

"No, it's not that."

"It is. And you're wrong. Nobody's perfect."

"Maybe nobody's perfect, but . . ."

"But what?" Jon demanded.

"Our behavior is just so bad."

"Oh."

"I said *our* behavior. I wasn't pointing any fingers. And the Wainscotts . . . when they talk about one another, there's just so much . . ."

"So much what?"

"Warmth. As if the other person really matters. As if things are perfect between them, the kind of perfect—"

"Damn it, what is it?"

She shook her head. "I don't know, I don't know what I'm saying. We're just so . . ."

"Julie!"

"It just seems that we're so *ugly* at times."

Jon just stared at her for a long moment. Julie felt her stomach twist painfully. What she had meant to say just didn't come out right. She didn't mean to be so hateful herself all the time. She didn't mean to be tired and aggravated and selfish. And Jon had looked at her a little bit differently when the night had started. They'd smiled; they'd talked, awkwardly, but it had been nice, and now . . .

Now he was looking at her with a cool, distant look in his eyes again. Removing himself, perhaps, she thought, from the reach of her claws.

"I'm willing to bet that even your perfect Wainscotts must have a few skeletons in the closet," he said. But he shrugged, lifting his hands. "We're probably ruining Clarissa's dinner. I mean, it's a bed-and-breakfast and we're paying, but I imagine that going down to eat the meal would be the courteous thing to do. Especially since we've had this conversation before. I'll go down. See if you can't hurry Ashley along."

Jon started down the stairs. Julie watched him go, filled with regret, but wondering if it were possible to go back far enough not to feel such terrible hurt all the time. "Jon!" she said, calling him back.

He stopped, a hand on the banister, and turned to her.

"I didn't say that *you* were ugly. I said that we were."

He shook his head, his eyes steady on her. "We're not."

She tried to explain. "It just seems that we're so hateful at times that we've even raised our children to be nasty to one another—"

"No, we haven't. Everyone has problems. Everyone. Siblings fight. That's life; that's the way it is. Tonight Christie and Jordan were wrong, and they know it, but they love Ashley, they didn't mean to hurt her, and whether you want to believe it or not, they wouldn't want to hurt one another, either." He hesitated just a second, then he walked back up the stairs to stand before her, not touching her, gripping the banister tightly as he spoke. "And I didn't mean to hurt you. I don't know how to say it any more meaningfully than that. I love you, Julie. I loved you when I married you, and I love you now. In my one great extramarital affair, the one you won't forgive me for, I withered like a damned dying bean pole because she wasn't you. All I remember from it was a lot of embarrassment and discomfort and misery in wondering just how many years my life would be a disaster if we didn't get back together. I love you, and I love my family. After all these years. But you know what? I refuse to go through what I went through before. So if you're so certain you want to call it quits, you just go ahead and do it now. Give up, throw in the towel. And good luck in your new life."

Chapter Fourteen

Christie wished that there was a phone in her room. She didn't dare go downstairs and ask if she could make a call. She hadn't seen a phone in the house, but her mother had called to make the reservations here, so there had to be a phone somewhere.

"Ashley?" she said softly.

Her little sister was curled against her, sound asleep. Ashley loved the house. And the vacation. She hadn't even stayed mad at Christie and Jordan; she had just talked excitedly about the attic during dinner, and Mrs. Wainscott had said that tomorrow they must all go up and find something to wear for the Christmas Eve ball tomorrow night. Dinner had been okay. Despite the fact that her parents hadn't said a word to one another during the entire meal. She didn't know where they were now. Her father had gone outside first, then her mother. But she didn't think that they were together. They wanted to be alone.

Christie turned on her back and sighed, wishing she could fall asleep. She smiled, thinking that she had liked Aaron Wainscott. Of course, he was older. And if Jamie hadn't been in her life . . . but Jamie *was* her life. Still, she liked Aaron, and she was glad he had asked her to come back and talk. She intended to do so. She wondered what Aaron and his father could possibly have disagreed on. Mr. Wainscott was wonderful. Tall, handsome, with something wonderfully gentle and noble about him as well. And Mrs. Wainscott was so lovely and so sweet. They were . . . perfect.

Something rebelled within her, and she reminded herself that her own father was a very handsome man, and noble, maybe, in his own way. He worked very hard. She knew that. She loved him. He was smart, he paid attention to her—he was just so damned pigheaded. Her folks had taught her all her life that there was no difference between people— religion didn't matter, race didn't matter, nationality didn't matter. But Jamie lived on the wrong street—as if he'd chosen his own address!—and so he was condemned.

She twisted in bed. Well, she'd like to compromise, as Aaron had said. But she wasn't giving

Jamie up, and if her folks didn't accept Jamie, next year she'd be gone.

And that was that.

She closed her eyes tightly. She wanted to sleep. The house was warm and beautiful at night, but Christie wanted it to be day again. She wanted to ride back out to the cemetery and talk to Aaron. She hadn't met a friend so easy to talk to in a very long time.

Just when she thought that she might have drifted off, she heard a gasping sound from the next room. She sat up in bed and listened.

"Jordan?" she called softly.

There was no answer. Ashley's little mouth was open and she was breathing deeply in her sound sleep. Christie slipped out of bed and walked into her brother's room.

"Jordan?" she whispered again. There was no light on in the room, but her own had been dark so her eyes had adjusted. Looking around, she saw that her brother was half on the daybed and half off it. He was on his back with his head hanging nearly to the floor.

"Jordan!" she cried, running across the room to him. She picked up his head, trying to put it back on the daybed. "Jordan, damn you, talk to me. Jordan, don't you do this to me. Jordan!"

His skin was cold. He wasn't responding. Christie panicked.

She leapt up and went rushing into her parents' room, throwing the door open.

But they weren't there. Neither of them.

"Oh, God!" Christie breathed.

But she didn't waste time just standing there; she rushed out into the hallway, gripped the banister, and screamed, "Help! Help me, please!" at the top of her lungs.

There was enough moonlight to brighten the property nicely.

Jon had left the house as soon as he could manage to do so courteously after dinner. Not that the meal had been unpleasant in any way. Jordan and Christie had been eager to make things up with Ashley since they'd all had such a scare. And Clarissa had talked about the ball, and how they must all dress up and enjoy the festivities. Julie had been polite but withdrawn, watching what went on rather than taking any part in it.

The pond drew Jon. Clarissa had told him earlier that there was a little shed near it where he could find skates that he was more than welcome to use. He hadn't been ice-skating in years, not since he'd been a kid and his folks had taken him north for the holidays each year. He'd been fairly decent at it in those days, though, and he was tempted to try again. The ice, the air, the night, were all inviting.

Jon went to the old wooden shed by the pond. The door wasn't locked, and he opened it. He wondered if he were crazy, coming out by himself in the night to try skating again. He wondered if he was in the middle of a midlife crisis, but he decided he had a few years to go before that actually happened. He was definitely trying to recapture something, though. Something clean and fresh—innocent, maybe. He wanted to believe again. In what?

Himself, maybe.

There was no light in the shed, or if there was, he couldn't find it. It was all right. Enough moonlight poured in so that he could see around him. All sizes of skates hung from hooks along one wall. There were what looked like sleds leaning against a far wall, and a table in the center of the small building seemed to be laden with all manner of tools.

Jon looked at the skates, whistling softly. Some of them were really antique, probably worth a bundle. Not wanting to take a chance on destroying what might be valuable property, he tried to find what looked like the most modern pair in his own size. Jesse Wainscott must skate, he thought, because there were plenty of men's skates in a size large enough for him.

Jon chose a pair, then walked down to the pond area. He found a tree stump to sit on, slid off his boots and laced on the skates. They were a fair fit, nice and snug.

Two steps out on the ice, he fell flat on his rear and slid along on it for about ten feet. He came to a halt, feeling like an idiot. Then he started to laugh. Well, what did he expect? He should have practiced skating again at a rink, where they had rails along the sides of the ice for inexperienced skaters to hold on to. He was on a pond.

But he could do this.

After a few failed tries, he came back to his feet. He balanced himself, and took a few tentative glides. It felt okay. He started to move along the ice in greater sweeps. The movement became natural and comfortable, and then it felt wonderful. He closed his eyes, feeling the cool air on the pond and the warmth his body created against it. His muscles felt great.

It was fun to play. Of course, it would be more fun if he weren't by himself.

He thought he heard laughter. He opened his eyes, looking along the pond where the moonlight glistened upon the ice. For a moment, he could have sworn he saw couples skating together on the ice. Men in high hats and frock coats, women in long woolen gowns, carrying fur muffs. Laughter seemed to fill the air again.

He blinked. The silence of the night came around him again. He was alone on the ice. He whirled in a deep circle, then paused.

He wasn't alone. Julie had come to the ice. She was seated on the stump where he had changed his shoes for the skates.

"Christie! What is it?" Clarissa Wainscott demanded worriedly, hurrying up the staircase toward her. In the darkened hallway, the woman moved with hauntingly beautiful grace in her period costume.

"Mrs. Wainscott, my folks aren't here. My brother —my brother—" Her brother might be dying; she needed to admit the truth. "My brother does drugs. He usually just smokes a little pot, but he's got some friends who have gotten him into pills as well and he's—he's in bad shape."

Clarissa Wainscott moved past Christie quickly, turning on the light as she stepped into the room and going to Jordan's side. She felt his forehead, then opened his eyes one at a time.

"We've got to get him up," Clarissa said.

"We need an ambulance—"

"I think we can handle this all right. An ambulance—an ambulance would take forever. We've got to get him moving right now. Help me. Once we get him up, I'll get something in him to purge his stomach."

They shouldn't have been in the boonies, Christie thought. They needed an ambulance badly. Her brother was heavy. Getting him up wasn't easy.

But Mrs. Wainscott did it. She had Jordan on his feet. "We don't want him to choke," she warned Christie.

"Is he really alive?" Christie asked worriedly. He was slumped between them. His eyes weren't open and his complexion was pasty white.

"He's alive, and honestly, he's not quite so bad as you think. Jordan!" she said, slapping Jordan's cheek. "Walk, now. Your sister is with you; walk!"

Then Clarissa Wainscott told Christie she'd be right back, and Christie was left with her brother.

"Jordan, I'm going to kill you!" she told him tearfully. Then she shook him. "Don't you die. Don't you die! Don't you dare die on me; I'll tear you right to pieces if you do!" She thought about the irony of her words and nearly started laughing.

"Please, Jordan, don't you die on me! I can't take Mom and Dad alone; you can't do this to Ashley. Jordan, please!"

He spoke to her at last. "Movin', Christie. I'm movin'. Walking . . ."

His feet were beginning to find the floor on their own. He was still an incredibly heavy burden.

Then Clarissa was back with them. She offered a steaming cup of something to Jordan. "Drink this, now, Jordan. Take a few sips."

She managed to get some of the hot liquid through his lips. He looked dead again for a second, then he suddenly came to life, gripping his stomach. "Bathroom!" he gasped, and on his own, he made it there.

Clarissa followed behind him, then stood at the sink, dampening towels to clean Jordan up when he was finished emptying his stomach. Christie just stood in the center of her brother's room, feeling helpless.

Then Mrs. Wainscott and her brother came back into the room. Jordan leaned heavily against Clarissa, groaning. She smoothed a cool, wet towel over his face.

"Is he going to be all right?" Christie asked anxiously.

"He's going to be fine."

Jordan groaned.

"Really?" Christie whispered.

"Yes. He can lie down now. Stay with him; I'm going to get him something to drink."

"Oh, no!" Jordan protested with energy. "No, please, no more—"

"I'm going to get you a cup of herb tea, young man, nothing awful again. It will settle your stomach."

Clarissa left them. Christie sat next to her brother, smoothing his hair back. Clarissa must have known what she was doing. Jordan might feel sick as a dog—which he deserved!—but his color was back.

"Christie?" Jordan said. He sounded so young. He was young. Just thirteen. Sometimes, she thought, they tried to grow up so fast that they didn't know how young they were themselves.

"I'm here, Jordan."

Tears started to trickle down his cheeks. "I messed up big, huh?"

"Yeah."

"Does Dad know? Is Mom here?"

"They're both still outside somewhere. And Ashley is sleeping."

"Man, it *is* Christmas!" Jordan sighed.

Christie stopped smoothing his hair and gave his cheek a sharp little rap with her fingers. "You little fool! You just cost me ten years of my life."

"I'm sorry, Christie. I'm so sorry. I'm quitting, as of this minute. I swear it, Christie. Don't tell Mom and Dad, please?"

"Jordan, they need to know—"

"No, no they don't. Not now, Christie. Some other time, yes. But now ... it could just make everything worse."

Christie stood, staring at him. "What did you bring with you and where is it?" she demanded.

He pointed to his backpack, just inside a closet. Christie dragged it out and dug through it. She found two vials of pills. She stared at Jordan, then walked into the bathroom and flushed the pills down the john.

"Thanks," Jordan said.

"Hey, it's not just me. You're going to have to clear this with Mrs. Wainscott."

"Oh," Jordan breathed.

They both looked toward the door because Clarissa Wainscott was coming in then with a tray. There were mugs of steaming tea on it, along with a plate of crackers.

"This should help some, Jordan," she said. "Christie, I thought you might like herb tea, too."

"Thank you," Christie said.

She and Jordan both stared at Clarissa awkwardly. "I think I'll try the tea," Jordan croaked. He swallowed some of it down slowly—and suspiciously. But the tea sat well in his stomach and tasted good.

He took in a deep breath.

"Mrs. Wainscott, thank you. I think you saved my life."

She shrugged. "I'm not sure it was quite so dire as all that. You would have been all right as long as you didn't get sick in the night and choke."

"Mrs. Wainscott . . ." Jordan tried.

Christie cleared her throat. "He doesn't want you to say anything to our parents. I mean, if they had come in, well, they would have had to know. But they haven't come back to the house yet. And . . ." Christie broke off, not sure how to go on herself.

Jordan picked up where she left off. "Please, please, don't say anything. It's not that I'm afraid of being punished; it's not that I don't deserve it. But things are a little awkward now."

"Real awkward," Christie said. "They're most probably going to split up."

"But maybe not. And I don't want them to think it's their fault. I mean, yeah, well, they're fighting a lot lately, but I wasn't trying to do myself in or anything because of them. I wasn't trying to do myself in at all. But if they knew . . . well, they'd feel really guilty and the focus would all be on me, instead of them trying to work out their marriage. They'd accuse themselves, they'd start accusing each other, and they'd feel worse, and it would just all be worse, and . . . please. I'm really okay. I'm going to be okay. Can we not say anything?"

Clarissa Wainscott was staring at Christie. Christie looked at her brother, reached for his hand, and squeezed it.

"Jordan, I understand what you're saying. But you have to think about you, too. It wouldn't be bad if you did need help out of this."

"Christie, I swear to you, I'll never touch another pill or roll another joint as long as I live," he vowed, and he meant every word he said. "And when it's right, I will tell Mom and Dad. I promise."

Christie looked at Clarissa. "I think he's going to be okay. I think he means it."

"Your folks really do have a right to know," Clarissa said.

"I'll tell them on my own, within the next few weeks, honestly," Jordan told her. She was watching him intently.

Finally, she nodded. She looked at Christie and smiled. "We'll trust you." She stood. "You need some sleep. Tomorrow your stomach will be sore, but I don't think you'll suffer any other symptoms. This time, you're going to be all right."

"There won't be a next time," Jordan promised.

"He does mean it," Christie said again.

Clarissa nodded. "Well, then, I'll leave you two to watch out for one another."

"Mrs. Wainscott?" Jordan asked as she started out of the room with a whisper of silk and the scent of violets.

"Yes?" she asked softly, turning back.

"Maybe we could not mention this to anyone. Maybe—maybe could your husband not know about this either?"

"Why?"

"I'm afraid that maybe he won't trust me so much. And maybe he won't let me be around the horses again."

She smiled. "He will. If I tell him it's okay."

"Will you do that?"

After a moment, she nodded. "Yes. I'll do that. Good night, now."

With that, she left him. Jordan closed his eyes. He felt Christie put another cool cloth on his head. It felt so good.

"Christie?"

"Yeah?"

"Thanks."

"Sure."

"Christie?"

"Yeah?"

"You really don't suck as a sister. And I'm sorry if I've given you a hard time over Jamie. I really do like the guy. And I owe you big. I'll help you in any way I can."

"Thanks."

"Christie?"

"I'll, umm, probably never say this again, but you should know that . . . that . . ."

"What?"

"I love you, Christie. If Jamie had been the type who'd hurt you, I'd want to beat the pulp out of him, even if he is older and bigger."

He sensed his sister's smile.

"I love you, too, you little rugrat. And you scared the shit out of me tonight."

She hit him in the shoulder.

His head rattled. He groaned.

"Don't you ever do that to me again," she charged him.

"Never," Jordan vowed.

Never, never, never.

"Hey," Jon said, startled to see his wife. "Want to come and skate?"

She shook her head. "I'm not very good."

"I can help you."

"I don't think so. I'm . . . afraid," she admitted.

"I'd be by your side."

"Thanks," she said. But she made no move to come out on the ice. He stretched out a hand to her, arching his brows. She smiled, but still refused to move.

"How'd you know I was here?" he asked her.

She shook her head. "I didn't. I thought I heard—" She broke off with a shrug. "I thought I heard people for a minute. Laughing, talking. I thought they'd be skating and that I could watch them for a while. I followed the sound and came here. I must have imagined it."

"Maybe not. I thought I heard something, too. Maybe there were people here. There have to be neighbors somewhere. There are neighbors; I know it. I talked to a couple of guys this afternoon." He stared at her for a minute. "Julie, do you want a divorce?"

She appeared startled by the abrupt question. "I—I don't know what I want anymore."

"That's fair," he told her.

"Maybe I do know what I want," she murmured.

"Oh?" He skated over to her, taking a seat beside her on the stump.

She gave him a rueful half smile. "I want to be Clarissa Wainscott."

"What?"

She shrugged. "You seem to like her. She's perfect. She always looks gorgeous; she lives this traditional Christmas of hers perfectly. . . ."

Jon reached for her hand, curling his fingers around hers. "Julie, I didn't do anything, did I? I mean, honestly, you're not jealous of her, are you?"

She shook her head. "No. Not in that way. I just envy what she has."

He arched a brow. "The house?"

Julie shook her head again, smiling. "It's something intangible."

"Maybe we could find it," Jon suggested slowly.

"Maybe," Julie agreed.

The night was really beautiful. Crystal clear and not too cold. The moonlight was shimmering down upon the ice in glowing ripples. For the first time in forever, it felt good to be together. Julie looked very beautiful, and vulnerable, and he thought back to the time when they had met, when they had fallen in love. And he bent his head to kiss her.

She leapt up. For a moment, he thought that she was going to strike him, that she was angry. But she wasn't angry, she was staring at him with her eyes wide and frightened. "Jon!"

"What? What?"

"There's something wrong."

"With what?" he demanded incredulously.

She shook her head a little wildly. "I don't know.

I just had an awful feeling. There's something wrong. We've got to get back to the house."

"Julie—"

"I've just had this awful feeling that something is wrong with one of the children. We've got to get back."

She raced by him. He wrenched the skates off, hopped into his boots, and came racing behind her.

The house seemed to be empty when they entered it. The downstairs area was lit only by a hall light and the dying embers of a fire in the drawing room. Julie was halfway up the stairs before Jon even closed the door. Once again, he raced after her.

The downstairs was not empty. Clarissa Wainscott sat before the fire, staring at the paintings on the wall. She watched the Radcliffs race by. Without bitterness, she envied them for the years that lay ahead of them, the laughter they might share in the future, happiness, even tears, life.

Then she looked outside, to the cold and the snow. And she consoled herself with the beauty of the scenery. She looked across the room. "My love, almost Christmas Eve!" she whispered.

It was amazing. Christie had just gone into her own room when the door burst open and their mom came into Jordan's room. She came to such a dead standstill that his father crashed into her when he arrived a few moments later.

"Julie, I think he's sleeping," Jon said softly.

But Jordan's mother walked over to him. She touched his forehead, and his arm. He kept his eyes closed, waiting.

His mom sighed with relief. "He's breathing," she whispered. Then, "The girls!" she said.

She burst into the next room. Jon followed. But Christie and Ashley were curled together once again. Jordan could hear his mother move to the bedside and touch them as well.

"Julie, everything's all right," his father said.

"I could have sworn that something was wrong!" she said.

Apparently, her tone disturbed Christie, because Jordan could hear his sister speaking then. "Mom?"

"Christie, is everything all right?"

"Sure."

"Ashley's been fine?"

"Sleeping like an angel. Mom, what's the matter?"

"I—I don't know. I was just so worried suddenly that something was wrong with one of you."

"Well, Jordan had a stomachache, but Mrs. Wainscott made him some herb tea."

"Jordan was sick?"

"Nothing major."

Jordan hadn't realized that he had opened his eyes and sat up until he saw in the darkened room that his father was standing in the doorway between the two rooms, watching him.

His dad walked over to him then and sat at the edge of the daybed by Jordan's feet.

"You okay, son?"

"Yeah, Dad, sure."

Jon nodded. "If something weren't okay, you'd tell us, right?"

He felt like a spineless jellyfish. "Right," he lied. Except it wasn't really a lie. He was going to talk to them about the things he'd gotten into. Just not now. He wasn't going to spoil Christmas for everyone.

It was unnerving the way his parents seemed to be some kind of aliens with strange antennae regarding their children. It was spooky, the way they'd come crashing back in here.

"I love you, Jordan," his father said. Jon leaned over him and kissed him on the forehead. Jordan suddenly felt the urge to hug his father.

"Good night," Jon told him. Jordan saw that his mother had come back in his room as well.

"Honey?"

"Yeah, Mom?"

"You feel better now?"

"I can't tell you how much better I feel."

Julie knelt down by the daybed, feeling his forehead, looking at him worriedly.

"Mom, I'm fine."

She nodded, stood, and walked to the window, looked out at the snow.

"Well, I guess we'll let you sleep then," Jon said.

Jordan knew that his father was watching his mother, but Julie didn't seem to notice. She still seemed perplexed and worried.

"Julie?" Jon said softly.

"I—I'll be along," Julie murmured.

Jon still watched her. He nodded after a moment. He tousled Jordan's hair, his fingers lingering for a minute, then he went into the next room.

"Mom?" Jordan said. "I'm really okay. You don't have to watch me sleep."

She laughed softly and came to the daybed. "Lift your head up a minute," she told him. She sat, and he laid his head in her lap. "Bear with me for a while, huh? I can't explain the feeling I had tonight. I do have to watch you sleep for a while tonight. All right?"

It was all right with Jordan. He just hoped it was all right with his father.

His mom just kept smoothing back his hair in a gentle, very maternal gesture. Guilt preyed upon him. Weird. It was just so weird. *How had she known something dangerous had been going on?*

It was as if his mom had suddenly gone psychic or something. Whoa, no. He hoped not. He'd really have to be careful in the future.

But he was pretty sure that his mom hadn't really changed any.

It was the house, he thought. This house. The whole place. It was different. Maybe special.

And very, very strange.

Chapter Fifteen

Julie awoke to the sound of laughter again.

When she looked out the window, it was like a replay of the day before.

The snowman was still standing in good shape. The kids were all bundled up, pelting each other with snowballs. They had Jon on the ground, and they were burying him.

She was tempted to come to his rescue.

But then she stepped back from the window. She wondered if he had thought that she was still trying to keep a wall between them last night. She had fallen asleep herself with Jordan on her lap, and when she had awakened and come into the bedroom sometime in the early morning, he had been sleeping himself. She wished she could have explained it to Jon; she had never experienced anything like that kind of fear before. Even this morning, watching Jordan below, she was worried. He still looked a little pale.

Julie dressed and came downstairs just as her children were coming in for breakfast. Once again, a full buffet was laid out in the dining room, and once again, there was no sign of their elusive hostess.

And now there was no sign of Jon. She poured herself coffee and arched a brow at Christie, who was piling an amazing breakfast onto a plate for herself. If nothing else, this place had restored her daughter's healthy appetite.

"Where's your father?"

"He didn't come in. I think he went back to the pond." She rolled her eyes. "He said you were probably going to want to go riding again. Oh, and Jesse said that we all needed to be sure to get up to the attic for a few minutes and find some clothing for the party tonight."

So Jon wasn't coming back to the house now. Had he gone to the pond? She could just go there herself and see. . . .

If he was alone?

No. She knew that he was alone. And it seemed that he wanted to be alone.

"I guess I do want to go riding," she said. "Ashley, you want to ride the horses again, right?"

"Yes, yes!"

"Jordan, Christie, you joining me?"

"I may go back to sleep for a while, Mom," Jordan said. Julie studied her son, then nodded.

"You're sure you're all right?"

"I'm sure I'm all right," Jordan said. "But it's Christmas Eve. I want to be awake tonight."

"Christie?"

"Oh, I'm going riding," she said. "But I'm going to go ahead, if you don't mind."

"Oh?"

"You can go with the older Wainscott, Mom. I'm going to go and meet the younger one for a while."

Jesse had already shown them the trails yesterday. But he'd been there at the stables again today when they came down, and though Christie mounted and took off quickly, Julie took her time, helping to saddle and bridle Midget and her own mount. When they were ready, Jesse offered to come with them again, and Julie found herself eager to accept. Ashley trailed behind her and Jesse a little, carrying on a full and private conversation with Midget.

"Your husband is getting good on the ice."

"Is he? I'm afraid there's no ice near us at home. He likes to rollerblade at home, though. Or he used to. When he had more time. He used to like to go out with Christie. He wanted me to try all the time."

"But you didn't."

"I'm scared," she admitted with a laugh.

"Well, he's getting awfully good. I'd trust him on the ice, if I were you."

"Maybe," she murmured.

"Your daughter was in a hurry," Jesse commented.

"She was off to see your son," Julie told him.

"Ah," Jesse murmured. "Well, I wouldn't worry about her. She's in good hands."

"Does Aaron live at home? Is he in school, or is he working?"

Jesse arched a brow at her. "Working, I would say. He's with the cavalry."

"Oh! The army? I didn't realize they still had a cavalry division." Julie surmised from Jesse's tone that Jesse wasn't happy about it. "I guess that's not what you wanted him to do. I'm sorry. I didn't mean to pry. I was just curious."

"You weren't prying. It's fine. No, I didn't want him to join up as he did, and we had some real words over it."

"So the situation is still tense," Julie murmured. "I'm sorry, I—"

"It's all right. He always comes home for Christmas. My boy always comes home for Christmas." He shrugged, then looked at her. "I've got to tell you, though, I wish that I could take back the words I said to him. I let the world, and my own sense of rightness within it, get in the way when I was talking to my son. I didn't wait to hear what he was thinking, how he felt. It's easy to do. Events kind of get like a carriage going downhill, brakes broken. You get all caught up in the ride, and forget why you're on the carriage to begin with." Jesse suddenly looked back at Ashley. "And you can't forget the little ones," he said softly. He winked at Julie. "They still believe in magic."

Julie glanced back at Ashley. Ashley was so happy. She was on her horse, content with the world. Her eyes were aglow and her cheeks were flushed.

"Hi, Mommy."

"Hi, Ashley."

"How's your son this morning?" Jesse asked suddenly, his eyes seeming somewhat piercing as he watched her.

"Doing well. But he was sick in the night."

"He'll be all right." Jesse looked at her. "I think you and your husband probably listen to your children. Listen good. You're still going to disagree sometimes. None of us has the power to control the world, just our little part in it. But no matter what, we've got to respect each other's opinions. Even when we think we're the parents so we must know what's right."

He was offering her a crooked smile that made

Julie's heart feel oddly as if it were cracking a bit. Jesse Wainscott seemed such a damned fine man. He so obviously adored his wife, and his son as well. He still seemed to be hurting from the argument.

"Surely, Jesse, you and your son can set things straight."

"My boy always comes home for Christmas," Jesse said again, as if that explained everything. He turned back to Ashley then. "Little Miss Radcliff! There's a fine clearing right ahead. I'll take you for a slow lope across it. If it's all right with your mother."

"Mommy?"

"As long as you listen to Mr. Wainscott," Julie said.

The two went dashing on ahead of her. Julie paused for a minute, listening as Jesse Wainscott gently instructed her daughter. He enjoyed her daughter, she thought. He enjoyed all her children. He took the time to listen to them. She paused just a minute, then urged her horse after them.

Christie was elated, riding out alone. And she was very proud of herself, because she didn't have the slightest problem finding the trail that led to the cemetery.

And Aaron was there, as he had said he would be.

"Christie! You came," he called to her, walking through the field of broken tombstones to reach her.

He held Shenandoah's reins as Christie leapt down from the horse.

"Well, you did invite me," she told him. She wondered why she had been so anxious to come. He was really attractive. And charming. She loved his smile, and the sound of his voice. She was in love with Jamie, she reminded herself. Maybe she had come just to make sure of that.

"I'm awfully glad of the company."

"Well, if you want company, you should come to the house. My family can be awful, but they're definitely all company. More company than you might want. My God, what a night!"

"Why? What happened," he asked, leading her horse as they walked idly through the graveyard.

Christie sighed. "Maybe it was good. But it was very strange. My airhead brother overdosed on some pills he was taking—"

"Pills?"

"Drugs. Downers."

"Oh," Aaron murmured.

"Your mother was terrific."

He smiled wryly, with a strange look of nostalgia in his eyes. "I imagine she was," he said softly.

"She made him throw up violently."

"Sounds wonderful."

"Well, it was, of course, because he was all right. But then do you know what happened?"

"What?"

"My mother suddenly turned into a witch—"

"She was angry, I imagine."

"No, no, I don't mean like that. My parents never knew what happened; they had been out. Your mom had everything under control by the time they raced back in, but the strange thing was that my mom came rushing into the bedroom in an absolute panic. As if she had known how much danger Jordan might have been in. Have you ever heard of anything like that? A psychic ability to feel someone else's danger?"

He smiled oddly. They paused, and she leaned against a tree, studying him. "I believe that strange things can happen, and that there are forces in the world we don't really understand."

"Well, this was strange. And Jordan said it got even stranger. I mean, my folks aren't stupid, so they probably have the sense to realize some of his friends are into dangerous substances, and so it's likely he might be, too. But Jordan told me this morning that neither of them lit into him; they were both rational, telling him that if he needed to talk or needed help, to let them know." She shook her head, mystified. "Damn! I wish they'd talk like that to me."

"Maybe they will."

Christie shook her head. "If you've never lived in

a place like Miami, you can't really understand. My folks are like the old guard. Natives—at their ages, that's kind of rare. And the city is a big mix of everything, and it's true that certain areas of the city can be dangerous, and there are a lot of crack houses and the like . . . and they just can't see past the street where Jamie lives."

"You've got to make them see what you see."

"I think that maybe I've got to give them a shock. Like just walking out when I turn eighteen."

"You don't mean that."

"I do. I'm telling you, you can't imagine how awful the last year has been. They don't even talk to one another; I can't imagine how they're going to talk to me."

"Do you love them?"

"Well, of course. We're just so damned messed up."

He looked off in the distance, toward the house. Then he looked back to her, reaching out a hand. "It could be worse. Come here."

He pulled her along to the center of the grave-yard, pointing in a direction that meant nothing to her. "That way," he told her, "is Washington, D.C." He spun her around. "That way is Dixie."

She arched a brow. "We are being traditional, right?"

"I'm showing you family problems. You know, of

course, that Wainscotts have lived on this property a very long time."

"I imagine that's why you all offer this quaintly traditional Christmas," she replied wryly.

He ignored her teasing tone. "Well, once, a long, long time ago, the nation was in turmoil. I grant you, it's in turmoil often enough, but this was real bad turmoil. Like nothing that's happened before or since."

"The Civil War?" she said, playing along with his story.

"Well, to folks in my uniform, it was the War of the Southern Rebellion. But the son of the house got into this terrible fight with his father. They didn't see eye to eye. And so the son rode away, angry. He took the time to kiss his mother quickly, and ruffle his kid sister's hair, but he never even said good-bye to his father. He rode away. And he killed lots of Rebs in gray, but not once in all the long days of war did he ever go into battle without a sick feeling of horror that he might kill his own father."

"Oh, God! He didn't, did he?" Christie cried.

"No," Aaron said. "But it was almost as bad. Oak River Plantation was taken over by Union forces. And some Southern cavalrymen had been taken— they were to be hanged. His father was among them. He'd actually escaped the lottery for the hanging, but there'd been a boy in his company who would have died if he hadn't stepped in. Anyway, the son rode up just in time for all hell to break loose."

"Oh, how awful. What happened? Did they get to see one another again?"

Aaron nodded gravely. "Just for a few seconds. People were converging with mixed loyalties; someone thought it was an attack; people started firing. There was an awful lot of bloodshed and many people died. And to make a long story short, the father and son never made up what had happened between them."

"That's a terrible story! So sad."

"I'm telling you, you can't imagine. The whole family had been up in arms against one another. Arguments over the big things—like the war itself. Then more arguments over the house, what people were doing. In the end, when they all tried to set it straight, they died trying to reach one another."

"Aaron, there is no war today."

"Doesn't matter. The best of lives can be a battleground at times."

"My parents' marriage is a battleground," Christie murmured.

"Well, the father and mother here died in one another's arms, hit with some of the same bullets."

"That's horrible; it's awfully sad. Don't tell me such terrible things—how can they help me?" Christie demanded.

Aaron grinned broadly, planting his hands on his hips. "Well, you don't part from people in anger, Christie. That's the point here. Think about it. Would you really want to walk away from your folks and possibly never get to see them again? You just don't know what can happen. There are no certainties in life."

"What if you can't get a point across?"

"Christie, I don't think you've really tried."

"I thought I had," she said.

"Maybe you should try again, a little harder."

She shrugged. "Maybe. But you're really exaggerating."

He smiled, shaking his head. He sat upon an above-ground tomb and patted the cold stone beside him. "I'm not exaggerating, believe me. But it's Christmas Eve. Sit down. Tell me what you want for Christmas."

She sat beside him. "I need a new compact disc player, a curling iron, and—" she broke off.

"And?"

"I want my folks to miraculously get along, I want my brother to quit being such a dope—and I want them to like Jamie."

"It can happen."

She glanced doubtfully at him.

"It's Christmas. I mean, it's the season for belief in the unseen, for blind faith, right?"

Christie nodded slowly. She smiled. "You still believe in miracles?" she asked.

His smile was very deep and charming. "I'm here every Christmas!" he assured her enigmatically.

The air was cool, but the sun was out. Christie lay back on the stone tomb, and they kept talking. It was nice to talk, nice to have a friend. Nice to tell him about Jamie. And nice to know, even in the company of this dazzling young man, that what she felt for Jamie was real. With Aaron, she could even spend the day believing that it could work out. As he said, it was Christmas. She'd believed in Christmas all her life. In blind faith.

"Keep telling me what you want for Christmas," he told her.

It was a great game. She told him all the petty little things she wanted, and went on to the bigger things. "World peace," she told him. "No more starving children anywhere. No more diseases. What do you think? Will I get my Christmas wishes?"

"We sometimes get more than we asked for," he told her.

She laughed. The afternoon passed pleasantly.

* * *

The house was completely decked in holly when Julie and Ashley returned to it after the ride. Clarissa Wainscott had been busy, Julie decided, but she wasn't anywhere to be seen now.

"We have to get costumes," Ashley reminded her. "In the attic."

"Yes, but Mrs. Wainscott isn't here right now."

"She told us just to go up. Come on, Mommy, please."

"Okay, let's check on Jordan first, though."

Jordan had been dozing. He woke up when his mother and sister came in. "Hey! How were the horses, Ash?"

"I love horses, Jordan."

"So do I, squirt."

"Jordan, did you help Mrs. Wainscott decorate with all that holly?"

"I'm afraid not. I fell asleep."

"You feel better?"

He nodded. To Julie's surprise, he hugged her. "Yeah, I feel real good."

"I'm glad, honey. Jordan, I'm not going to push you right now, but you've got to promise that if you're having problems with anything, you'll let your dad and me help you."

"Together?" Jordan asked softly.

"Jordan, no matter what, we both love you more than anything."

"Sure," he said quietly.

"By the way, have you seen your dad?"

"Not since this morning."

"We're going to go up to the attic and find some costumes, and you're coming," Ashley told him.

"Oh, I am?"

Julie nodded. "Sure. Let's go find stuff and get all dressed up. It will be fun."

She, Ashley, and Jordan went up to the attic. Ashley seemed to know her way around. There were trunks everywhere with all manner of apparel in them. Jordan, who had at first seemed to think it was babyish to dress up, began trying on jackets, frock coats, and high hats with great enthusiasm. Julie found a dress for herself, and a handsome old-fashioned pin-striped jacket for Jon.

Christie arrived, happy and flushed from her ride, when they were still digging into trunks.

"Christie, we're finding costumes."

"I know. I was out with Aaron. He told me to come back and find something to wear. It all starts at sunset, he told me. Mom! This stuff is great! Look at this dress . . . can I take this one?"

"I imagine so," Julie said a little uncertainly. "You all must be very careful with these things."

"We will, Mommy. Promise," Ashley vowed solemnly.

"Think your dad will like this?" Julie asked the kids.

"Sure," Christie said. She glanced at her watch. "Where is Dad? It's getting late."

"I guess he's been out on the ice all day," Julie said.

"Maybe you should go out and find him, Mom."

"I need to get Ashley cleaned up and dressed—"

"I'll help Ashley," Christie said.

"Jordan could go—"

"I'm still a little shaky, Mom. I'm trying to keep my strength up for the party tonight," he improvised.

Now that was a truckload of bull, and Julie knew it. But all three of her children were looking at her. She didn't know how to tell them that she wasn't angry at their father then, she was just feeling awfully awkward around him. Wanting to try, maybe, but afraid to do it.

"I want Christie to help me dress," Ashley said stubbornly.

"Mom, please go find Dad," Christie said quietly.

"Sure. Sure. You all get ready, and whenever it starts, go on down to the party. Dad and I will be along. And you, young lady—Ashley Radcliff—you stay with your sister and brother."

"I will."

"And you two keep an eye on her."

"Promise," Christie said.

Julie left the house, hugging her arms across her chest. It had gotten colder since she had come in. It was going to be dusk fairly soon, and after that, it would be dark almost immediately.

She walked briskly, coming down to the pond area. Jon was still there.

Alone.

He was skating beautifully. Around and around the pond. Skating came naturally to him, and in the last two days he'd managed to make himself look like a pro. Julie stood by the ice, watching him, for a very long time. Once, she had been far more adventurous.

More fun.

She would have been out there with him.

Christie was wonderful that night. She ran a shower for Ashley, helped her into the old-fashioned dress, and was gentle with her hair. "Okay, squirt, Jordan is dressing, and it's getting late. Can I trust you for just a minute while I get dressed?"

"Can I sit on top of the stairway and watch for people to come?" Ashley asked.

"Sure! Just don't move until I come for you."

Ashley raced out along the hallway and plopped down at the top of the stairs.

Mary was coming tonight, and she was anxious to see her.

As she sat, she could see how shadows fell even inside the house while the sun was setting. It didn't seem that the electricity was on; maybe it wasn't needed. Someone had set out a zillion candles and they seemed to burn brighter as the sun fell.

Suddenly, the front door burst open. Jesse Wainscott, very handsome in his rakish hat and frock coat, came in the front door.

"Clarissa!" he called hoarsely.

Mrs. Wainscott suddenly appeared at the door of the drawing room where they had come the first night. The two looked at each other. They looked at each other in such a way that Ashley realized she wasn't breathing. They looked at each other with so much hurt, and so much happiness.

Then they went rushing toward one another. Gliding, flying . . . racing.

He swept her into his arms and kissed her.

"Excuse me," Ashley heard, and she turned. Mary was there. Mary put a finger to her lips as she tiptoed past Ashley down the stairs.

"Mommy, Daddy?" Mary called at the landing.

And then she went racing to them, too, just as the door opened and a young man came in.

The brother, Ashley knew. Christie's friend, Aaron.

They greeted one another, laughing, hugging, talking, hugging again. . . .

"Our guests will be here any minute," Clarissa said.

"Yanks arriving," Jesse said with a grin.

"Rebs all over the place," his son answered with mock sadness.

They laughed, and Ashley found herself leaping up just as the door opened and a host of people entered the room. They came from the night, from the darkness, and in minutes the house seemed to be full, and music was playing and handsome men and women were sweeping the floor in beautiful circles as they danced and danced. . . .

"Whoa, squirt! Will you look at all that?"

Jordan had come to the landing. He reached down for her hand. "Come on, Ash, let's go see if we can try to dance to that, huh?"

She didn't answer him. She just followed him down to the party.

"Jon!"

Jon had spent the entire day on the ice. Thinking. Wishing. Praying.

It was Christmas. Maybe a man never got too old or too worn out to pray for the best on Christmas.

He heard his name called and turned, saw Julie, and smoothly glided over to where she stood.

"Hey! How was your day?" he asked her.

"Great! But the day's almost over. I picked out a costume for you; is that okay?"

"That's wonderful. Thanks."

"We should go in and clean up now. It's almost dark."

"Almost. Not quite."

"You've gotten good."

He gazed at her, brows arched. "Thanks. Why don't you come out with me for a few minutes."

"I told you . . . I'm afraid."

She was afraid, but she hadn't said no. Jon suddenly felt that it would be very important for them to spend time together, alone, now.

Afraid, but leaning on one another.

"I was hoping you'd come out," he admitted to her huskily. "I left some skates for you by that tree stump at the pond's edge."

"Jon—"

"Please."

He turned away from her, gliding swiftly out on the ice, spinning around the center.

"If I come out, will you come in?" she shouted.

"Yes!"

Jon could hear Julie muttering to herself. She walked around to the fallen tree where they had sat last night. She found the skates he had brought.

She laced them on as Jon slowly glided back to her.

She looked up at him, blue eyes very soft and pretty as she warned him, "You're going to owe me for this one."

"It's almost Christmas. Give me this present, for old time's sake."

She hesitated and repeated, "I'm afraid."

"We're all afraid. Take a chance. On me."

"If I stumble—"

"I'll catch you. Trust me," he told her.

She smiled hesitantly, then stood and accepted the hand he offered her. She wobbled out onto the ice. She started to slip. He held her securely. She was all right.

"You're not bad," he told her a second later as they moved over the ice. "Not bad at all for a Florida girl."

"Thanks."

With one arm around her steadying her, Jon carefully followed her strides with his own. In a few minutes, they were synchronized as they moved across the ice.

"You okay?"

"Sure."

"Really?"

"No. I'm going to fall on my butt any minute."

"I'll let you in on a little secret. I already did that."

"Jon?"

She was very serious then, her eyes wide and magical and very young, and he hadn't thought that he'd ever live to see her looking at him the way she was looking at him now.

"Yes?"

She was going to speak, but suddenly her face went pale. He thought she was having one of her premonitions again, that she was going to panic and say that something was wrong with the children. And of course he'd agree, because there had been something last night. Something far more serious than Jordan had admitted. He just knew it.

"The kids?" he whispered.

"The ice!" she cried out.

Then he heard it. A splintering, cracking sound.

He couldn't believe it. He had been on the ice all day. It had been as solid as granite.

But it wasn't now.

Before he could even begin to move, Julie was suddenly screaming and the ice was giving way right beneath her.

She went down so fast that he wasn't able to stop her. Her head went under the pool of water that formed in the great crack of ice. Jon shouted, falling flat down against the ice, desperately reaching for her. He just caught her wrists before even her hands could disappear into the dark void of water beneath them.

Chapter Sixteen

"Julie!" Her glove came free in his hand. He swore, catching her fingers again. "Julie, Julie!"

Her head bobbed to the surface. Her lips were blue; she was shivering. Her eyes met his in panic.

"Jon. Oh, God, Jon . . ."

"Julie, hold on, I've got you. I'm just inching back on the ice. I'll drag you. Slowly, okay? We can't crack any more of this, understand?"

She nodded. He moved backward. They heard a cracking again. He went still, then pulled very hard on her arms, trying to draw her body back up while he inched back toward the shallower shore area of the pond where the ice would be the firmest.

"Jon!" she whispered.

"Yeah."

"You've got to let me go. This is all going to crack up in a minute."

"I'll never let you go."

"You can't let the kids be orphans!" she whispered.

"Julie, I told you to trust me."

She nodded, keeping silent. He suddenly pulled himself up on his knees, and in doing so, managed to drag her out of the icy pool of water, and hard against him.

Soaking wet, shivering, sobbing, she leaned up on his chest. "You did it, you did it—"

"I told you to trust me!" he said, cocky now.

She smiled. And she kissed him with the coldest lips he had ever tasted. It didn't matter. It was a great kiss. Warm on the inside. Passionate. Grateful. Tender. Wonderful. Yet even as enwrapped as he was in that kiss, the sound of cracking ice was an instant warning that drew him from her.

"Jon," she murmured, "I'm sorry, I shouldn't have—"

"Julie, shush, will you? You should have, but the ice is cracking up more."

"Hey, out there!" came a cry. It was Jesse Wainscott, Jon realized. Jesse and a group of friends. His guests had apparently arrived; his party was under way. The friends with him were all dressed up. Some in Union uniforms, with dark frock coats and slouch hats, some in Confederate gray, and some in simple old-fashioned dress. There must have been at least twenty people now hurrying from the slope that led down to the pond from the house.

Help was coming.

"Julie, hold very, very still," Jon told her. "Listen. I'm easing you to my side. Look, there's Jesse with a rope. Grab hold of it as soon as you can reach it. . . ."

Julie did as he told her. She rolled away from him, easing some of the strain from the ice as their weight evened out on it.

"Julie!" Jesse called to her. "Get the rope!"

Julie caught the line he had tossed her. "Slip it around your waist so that they can't lose you," Jon told her. She did as he ordered without question. Jesse and a friend started slowly pulling Julie in. The ice suddenly let out something like a shriek and began cracking again.

Jon tried to balance, but the sheet of ice on which he lay suddenly went completely vertical.

He felt the slashing pain of the cold water against his flesh. And he started to go down.

He couldn't go down. He couldn't risk losing the opening. He began to pray. *God, forgive me for bitching! Give me a chance, please, God, one more chance.*

He jackknifed his legs to shoot to the surface in the opening of the ice. He reached out a hand, and it was taken.

Julie. Julie had his hand.

"Julie!" he gasped out. He was shaking. Blue.

Freezing, drowning, and dying, probably. And he could still hear cracking ice.

"Julie, get out of here—"

"Trust me," she told him.

He thought she smiled. She was trying to hold him so tightly. She couldn't possibly have the strength to hold him much longer. . . .

She didn't have to. Jesse was there. The men had rigged up more lines.

"Around your waist, Radcliff, you know the drill," Jesse Wainscott told him cheerfully. "We'll get you to the house and warmed up in no time."

And miraculously, he was out of the ice. Men were cheering, laughing. He was being clapped on the shoulder. He was covered with one gray frock coat and one blue one, and then Julie, encompassed herself in borrowed wool, was at his side, and they were making their way back to the house with Jesse introducing him to his friends all the while.

The house looked wonderful. Warm.

Alive.

It was ablaze with lights. Candles burned everywhere. Couples danced across the polished floors to the cheerful sound of a half-dozen fiddles being played upon the stairway. Tables had been set up with punch, crystal cups, and all manner of fine food: hams, fowl, casseroles, cakes.

"Mommy! Daddy!" Ashley shrieked as they

came in the front door. She came running to them, throwing herself against them. Jon and Julie hugged her instinctively in return; hugs never felt so good, Jon thought, as they did when they came right after you thought you'd never feel another hug again.

"Ashley, baby, you'll get all wet and cold," Julie said at last, easing Ashley away.

The fiddles stopped.

The dancers all paused and looked at them in surprise.

Clarissa came forward. "Julie, Jon! What on earth happened?"

"The ice, my dear," Jesse informed her. "It cracked."

"Oh, Jesse, how could such a horrible thing have happened here?" Clarissa cried with dismay.

"No harm done, my love. They're a bit wet, and very cold, but alive and well," Jesse said.

Christie had come over with a handsome young man in a Union uniform, who was quickly introduced as Aaron Wainscott. "Mom, Dad! Didn't you even think to test the ice?"

Jordan stood next to her, shaking his head. "Parents can be so irresponsible! Didn't you two think?" he demanded. "What did you think we'd do without you?" he asked softly.

Jon grinned sheepishly at his son. "I'm sorry,

truly sorry. We'll never do anything so careless again."

"Never," Julie vowed.

"Sorry, folks!" Jon said. "We certainly don't mean to put a damper on the party."

"Just go on up and get into a hot tub and get changed and we'll have warm whiskey for you when you get back down," Jesse said.

"Thanks," Jon said. He looked around. It was a strange party, all these men dressed up like Yanks and Confederates and milling around together. What the hell, it was northern Virginia. "Thanks, you guys, all of you." He saw that the two men he'd met by the oak the other night were two of the ones who had helped pull him and Julie out of the pond. "Thanks—you saved our lives."

"Our pleasure," one man replied. "Get on out of those things before you freeze your missus!"

Jon nodded. He and Julie doffed their borrowed wool coats and hurried up the stairs. Jon was already stripping off his clothing as he closed the door. Shaking, shivering, their teeth chattering as they told each other how scared they'd been, they finished discarding their icy wet garments in the too-small old-fashioned bathroom. Jon turned the shower on hot, insisting Julie get in.

"You get in."

"You can go first—"

"Julie, go."

"No, Jon, you're bluer—"

"Julie—"

He paused, determined to dispense with the argument. There were times when it was quite convenient that Julie was fairly small and slim. He picked her right up and stepped into the shower stall with her.

Steam rose around them and hot water pelted deliciously down upon them.

"Okay?" Jon asked her as the water sluiced over them both.

"Okay," she agreed, smiling. "Jon?"

"Yeah?"

"I'm sorry," she said.

"For what?" The water ran through his hair, down his face, over his back. It was so damned good to be alive. "Julie," he said, "I was the guilty party, remember?"

"But it's Christmas, right? It's all about forgiveness. It's so amazing, the amount of things you can think of at once when you think you're dying! I've been horrible, too self-righteous to forgive you— and you were right in a way! We had split up; I was naive to think that you'd become celibate because we weren't together. It was just that you were so special to me—"

"Julie, Julie, you were special to me, too. That's

why it didn't work with anyone else." He grinned. "Literally," he admitted.

"But it's not just the past—"

"No, it's the future," he said. He took a deep breath. "Julie, we can't change the world. Modern life is hard. Life is always hard—it's part of the greater scheme, so it seems. We can't change bad things, but we can help each other through them."

"Jon," she said breathlessly. "You hate your job."

"I'm quitting my job. If you think we can make it if I do."

"Jon, we made it before. It's just scary—"

"You trusted me tonight, right?" he asked her.

"Yes, but—"

"All right, so the ice broke," he said ruefully. "But we got out of it together. You trusted me. Well, I'm going to trust you, too. You are a good realtor. I hate my job. I really hate it. I have to change it. What do you say?"

She stared at him, blinking against the water. "Do you really think that I can make my half of a living?"

"Assistant D.A.'s aren't paid all that badly, and I think that you can make a hell of a living. Julie, things were wrong between us because of what I did. They were also wrong because we lost each other. When we first fell in love, it was you and me against the world. I was your best friend, not your worst enemy. We let life get in the way of living. If you still love me, Julie, let's try to go back and remember that life is supposed to be about people, children, laughing, getting along—love! It's not about the traffic on U.S. 1, candy sales, the Bobo Vinzettis of the world, or the rat race in any way. Julie . . ."

He couldn't tell if she was crying, or if it was just the spill of water on them both. But she was suddenly in his arms, her face buried against his chest, and it was the most wonderful feeling in the world.

"I've been a horrible mother," she said.

"You've been a busy mother, Julie. That's all."

"An awful wife."

"The best wife in the world."

Julie looked up at him. Her heart did a strange little skid and slam, like it hadn't done since she had first met Jon. He was looking at her, too. Gazing down at her in a way that made her tremble. That look was in his eyes. That look she had envied so much when she had seen Jesse Wainscott's eyes light up when she had mentioned his wife, Clarissa.

She had wanted warmth for Christmas.

She'd been given much more.

They'd missed quite a bit of the party, but it didn't seem to matter. Once they were dressed in their borrowed finery and came back downstairs, the ball was back in full swing, the fiddles playing madly and folks milling about and dancing and talking. The house was ablaze with light and laughter. Clarissa remained on Jesse Wainscott's arm throughout the night, dancing with her husband, talking with him—enjoying her guests, but never leaving her husband's side. Seeing Jon and Julie, Clarissa and Jesse drew them into the party, where their children already seemed to be quite at home. Christie danced the night away with Aaron Wainscott, who politely shared her with some of the other young men, but only on occasion. The Wainscotts' young daughter was there as well. Julie met her when she paused to pour a cupful of punch for herself. "Hello," the girl said gravely.

Julie had a strange feeling she'd seen the child before.

"Hello," the youngster said again.

"Hello."

"I'm Mary. Mary Wainscott."

"Mary. How nice to meet you."

"I'm the daughter," Mary said.

"How nice. Of course—that's why you look so familiar."

"You've seen my painting, maybe."

"Oh, of course, that painting is of you, all dressed

up in traditional Christmas finery!" Julie said, smiling. "You look like your mom."

She nodded.

"Where have you been?" Julie asked her politely. "We've missed seeing you."

"Oh, I spend time with relatives," she said vaguely. "But I'm always home by Christmas Eve."

"That's wonderful. It's always good to be home for Christmas."

"You're not home."

"Yes, but—" Julie said, then paused and smiled. "You're home with your family, Mary. I'm with my family. And we're all together, so . . . well, I guess wherever they are, I'm home. Does that make any sense?"

Mary nodded quite gravely. "Indeed. Excuse me, please. I see a friend I'd like to introduce to Ashley."

There was a young teenager standing just inside the door to the foyer. He was splendidly costumed as a Confederate drummer boy. Julie smiled, glad to see that the Wainscotts had young friends to dress up and visit for their children as well.

"Mrs. Radcliff!"

She swung around. Aaron Wainscott was at her side, bowing to her politely. Christie remained on his arm.

"I was going to dance with Dad," Christie said. "And I thought maybe—"

"Aaron, you do not have to dance with me," Julie said.

"Madam, the pleasure would be mine," he assured her.

It was a wonderful Christmas Eve. She was swept around the floor by the handsome young man in Union blue while she watched with pride as her daughter danced with Jon. Ashley was even whirling around the room with the very polite drummer boy. And Jordan . . .

Jordan was having a wonderful time. He was surrounded by three very lovely young ladies who giggled at his every word.

"Have you enjoyed your stay?" Aaron asked her.

Julie smiled. "I could never tell you how much," she told him quietly.

"I'm glad. Your daughter is very special."

"Thank you. She's . . . she's got a boyfriend, you know."

"Of course. She's told me all about him. She has a good head on her shoulders, Mrs. Radcliff. You and your husband have taught her well. She looks into the hearts of people; she doesn't prejudge them."

Watching him, Julie felt a flush rising to her cheeks. Why hadn't she and Jon ever looked, really looked, at the boy their daughter loved?

The music stopped. "Thank you," Julie told Aaron.

"You are very welcome, Mrs. Radcliff. I truly enjoyed the dance."

"No. I meant thank you for a lot more."

Aaron nodded, kissed her hand, and deserted her to find Christie. Julie saw her husband coming for her, and smiled. The next dance was a slow ballad. Jon drew her against him.

"Jon?"

"Hmm?"

"When we go home, we have to have Jamie over for dinner."

"Mmm," he agreed.

He was moving her in a particular direction, Julie realized.

They were underneath the mistletoe.

He kissed her.

And the fiddles played on, and countless couples whirled around and around them, and the sands of this Christmas Eve trickled through the hourglass of time.

In the wee hours of the morning, the guests were at last gone, and the Radcliffs were in bed.

Ashley awoke suddenly. Christie was sleeping at her side. Ashley slipped out of bed. Quietly, she opened the door to Jordan's room.

Jordan was sound asleep. Still smiling. He'd never had so many pretty girls to flirt with in his whole life. Ashley, feeling like a very mature six, shook her head and tiptoed to the door to her parents' room. She cracked open the door. Mommy and Daddy were sleeping, too. All curled up together. They looked very warm and snuggly, and Ashley was so happy she had to sniff back a tear. Somehow, things were right now.

She wasn't ready to go back to sleep. She went out to the hallway and sat down on the top stair.

As she sat there, she suddenly saw Mr. and Mrs. Wainscott. She was about to call out to them, but something stopped her.

Maybe it was the way they were looking at one another. Mrs. Wainscott seemed to move very, very gracefully to her husband, almost as if she floated on clouds. He took her in his arms. Very, very tenderly.

Ashley was embarrassed. She shouldn't have been watching. She was about to leap up and hurry away, but then she paused.

Aaron Wainscott entered the foyer from the left side of the house. He paused by the doorway, watching his parents.

Ashley looked to the right side. Mary was standing there as well, looking at her brother.

Aaron walked across the foyer and took his younger sister's hand.

They walked to their parents. They all put their arms around each other and hugged very tight.

Then Ashley blinked.

And they were gone. Not completely; something of them remained, but they seemed to fade away.

Ashley saw that daylight was just starting to break.

She was surprised to realize that she wasn't afraid at all. She stood up and went racing downstairs and into the drawing room.

Just as she had expected, they were all back in the paintings.

She stared at them. More and more daylight crept into the room.

She turned, racing up the stairs. It was time to wake Mommy and Daddy. They'd open presents.

They'd wonder where the Wainscotts were, but they wouldn't see them.

When they had opened all their gifts and eaten breakfast, Mommy and Daddy would start wondering where to find a church. And because they couldn't find the Wainscotts, they'd probably be completely confused, but they'd leave a check for their bill and head back to Washington, D.C.

And Daddy would drag them through all the museums again, but that would be okay.

They would probably never know. . . .

Ashley stared at the paintings.

"Good-bye. Merry Christmas!" she said softly.

And she turned around to race upstairs. She wanted her own family now.

Epilogue

Christmastime
One Year Later

The car bumped along the road and Jon Radcliff swore softly, running his gloved hand over the windshield. He grimaced at Julie.

"Finding the place sure hasn't gotten any easier!" he muttered.

"Well, it's here. Somewhere. We will find it," Julie told him. She turned around to look at the kids in the back.

They had rented a minivan at National Airport this year. They'd had to, because Jamie Rodriguez was with them. Jordan and Ashley were in the bucket seats in the middle row; Christie and Jamie were all the way in back. All four kids were dozing now. It seemed that they had been driving for hours.

Julie smiled, glad that they were all together.

During the past year, Jon and Julie had both

made a concentrated effort to get to know Jamie. The kid from the wrong side of the tracks had won himself a full scholarship to the University of Miami School of Education. Christie, naturally, enrolled there as well, and applied herself throughout the first semester with a drive and enthusiasm that had made both her parents proud.

It had been a good year. Not, of course, without a few pitfalls, because that was life. Jon had left his moneymaking prestigious law firm and returned to work at the D.A.'s office. He remained overworked and harassed, but he was happily harassed. He was doing what he wanted to do, and his heart was in his work. He was also able to give Julie some more leeway and time, and Julie was thriving as a realtor. Sometimes they both still had to step back and breathe and look around and think about priorities, but for the most part, they were doing well.

When they'd come home from last year's holiday trip, Julie and Jon had both been shaken when Jordan had admitted to them that he'd had a drug problem. Christmas hadn't changed everything; they'd both felt guilty as hell. But there hadn't been any screaming, any accusations. They got Jordan into a drug-abuse program, and they both made a point of knowing what went on with their son, not just in his special program, but in his life in general. In October, one of Jordan's best friends was in a car accident with an older cousin. Both kids had been high. One had walked away, one hadn't; he was paralyzed from the waist down. That night, Jordan had called Julie to pick him up at the mall when he had said earlier that he was going to get a ride home. When she'd heard about the accident, she'd hurt desperately for the families involved, but she'd also been incredibly grateful herself. Then, looking at Jordan, she'd realized that her son had had the good sense to realize that his friends were in no shape to drive. He hadn't been able to stop them, but neither had he been driven by any peer pressure into stepping into the car. She hadn't said anything at all to Jordan; she'd just started to cry and they had hugged one another for a very long time.

Ashley had involved both her mother and father in the Christmas Chocolate Torture, as Julie called it. Jon had managed to make quite a few sales at the D.A.'s office, so Ashley was a very happy little camper. But then, Julie quite frequently thought that Ashley was the one who might have really held them all together. She'd still been young enough to believe in magic, to accept the very strange as normal, and to believe that love was the strongest power in the world. Even the modern world, where commercialism ruled and the rat race had become the customary way of life.

Then there was Cruddy-Disgusting-Joe. . . .

"Hey!" Jon said suddenly, softly. "Talk to me, huh? Keep me sane in this darkness."

She smiled. "Talk about what?"

"Your thoughts. A penny for them."

Her grin deepened. She hugged the small car pillow she had been holding to her chest. "I was thinking about our year since last Christmas."

"Yeah?"

She nodded. "Specifically, at this moment, of Cruddy-Disgusting-Joe."

He arched a brow. Upon their return home last winter, Julie had dug around the house until she'd found two good blankets, a couple of warm flannel shirts, and some still good jeans Jon didn't wear anymore. Then she'd gone out and bought gift certificates to some of the restaurants in the area of her work. She'd been nervous, and she'd made Jon come with her to give the things to a smelly old fellow, from one of the halfway houses, who wandered along the streets.

"Well, honey, you didn't really think that you could change the man into a rocket scientist with a few blankets and Big Macs, did you?"

Julie shrugged. "I thought maybe he'd take a bath."

Jon laughed. "Okay, so he didn't take a bath, and he wore out the things you gave him in a matter of weeks, as if he'd purposely rolled in mud and rocks with your donations on his back. He didn't change. He's apparently happy muddling along the streets on his own."

"I thought maybe he'd get a job," Julie said regretfully.

"Well, he did keep your car from getting stripped that day in August."

That was true. A gang of car strippers had run around her work area for a few months in summer, blazing a little trail of gutted cars. They'd come for Julie's car, and Cruddy-Disgusting-Joe had let out such a holler that the police had been called. A week later, with Cruddy-Disgusting-Joe's descriptions, the police caught the thieves.

"You're right. This year, he isn't getting your cast-off clothing. I'm getting him a few new outfits to destroy straight from Macy's," Julie said. Jon, smiling, reached out and squeezed her hand.

"Dad?" Christie called from the back in a sleepy voice.

"Yeah, honey?"

"Are we almost there?"

"Sure. Yeah. Almost," Jon called back. He glanced at Julie again. "Where *is* this place?"

"It's got to be here somewhere."

"We should have called."

"I couldn't find the number. I didn't see their advertisement this year."

"They must have booked up early."

"Yeah, maybe.... I was just planning on stopping by, to say thank you, I guess, but now we're going to have tired, starving kids on our hands," Jon said apologetically.

"Well, if worse comes to worst, there's that little Ma and Pa restaurant just off the highway. And once we're at the highway, it isn't an hour back to the hotel in Crystal City."

"Dad!" It was Jordan this time.

"Yeah?"

"Are we near a gas station?"

"I don't think so, but I have plenty of gas."

Jordan groaned.

"Dad," Christie said, giggling, "get serious. Jordan doesn't care about gas, he has to *go*."

"Oh. Well, fine, there's the snow," Jon said.

"Cool," Jordan said with relief. As Jon pulled the car onto the shoulder of the road, Jordan leaned forward and grinned to his mother. "Can't help it— I'm a Southern boy, Mom, from the land where the sun always shines. It's *neat* to see the snow melt when you—"

"I get the picture, Jordan," Julie told him.

Jordan nodded and slipped out of the van, walking toward a clump of trees on the right side of the road.

"I guess I'll go watch the snow melt, too," Jon said, following his son out of the car.

The cold air that came into the heated, enclosed van when the doors were opened felt good.

"I'm going to stretch my legs for a minute, Mom, okay?" Christie asked.

"Sure. Just be careful," Julie told her. "Is Jamie—"

Christie laughed. "Jamie was up studying every night before we came on this trip; he has to keep his average up so high. He's sound asleep. Like Ashley. I should put the two of them together back here."

Christie crawled out of the car, stretching. The minivan was comfortable, but still a tight fit. And the night was beautiful. Very dark, except where it was illuminated by the minivan's headlights. Snow lay on the ground in soft, clean white drifts. It crunched beneath her feet. The air was cold and crisp and felt good in her lungs.

The lights reflected off an object in the woods to Christie's right. An overgrown trail seemed to lead deep into a copse of trees. Not too deep. Curiously, Christie determined to explore.

She shoved her hands into the pockets of her hooded parka and started walking. The light from the headlights faded somewhat, but she could still see easily enough. A little cry of delight escaped her as she realized that they were near the Wainscott home. The headlights had been reflecting on one of the snow-frosted headstones in the old family cemetery they had ridden to on horseback the Christmas before.

Christie wasn't at all afraid; she felt almost as if she had come across some well-known landmark or a very familiar trail. She walked into the copse, spinning around on the soft snow, smiling at the sculpted angels with their eyes cast toward the heavens.

"Christie!"

The voice startled her, and she spun around again. A smile lit up her features. "Aaron! Aaron Wainscott! Is that you?!" She ran toward him without a moment's hesitation, hugging him like a long-lost brother, then drawing away. He was ready for the traditional Wainscott Christmas again, dressed in his Union cavalry gear, and she shook her head, smiling. "At it again, I see. You all are so very good at this!"

"Christie, you look wonderful. Things are working out? What's going on? You're with your folks? And everything is great? Okay? Awful?"

Christie laughed. "I'm with my folks. Let's see, math is a bitch, and I have a history teacher who is truly straight from hell. But Jamie is here with us this year. I am going to marry him eventually. My folks are being really good about him. They're trying." She smiled. "I think, thanks to your folks, they're getting along a lot better with each other, and that kind of makes things look better, you know? Have you heard that expression about a glass being either half-full or half-empty? Well, you know, it's not that the glass got any more water in it, but we're all starting to look at it as if it's half-full!"

"That's great."

"How about you? How are things?"

He smiled, touching her cheek. "Well, you know how the country can be. Things are pretty much the same. I'm happy, though. It's almost Christmas Eve."

"You really like Christmas, don't you?"

"It's everything to me."

Christie laughed suddenly. "So why are you always hanging out in the cemetery? Come on with us. You can show us the way to your folks' home."

He took both of her hands in his, staring at her fingers as he touched them. "Christie . . . you're not going to find my Oak River Plantation this year. You found it last year. There are other guests now. You—you and your family don't need the old house anymore."

"Aaron, we're not staying, we just want to say hi and thanks!" Christie assured him, frowning. She was tempted to pull her hands away, except that, though he was certainly being odd, he wasn't being mean. His hands on hers were very warm, and was his smile.

"You don't need to say thanks," he told her.

"Listen," Christie said with frustration, "I'm getting my mom. She'll be so happy to see you. And she'll talk you into getting in the car with us and getting us up to the house and a nice warm fireplace. Don't move a muscle."

She started to walk away.

"Christie!" He caught her hand, pulling her back.

"Aaron, I'm just getting my mom. I'm coming right back."

He nodded. "Sure. Just Merry Christmas, huh? Happy life. Don't ever throw any of it away, okay?"

She stared into his eyes, his handsome face. Shook her head. "Merry Christmas to you, too. I know Jamie won't mind if I kiss an old friend," she told him. She stood on tiptoe and gently kissed his lips. "I'll be right back!" she whispered.

Christie went tearing back through the trees, calling out as she went. "Mom, Dad! I've found it! I've found the old cemetery. Aaron Wainscott is here; he can show us the way."

Julie had been standing outside the van, leaning against it, Ashley, awake now, hugged to her. Jamie, too, had awakened. His dark hair was a little mussed—sexy, Christie thought, but she'd keep a lid on it. Jon and Jordan were still staring at a deep pile of once-white snow. They all turned at the sound of her cries.

"Aaron's there? At this hour?" her mother said doubtfully. "Why didn't you bring him out here?"

"Couldn't talk him into it. He's a little strange tonight, but I know you'll set him straight. Jamie, I really want you to meet him. Come on!"

Christie led the way back to the cemetery. "Aaron! Aaron!" she cried out.

Her family all wandered into the copse with its crooked, broken headstones and beautiful angels. They all looked around, then looked expectantly back to Christie.

"Well, he was here. I didn't just imagine it," Christie said.

"You did find the cemetery," Jordan said grudgingly.

"So where did your friend Aaron go?" Jamie asked Christie.

"He's disappeared because he's a ghost," Ashley said matter-of-factly.

"Oh, honey!" Julie laughed. "Aaron is no ghost! He's Mrs. Wainscott's son."

"Mrs. Wainscott is a ghost, too," Ashley said. She looked at her father very seriously. "And that's why you can't find the house. It's even a ghost."

"Can houses be ghosts?" Jordan asked.

"They can be haunted," Jamie offered.

"People are ghosts," Christie advised her sister.

"People aren't ghosts!" Julie protested. "Aaron must have just decided to go to the house on his own, or else . . ."

"He is a ghost," Ashley insisted. "And he steps out of the picture when he's allowed to haunt the house. Mostly, he has to haunt the cemetery. I think it's because he must have actually died near here or something. I don't know. All I know is that they step out of the paintings when they're free to haunt Oak River Plantation, and then they go back into the paintings when they're not. They must have had some kind of a really terrible fight, because Mrs. Wainscott haunts the place by night, and Mr. Wainscott haunts the place by day. Didn't you notice that we never saw them together? They only get to see each other all together on Christmas Eve. And I think that they get to do that because they really did love each other, they just let that war kind of get in the way."

A pin could have been heard, dropping in the forest. They all just stared at Ashley. Blankly. Several seconds passed. She was seven now, of course. But still, such an assured and detailed display of imagination!

"Ashley—" her mother began at last.

"Mom, Aaron said that we wouldn't find the house," Christie said a little uneasily, staring at her little sister. "He said that we'd been at the house last year; someone else would be there this year. He said that we didn't need the old house anymore, we didn't need to say thanks."

"Hey, want to know what's weirder?" Jordan demanded suddenly. He sounded a little spooked.

"What?" Julie asked him.

"Look," Jordan said, and he pointed toward one of the lichen-covered tombstones. Snow dusted it, and he went down on his knees in front of it to wipe away the snow. It read:

CAPTAIN AARON WAINSCOTT, ARMY OF THE POTOMAC
BORN JULY 20TH, 1842 / DIED DECEMBER 24TH, 1862
BELOVED SON AND BROTHER
TRAITOR TO THE SOUTH
BUT LOYAL TO HEARTH, HEART, AND FAMILY
MAY HE REST IN PEACE

"Aaron must be a common family name," Julie said.

"Aaron told me a story last year," Christie said uneasily. "He told me about this Aaron." She grimaced at her parents. "I was saying that we didn't get along, and he told me about this family, and how the son had fought for the Union and the father had fought for the Confederacy. And they both died. Here. Or somewhere near here."

"So your Aaron must have been named after the young man who died," Julie said to Christie.

"Yeah, sure," Jon said suddenly. His voice sounded strange. He reached out a hand toward Julie without really looking at her. He seemed to be desperately grasping for her. She took his hand, and let him draw her next to him. He was staring at another tombstone. A larger one. "Can you read that?" he demanded. "I'm a few months older than you are. You may still have more vision left. I think I'm seeing things. Julie, read!"

Julie stared at the tombstone, reading silently.

HERE LIE INTERRED THE BODIES OF
CAPTAIN JESSE WAINSCOTT,
A BRAVE AND COURAGEOUS SOLDIER,
EVER LOYAL TO HIS CAUSE
BORN APRIL 18TH, 1819 / DIED DECEMBER 24TH, 1862
CLARISSA WAINSCOTT, BELOVED WIFE AND MOTHER
BORN MAY 10TH, 1823 / DIED DECEMBER 24TH, 1862
MARY, PRECIOUS DAUGHTER
BORN NOVEMBER 8TH, 1850
DIED DECEMBER 24TH, 1862

Jordan came by his mother's side and read the words out loud. "Wow!" he said. Then he added, "Hey, this must be some kind of a prank. These stones are really easy to read in an otherwise awfully neglected little cemetery."

"The cemetery isn't neglected," Christie protested. "Someone obviously tends this place."

"Of course, the Wainscotts take care of it," Julie said. "And this . . ."

"They all died on Christmas Eve," Jamie said, kneeling down by the large tombstone, pulling off a glove and running his fingers over it. "Looks real," he said, glancing up at the Radcliffs. "Don't you think, Mr. Radcliff?"

"Okay, so it's a real old tombstone; someone has just played a few games with it," Julie said.

Jordan started humming the theme song to *The Twilight Zone.*

Christie hit him in the arm. "Stop that!" She looked at her folks. "This is weird. Really weird. And I'm freezing. Dad, could we please go back to that place and get some hot chocolate?"

"Yeah, sure. What do you say, Julie? We'll have hot chocolate, get something to eat, and get warmed up, and then, if everyone is up to it, we'll make one last try to find the house. How's that sound?"

Julie just nodded stiffly. "Mmm. Let's do that," she murmured. She set an arm around Ashley's shoulders and stared down at her daughter, walking quickly away from the cemetery as she asked her, "Ashley, honey, what pictures were you talking about?"

"When we were at the house, Mommy. The pictures—"

"The paintings in the parlor?" Jon interrupted.

"Right. Those paintings, Daddy. And when we first got to the house, they were all in the paintings. Mr. and Mrs. Wainscott were in one; Aaron and Mary had their own. Then, first, Mrs. Wainscott was missing from a painting. And the next day, I saw that Mrs. Wainscott was back, but Mr. Wainscott wasn't in the painting anymore. That was because he was with me. But it was a secret, and I knew it was a secret, so I didn't say anything."

They had reached the road and the van. Julie looked at Jon. "She's really been doing an awful lot of reading for that literacy project at school," Julie said.

"She's—gifted!" Jon replied, seeking an explanation, the same as Julie was.

"Oh, I am not!" Ashley protested. "I'm telling you what happened! No one ever believes you when you're seven!" she said unhappily.

"I believe you, Ash," Jamie Rodriguez told her, tugging lightly on her hair as they crawled back into the car. She smiled at him. Jamie was nice. She was glad to have him around, now that everybody wasn't fighting all the time.

"I'm telling the truth," Ashley assured him.

"Ashley," Christie murmured, "I think that you are telling the truth, and it scares me!"

Ashley looked at her. "It shouldn't scare you. It never scared me. And I knew they went in and out of the pictures. They did it to help us. So that we wouldn't have to be lonely forever, only getting to see each other on Christmas Eve."

"Ashley!" Julie cried. "Honey, you can't really believe in such things!"

"Why not?" Ashley asked stubbornly. "I believe in Christmas."

The others remained silent then. Jon had no trouble retracing the road to the little restaurant, and they all piled quickly out of the car and into the wood-frame building. There was a long, old-fashioned counter directly in front, and by silent, mutual agreement, they all climbed onto the counter stools.

The restaurant was all but deserted, except for a young couple with twin babies who were just finishing up their dinner in front. A very old man, surprisingly sprightly for his tall, bony frame and wispy gray hair, came walking out from a back room, drying his hands on a clean white bar towel. "Howdy, folks. I'm afraid I was just closing up for the night, but I'll help you with what I can."

"Thank you, we'd really appreciate it," Jon said.

The fellow nodded, looking them all over. "Nice-looking family you got here. You, too, young fellow," he told Jamie. "You adopted?"

Jamie smiled. He shook his head. "I'm Christie's boyfriend."

The old man nodded. "That's mighty fine, young feller. Mighty fine. Now, what can I get for you?"

"Hot chocolate all around, if you don't mind. And anything at all that you might have left to eat."

The old man nodded. "Got stew. Will you eat stew, young lady?" he asked Ashley.

Normally, Ashley would have wrinkled her nose and echoed, "Stew!"

But she didn't. She nodded.

"There's just me, so if you want faster service, someone step on back here. Mugs are there, hot chocolate machine is there, pours out a cup exact. What will they think of next? I'll be right out with the stew."

He disappeared back into the kitchen. Jon and Julie stared at one another and smiled. "I'll get the hot chocolate," Julie said.

"I can do it if you want."

Her smile broadened. "I want to get hot chocolate for my family," she said. Jon, smiling as well, nodded.

The old fellow managed to get bowls of stew out to them in a matter of minutes, accompanied by big, fluffy dinner rolls. The cold had made them very hungry, and they all started eating right away, complimenting the old man.

"Glad you like it," he told them, leaning on the counter. "Don't usually get strangers by here this time of night. Except the occasional lost motorist."

Jon stopped chewing on his roll and swallowed. "Well," he said ruefully, "I guess I am your occasional lost motorist. I thought I knew where I was going. Maybe you could help us. We're looking for a place called Oak River Plantation."

"Oak River Plantation?" the old man said, his bushy salt-and-pepper brows arching high.

"Right," Jon said.

The man smiled. "You're fooling with me, mister."

"We're not, honestly," Julie said. "Why?"

"There ain't no Oak River Plantation. Not anymore. Place burned right to the ground way back in the middle of the Civil War, well over a hundred years ago."

"Someone rebuilt it, because we were there," Jon said politely.

"No one rebuilt it," the fellow said.

"But—" Julie began.

"How can you be so certain?" Jordan exploded.

The old man smiled. "I'm certain, young man, because my name's Wainscott, and I own the property it sat on. My great-grandfather was younger brother to the captain who owned the place when it all went up. No one ever rebuilt there."

"Well, then," Jon said, "someone nearby is pirating the name. It's been done really well, but—"

"Mr. Wainscott," Jordan said, not intending to interrupt his father but doing so anyway, "are you the one who keeps up the old family cemetery?"

"And my granddaughter, Mary, there, with her husband and boys."

They all turned to the young couple near the door with the twins. The woman was very pretty, and had a great smile. "Hi, folks." Her husband nodded a polite greeting; one of the twins burped.

Everyone laughed. A building tension seemed to ease from the room.

"The tombstones are all tended; they're very nicely legible for being so old," Julie said.

"Clear as rain. Mary went to a highfalutin art school up North and studied grave markers; can you beat that?" the older Mr. Wainscott said, obviously still astounded by such an idea.

"Funerary art," Mary said, smiling indulgently at her grandfather. "There are some really beautiful pieces in my own backyard."

"And some interesting gravestones," Jon said.

He shook his head. "Something awful must have happened; the whole family died on Christmas Eve, 1862."

Old Mr. Wainscott snorted. Mary glanced at her husband, who nodded to her with a bemused shrug. She came to the counter. "Jesse Wainscott was supposed to be one of the most extraordinary men to ever serve with the Confederate marauder, Mosby. He and his men hit the Union troops so often that Custer put out an order that captured men were to be hanged. Jesse was captured, and though he wasn't to hang originally, a young boy in his company was supposed to die, so Jesse determined to take his place."

"Oh, my God!" Christie breathed.

"Shush!" Jordan commanded.

Jamie reached for Christie's hand, squeezing it.

Mary continued. "But Jesse happened to be a Freemason as well, and he gave a distress signal to a Union commander who was obliged, as a Mason, to answer that call. Jesse might have walked away from the hanging." She smiled, then glanced at Christie and Jordan. "But talk about your dysfunctional family! Jesse had had this terrible row with his son, who had decided to fight for the Union. And he'd had words with his wife, because she was sick and tired of the fighting. But, anyway, when the wife and son heard that Jesse was in trouble, none of the past mattered. They came riding to his rescue. Their daughter was supposed to be safe with relatives, but she wasn't. She saw her mother leave and followed her. Clarissa raced her horse all the way from Front Royal to Oak River Plantation—"

"Hear the horse died, too," the old man put in.

"Clarissa had a gun," Mary said, narrowing her eyes at her grandfather for his interruption of her story. "Aaron Wainscott's command came in at just about the same time. Shooting started and panic rose. The Union boys thought that Mosby was coming after them with demons straight from hell. It was a slaughter. So much gunfire. Jesse and Clarissa were killed straight away, right in one another's arms. Aaron was wounded and died, and even the young girl got caught up in it and was shot and died as well. The whole family. And more. Union men, Rebel men . . . and somehow, a cannon was fired, the house caught fire and burned right to the ground. Naturally," Mary added, her eyes alight with a twinkle, "with such a history, our property is supposed to be very haunted!"

"Naturally," Julie agreed in a whisper.

She stared at Jon. She felt a little hand slipping into her own and turned to see that Ashley had come to stand beside her. "I told you, Mommy."

Ashley had told her, of course.

But she was still a grown woman and it was impossible to believe. There had to be a rational explanation.

Behind the counter, old Mr. Wainscott chuckled. "Legends!" he said. "We're close to D.C. here, all right, you know, but at night sometimes the ground fog is neck-high, the wolves howl like banshees, and the wind sounds like a woman's cries when it whistles through the trees. Folks around here tend to the fanciful, you know? Rumor does have it that Jesse gets to come alive by day, 'cause he was such a fine, brave fellow. Like his boy. The boy's supposed to haunt the cemetery, isn't he, Mary?"

"Yes. Legend has it that he was all shot up; he had tried to reach his folks when the bullets were flying a million miles an hour. Some of his men tried to get him away from the action, and they brought him to the cemetery with a company surgeon. He died on one of the graves. He's still supposed to be there, of course," Mary said with a smile. "But he hasn't talked to me yet!"

"Clarissa gets the nights, they say, for all those nights she waited up, cold and alone, for her man to come home. Women waited, so she waits with her daughter," old man Wainscott told them. "The girl was shot and afraid, and she tried to crawl up to safety."

"Up—to the attic?" Ashley whispered.

"Why, yes. She was mortally wounded, and died there," Mr. Wainscott said, surprised that Ashley had guessed such a place.

"But the good part is that once a year, on Christmas Eve, they're all allowed to come back together. Because they were all wrong, you see, to let the outside world intrude on their love for one another. Still, that love existed. So they get their one night a year to dance the hours away. It's a great legend," Mary said.

The Radcliffs and Jamie Rodriguez just stared at Mary. She smiled a little uneasily. She must have thought, at that moment, that the people alone with her in this tiny place with her precious babies were awfully damned strange.

"Great legend," Christie echoed.

Julie suddenly swung around on her bar stool, still a little white. "This was wonderful stew. What do we owe you for it?"

"Well, now, it's nearly Christmas . . ." he murmured, scratching his chin. "Don't think I can charge you folks."

"You have to charge us!" Jon insisted, laying some bills on the table. "You've got—" He paused. "A cemetery to keep up."

"Oh, rest assured that cemetery will always be kept up!" he said, and winked at Mary.

Julie managed to thank him; the kids all choked out something of the same.

They offered weak good-bye smiles to Mary and her family, walked numbly from the restaurant, and piled back into the van.

"It's a conspiracy!" Jordan exclaimed as his father revved the engine and brought them back out to the road. "That's it! In the Cold War—"

"In the Cold War?" Christie interrupted incredulously.

"Maybe . . ." Jamie said thoughtfully, "maybe your brother has something there. There could be a group of people out here who want to be on one of those television programs about the occult, or legends or the like, and so they staged it all."

The Radcliffs just stared at him.

"Well, I was just trying to offer an explanation!" he exclaimed.

"The Wainscotts are ghosts, and I told you so!" Ashley said determinedly. "Nice ghosts, special ghosts. And we got to see them because . . . I guess because we needed them!"

Julie had been sitting in silent shock. She suddenly realized that she was staring at a stopped car on the side of the road, where a man was struggling to change a flat tire in the cold and snow. She reached out and touched her husband's arm. "Jon, wait! Look, those people are in trouble. They've a flat. They have two little kids—the baby is crying. We have to stop."

Jon nodded, still a bit dazed himself, and pulled off the road. Again, the entire family piled out of the van, and approached the stopped vehicle.

"Can we give you a hand?" Jon called.

The man struggling with the tire was young, but he looked very tired. His wife was standing at his side, trying to rock the screaming baby. A four- or five-year-old child was kicking up the snow around them.

"I told you to bring another bottle!" the man was saying with exasperation.

"You told me to breast-feed!" the wife replied, her tone conveying that she was at her wit's end as well. "Michael, damn you, stop that now!" she cried. "I told you to get the tire fixed before we left!" she admonished her husband. She was both angry and very close to tears, and when she looked up and saw the Radcliffs coming near her, she was embarrassed as well.

"Hi, folks, we thought you could use some help," Jon called.

The husband stood, wiping his right hand on his jeans before accepting the handshake Jon offered. "Jon Radcliff, my wife Julie, son Jordan, daughters Christie and Ashley, and friend Jamie Rodriguez.

Between us, we should be able to help with that tire."

"Let me take a look," Jamie offered. "I'm good at this; I've worked with cars a lot."

"Thanks. I don't know if you can help or not—that bolt there seems to have stuck."

Jamie was on the ground with the tire. "Hand me that wrench, Mr. Radcliff, please?"

Jon did so. Jamie began getting the tire situation under control.

The woman with the crying baby had long auburn hair and big green eyes. She was pretty, but thin and frenzied. The baby was still crying. Julie reached out for the child. "May I?"

The young woman's relief was evident. She just needed to put that baby down for a minute.

And the baby . . . maybe she needed to not feel so much tension in the arms holding her. She quieted down with a little whimper in Julie's arms.

"Thanks. Thanks. I—" the woman began, then paused, growing a little red as she looked at Julie's children. "I'm breast-feeding, but in a car all day it's just impossible, and she hates the bottles, so I wind up having to get rid of her milk before she gets full. Oh, I am sorry. I'm Lauren Granger, my husband Mark, Michael there," she said wryly, indicating the restless, snow-kicking youngster, "and the baby is Sarah."

"Sarah is adorable," Julie assured the woman. "We have those little boxes of apple juice in the car, if you'd like to try that."

"Yeah, thanks—"

"Doesn't she get sick on juice?" Mark demanded of his wife. His voice was like a growl, but he immediately seemed to hear his own tone, and regret it.

"Only when *you* bounce her around, Mark," Lauren said.

"Wow, folks, I'm sorry. You're being so helpful, and I'm so rude," Mark said. He lifted his hands and let them fall to his side. "We'd like the juice very much. Thanks." He shook his head, seeking some kind of explanation for his mood. Or maybe for life in general. "We've just been driving forever. The kids have been screaming the whole way. My boss nearly bit my head off for leaving." He glanced at his wife reproachfully. "You know how it goes. Bah, humbug. Merry Christmas. And we're just as lost as can be."

"I know the area fairly well," Jon said, hesitating as he felt Julie's stare. He stared back at her with a little frown. "Where are you going?"

"Some place Lauren found in a magazine advertisement. It's called Oak River Plantation. It's supposed to offer this really wonderful, old-fashioned Christmas. It—"

He broke off, because Julie had started laughing. "What is it?" he demanded.

Julie quickly sobered, looking at Jon. "It's nothing. I'm sorry. It's a wonderful place."

"You've been there?" Lauren said, glancing at her husband with a sigh of relief. "So it does exist?"

Julie hesitated just a second, looking around at her family. Her eyes focused on Ashley's. She smiled. "Yes, it exists. We could drive all night and never find it again, but if you just go straight down that road . . ." She indicated the way, along the road with the old cemetery shrouded in the trees to its left. She looked back to Lauren and Mark, their crying baby and cantankerous son. "You'll find it. In just a matter of minutes."

"Tire's all set!" Jamie said, rising cheerfully.

"Thanks . . . thanks, young man," Mark said.

"My pleasure."

Christie, who had run back to the van, brought a handful of little boxes to Lauren. "Juice!" she pronounced.

"I guess I'd better give the baby back," Julie said. "Congratulations. She's lovely."

"Thanks," Lauren whispered. She started walking around her car, looking back at them. "Thank you. Really. Thanks so much."

"Our pleasure," Julie said.

"You're a godsend," Lauren told Jamie.

Jon set a hand on Jamie's shoulder. "He is a great kid, huh?"

Jamie shrugged uncomfortably.

Lauren smiled, and turned away.

The Grangers drove off into the night. Jon reached out for Julie's hand. She reached out in return, and their fingers entwined together.

"Get in the van!" Jon said suddenly. Tugging at her, he dragged her along.

"Where are we going?"

"That big grocery store back toward D.C."

"A grocery store!"

"We have to hurry! It's getting late."

"Jon, are you all right?"

"I'm fine."

Christie stared at her mother as the car shot onto the highway. Jordan stared at Christie. Even Ashley seemed to think that her father had finally completely lost his mind. Jamie had the good sense to remain silent.

The ride took about fifteen minutes—Jon was definitely exceeding the speed limit. But no matter how they questioned him, he had no answers—until they reached the store. There, he found a clerk, demanded to know if they had any kind of flowers anywhere in the store, then rushed to the aisle where the clerk said they could find what was left.

Flowers were in the produce section.

The lettuce looked much better.

The pickings were poor. It didn't matter. Jon was determined to buy as much as he could, the very best that he could find.

Then they were back in the car. And Julie wasn't surprised when she found that their return trip brought them back to the old Wainscott family cemetery.

"Place the flowers everywhere," Jon said, laying exorbitantly priced roses on Aaron Wainscott's grave. "Everywhere." At last, he looked at Julie. Really looked at her. "All right?" he asked softly.

She smiled and nodded. In a few minutes, the flowers were all laid upon the graves.

"I need another rose over here. For Clarissa!" Jordan called.

Christie decided to throw him one. She threw a bunch of snow as well.

Jordan retaliated.

Suddenly snow was flying everywhere. Jon was pelting Julie. She pelted him in return, then turned to run. She was laughing hysterically when she tripped over a broken footstone and fell into the soft cushion of snow. Jon fell on top of her. She looked up at him and smiled. And she kissed him in the snow, and it was cold all around, but it was very warm, and very good, to be kissed.

"We had to thank the Wainscotts. For Christmas," he told her.

"I agree. Do you think that the Grangers will find Oak River Plantation?" she asked.

He nodded. "I'm certain of it. All the right elements are there. They've just been so busy living that they . . ." He shrugged. "They forgot how to love."

"And it's really, really wonderful to remember, isn't it?" Julie whispered.

He nodded, lying beside her in the snow, in the dark, heedless of the gravestones around them. "Wonderful!" he whispered.

"The Grangers will make it," Julie mused. "That baby of theirs is just adorable."

"Yeah?" Jon said, arching a brow. Then his eyes narrowed. "Were you thinking . . ."

"Well, I don't know. Maybe. What do you think?"

Jon raised himself over her again, and his smile was rueful and deep. "Want to go back to the hotel and fool around and see what we get next Christmas?"

Julie laughed. "Sure!" she told him.

He rose, then helped her out of the snow. "Hey, kids! What are we, a bunch of crazies, having a snowball fight in a graveyard? Let's get back to some warmth."

"And video games," Jordan said agreeably.

Ashley took her father's hand as they started out of the cemetery.

Julie paused, just a few steps behind the others. She saw a tall figure leaning against one of the trees, wearing a slouch hat and old-fashioned frock coat.

Union style.

He lifted a hand to her and waved good-bye.

It couldn't be. It really couldn't be.

"Merry Christmas, Aaron Wainscott," Julie whispered. "Merry Christmas. And thank you!"

Again, he waved.

Then he seemed to fade into the night. Julie waited just a second longer, then smiled and followed her family back to the car.

Journeys of Passion and Desire

☐ **TOMORROW'S DREAMS by Heather Cullman.** Beautiful singer Penelope Parrish—the darling of the New York stage—never forgot the night her golden life ended. The handsome businessman Seth Tyler, whom she loved beyond all reason, hurled wild accusations at her and walked out of her life. Years later, when Penelope and Seth meet again amid the boisterous uproar of a Denver dance hall, all their repressed passion struggles to break free once more. (406842—$5.50)

☐ **YESTERDAY'S ROSES by Heather Cullman.** Dr. Hallie Gardiner knows something is terribly wrong with the handsome, haunted-looking man in the great San Francisco mansion. The Civil War had wounded Jake "Young Midas" Parrish, just as it had left Serena, his once-beautiful bride, hopelessly lost in her private universe. But when Serena is found mysteriously dead, Hallie finds herself falling in love with Jake who is now a murder suspect. (405749—$4.99)

☐ **LOVE ME TONIGHT by Nan Ryan.** The war had robbed Helen Burke Courtney of her money and her husband. All she had left was her coastal Alabama farm. Captain Kurt Northway of the Union Army might be the answer to her prayers, or a way to get to hell a little faster. She needed a man's help to plant her crops; she didn't know if she could stand to have a damned handsome Yankee do it. (404831—$4.99)

☐ **FIRES OF HEAVEN by Chelley Kitzmiller.** Independence Taylor had not been raised to survive the rigors of the West, but she was determined to mend her relationship with her father—even if it meant journeying across dangerous frontier to the Arizona Territory. But nothing prepared her for the terrifying moment when her wagon train was attacked, and she was carried away from certain death by the mysterious Apache known only as Shatto. (404548—$4.99)

☐ **RAWHIDE AND LACE by Margaret Brownley.** Libby Summerhill couldn't wait to get out of Deadman's Gulch—a lawless mining town filled with gunfights, brawls, and uncivilized mountain men—men like Logan St. John. He knew his town was no place for a woman and the sooner Libby and her precious baby left for Boston, the better. But how could he bare to lose this spirited woman who melted his heart of stone forever? (404610—$4.99)

*Prices slightly higher in Canada

Buy them at your local bookstore or use this convenient coupon for ordering.

PENGUIN USA
P.O. Box 999 — Dept. #17109
Bergenfield, New Jersey 07621

Please send me the books I have checked above.
I am enclosing $_____ (please add $2.00 to cover postage and handling). Send check or money order (no cash or C.O.D.'s) or charge by Mastercard or VISA (with a $15.00 minimum). Prices and numbers are subject to change without notice.

Card #_____ Exp. Date _____
Signature_____
Name_____
Address_____
City _____ State _____ Zip Code _____

For faster service when ordering by credit card call **1-800-253-6476**

Allow a minimum of 4-6 weeks for delivery. This offer is subject to change without notice.

TOPAZ

WONDERFUL LOVE STORIES

☐ **SECRET NIGHTS by Anita Mills.** Elise Rand had once been humiliated by her father's attempt to arrange a marriage for her with London's most brilliant and ambitious criminal lawyer, Patrick Hamilton. Hamilton wanted her, but as a mistress, not a wife. Now she was committed to a desperate act—giving her body to Hamilton if he would defend her father in a scandalous case of murder.

(404815—$4.99)

☐ **A LIGHT FOR MY LOVE by Alexis Harrington.** Determined to make the beautiful China Sullivan forget the lonely hellion he'd once been, Jake Chastaine must make her see the new man he'd become. But even as love begins to heal the wounds of the past, Jake must battle a new obstacle—a danger that threatens to destroy all they hold dear.

(405013—$4.99)

☐ **IN A PIRATE'S ARMS by Mary Kingsley.** They call him the Raven. His pirate ship swoops down on English frigates in tropical seas and he takes what he wishes. Taken captive while accompanying her beautiful sister on a voyage to London, spinster Rebecca Talbot is stunned when the handsome buccaneer winks at her and presses her wrist to his lips. She daringly offers to be the Raven's mistress if he will keep her sister safe.

(406443—$5.50)

*Prices slightly higher in Canada

Buy them at your local bookstore or use this convenient coupon for ordering.

PENGUIN USA
P.O. Box 999 — Dept. #17109
Bergenfield, New Jersey 07621

Please send me the books I have checked above.
I am enclosing $_____ (please add $2.00 to cover postage and handling). Send check or money order (no cash or C.O.D.'s) or charge by Mastercard or VISA (with a $15.00 minimum). Prices and numbers are subject to change without notice.

Card #_____ Exp. Date _____
Signature_____
Name_____
Address_____
City _____ State _____ Zip Code _____

For faster service when ordering by credit card call **1-800-253-6476**

Allow a minimum of 4-6 weeks for delivery. This offer is subject to change without notice.